AUDIENCE PARTICIPATION

EVAN CLOUSE

COVER IMAGE ILLUSTRATED BY
GABE PEREZ

Contents

Acknowledgments

I would like to thank every person who has supported me and understands just how important this work is to me. Thank you for reading. Thank you for your input. Thank you for caring. You know who you are.

CHAPTER 1

INTENDED CASUALTIES

"Ah shit! You can call off the search! I found her! The fucking bitch offed herself!" Pug Homleyman yelled out after entering the theatre's projection booth. Globs of fat oozed under his sweat-stained white shirt as he waddled his way to the middle of the booth and looked down at his latest deceased starlet. Her elegant white gown was saturated by her own blood. As was the reel of film that laid under her stiffening body.

"Ah, Jesus Christ!" the head of the movie studio exclaimed as the twelve other men who had been invited to that evening's private film screening came bustling into the room. "Just look at this mess. She musta slit her wrists with that straight razor over there. And this bitch laid there and bled out. But why in the hell did she have to bleed all over the fuckin' film?"

He pulled the large, metal reel out from under the starlet causing her head to land on the soiled floor with a heavy thud. He wheeled the reel over to the projector and began inspecting the infected print. "Oh, man. Look at this. Blood all over this thing. But it's kinda weird. There are parts of the film that are just fine and others that are covered in her blood. It's like the blood seeped through the film and impacted just certain frames. Really fuckin' weird. Fortunately, we have several other pristine prints, so this won't affect our distribution."

"No, it won't," the thirty-eight-year-old Ezekial Winthrop III responded in a sorrowful tone. He straightened his red tie under his black, form-fitting suit jacket as he continued. "But it does put a damper on our little party tonight, now, doesn't it? The only reason that I put my daddy's money into producing these films is for our little screening parties. Oh sure, it's nice when they turn a profit. But it truly is worth the millions that I put into these sordid little stories to have our latest starlet screen the film with us. Oh, how my heart swells as I watch her screen presence mirrored in her enthralled eyes as the film plays. It is a thrill to watch our latest little starlet's dreams come true. And it is so satisfying to know that we were her golden ticket to fame. We gave her this opportunity, and they always glow with appreciation as their image flickers on the big screen. This is quite unfortunate. I so wanted to see her glow tonight."

"I wanted to see her legs spread while we each fucked the shit out of her," the Casting Director, Bob Lemmings stated as he smoothed his greasy comb-over on the top of his pasty head. "Well yes, of course," Ezekial agreed. "What would our little soirees be without the celebratory gang bang? Just as I love to see them glow as they watch themselves on the screen, I love fucking that gleam in their eye right out of them. I just love that moment when they realize what is about to happen to them as the credits roll.

"They scream. They struggle. They weep. And while I'm forcing myself into them, do you know what I'm doing? I'm watching their dreams die in their eyes. What were once sparkling blue sapphires under their lush lashes turn lifeless. Grey. Hopeless. I absolutely love the power to give these women their dreams on a golden platter. And I love turning those dreams into a horrific nightmare just a few minutes later. I love watching the fight drain from their souls as every principle on the film takes turns making them do such degrading things. And painful too, I would suspect. Each of us taking turns over and over until they are completely stripped of their dignity and self-worth and wilt into nothing but our little puppets. Puppets that we place in the corner until we need them again. And then, we pull their strings and produce another movie with them. Sometimes the movies are for public consumption and sometimes they are, um, for our own *personal* use, heh, heh, heh. They are shattered after their initial screening and do everything that we demand. Well, until they can't take it anymore and they do something silly like this. And then, the box office receipts come pouring in. And the DVD sales. And the merchandising. Everybody loves to build up a starlet. And everybody loves it when that starlet comes crashing down to Earth. They will pay and pay and pay to watch her final on-screen smiles, laughs, and gasps. The poor unfortunate soul who had such a promising career but could not handle the rigors of fame. So, we have an overdose. Or drunken car accident. Or suicide in the bathtub. But this is a new one. Suicide even before she saw her big-screen debut. I wonder why she did herself in before we even had our little party with her?"

"She did herself in," Pug grumbled, "Because she knew somehow. She knew what was going to happen tonight. I received a phone call from her this morning. She said that she wasn't coming to the screening. I told her it was in her contract. That she *had* to show up. She said she didn't care. That she'd been doing research and found out that every starlet that was signed to our studio, DL Pictures, ended up dead after their big break. Sometimes it was right after their big debut, sometimes a few films in. But each and every one of them died under mysterious circumstances. And usually pretty gruesome. I tried to explain to her that it was all a coincidence. That this is a difficult business that some girls just aren't equipped to handle.

"And that's when the conversation turned fuckin' weird. She said that it wasn't that at all. She said that she knew that it was because we raped and brutalized each and every one of them. That each girl was treated so badly by us, that they lost all hope and decided their only escape was suicide. I just laughed and asked her how in the hell she could possibly know that. And do you know what this stupid bitch said? Get a load of this! She said that she knew because she had communicated with each of the dead girls! She said that she spoke with all eleven of our deceased little beauties.

"I just kept laughing. Until she started going into details. She told me about Ginger and how she had been gang-raped at her premiere and that she felt so degraded afterwards that she rammed her car headlong into a tree. That was a damn shame. Her fuckin' red head just exploded around that oak. The tabloids were all over that one. But holy shit, did we cash in! Ginger's debut motion picture, *Tomorrow's Sunset* was the third highest grossing film that year. I think it was worth our "seed" money don't you, boys?

"She then talked about her supposed conversation with Violet. Oh man, *she* was a feisty one. Remember how we had to keep her chained up in the basement of my mansion until it was time to shoot her scenes? But as soon as we got her on the set, she tore the hell out of everything. I still have the scar on my cheek from that bitch's fingernails. She was completely unusable. But we made just about as much off her snuff film than her *Amazonian Fury* trilogy. And this bitch knew all the details of the snuff film. She described the beatings with the chains then how we suffocated her with a clear plastic bag while being raped. How the fuck could she know that? We must have a snitch somewhere. Regardless of how she knew, I stopped my laughing and just listened to her as she talked about all eleven of them and tried to figure out how she knew such intricate details.

"Sophia was the next one she talked about. Weighted herself with heavy chains and jumped right off of my yacht right after we screened her third feature, *The Black Tide*. Then it was Virginia who made herself a little arsenic cocktail at our bar right after we screened *Know When To Say When*. Oh shit, the dumb fuckin' Christian crowd really loved *that* sappy, self-righteous piece of shit and Virginia became their poster child for abstinence from alcohol. Well, I'll drink to that!

"Then Claudia. Oh, poor Claudia. Hung herself right after her biggest film debuted. Yeah, the box office for *Jagged Lies* really took off after it was reported that not only did she hang herself, but she did it with razor wire, so by the time the cops found her, she was completely decapitated! Cool way to go, I guess. And great publicity for the flick.

"I have to admit, I got a chill when this bitch told me she had actually spoken to Simone. Even if she *could* actually commune with the dead, which is horseshit of course, how in the hell would she talk with *Simone? That* crazy bitch cut out her own tongue. And eyes. And ears. Then just bled out all over her floor. I still have her eyes preserved in a jar around here somewhere. Yes, her mahogany eyes sparkled on the screen. Which made her the perfect lead for *Speak No Evil, Hear No Evil, See No Evil.* Completely unoriginal title with a completely unoriginal story that did crazy business all over the world. Of course, that one was our last international release. The rest of the world quit importing films and pretty much everything else from this country in retaliation for our tariffs. Oh, and, y'know. Trying to confiscate their land for their natural resources. Yes, we have become quite the international pariah, now, haven't we? But fuck the rest of the world! We'll be in their markets again soon enough. All we need is a little World War, then The Regime, and our films, will dominate the world stage once again!

"In the meantime, we've had to rely on *this* country's audiences. And as poor as these dumb bastards are, they still scrape up enough money to pay for their TV and movies, now don't they. Just a bunch of sad sack lemmings being numbed from the harsh reality of life under The Regime by our little offerings. And I'm telling ya, we couldn't have scripted a better domestic-only release to get everybody's patriotic hackles up. Yeah, *Star Spangled Firing Squad* starring our very own blonde girl-next-door, Skipper. What a fun little romp about rounding up illegals, lining them up, then putting them in front of a firing squad. Yeah, Skipper sure took it hard when she found out that our illegals weren't actors. And we weren't using blanks in the rifles. But not as hard as she took it from *us,* right boys? Too bad she ate her own bullet. And I have to admit. I always said that she had no brains. Well, I stood corrected when I saw her brains splattered across her movie poster outside the downtown cinema.

"Our next release starred Veronica. And *this* bitch knew every detail of her story. But that kinda makes sense. Her death was the exact plot of *Meatgrinder Mayhem.* She probably just saw the movie and put two and two together. Goddamn, Veronica had cute little tits.

And I do mean *had*. Jumped right into that meat grinder at a nearby packing plant. Yeah, she had cute little buns, too. After that, all she was good for was to be *served* on cute little buns. Medium rare, with some mustard and pickles of course. She was a bit gamey, but really moist. One of the better burgers I've had, actually.

"Then she told me that she had spoken to Ursula. According to *this* crazy bitch, Ursula told her how she tried to play along with us for over two years and released five films in that time. The more she succumbed to our will, the more brutal we became. After all, what's the fun if they don't scream, right boys? Anyway, she said that Ursula said that after her fifth film, *Blind Bondage*, she just couldn't take it anymore. She climbed out of her twenty-third-floor balcony, put on a blindfold and just walked around on the ledge until, well, you know. Geronimooooooo! SPLAT!

"Now, Candace was fun. What a little partier *that* one was. She was up for anything, which made her the perfect choice to star in *Skin Tight, Up All Night*. A fun little soft-core T&A flick about a young girl who gets caught up in the big city party lifestyle. Drugs, booze, sex. This one had it all, which would have made it perfect for the overseas market. Ah, well. What we lost in revenue over *there* was *more* than made up for from the streaming by the so-called Christian men. Those motherfuckers talk piety and live depravity, which is just fine for our bottom line. Take the family to our more wholesome features, then stay up late and jack off to our disgusting shit. Those stupid fucking Christians are a win-win for us, boys. I've heard the Speaker of the House watches our more twisted shit all the time. With his porn buddy, whatever the fuck *that* is. What a fuckin' hypocritical worm that little asshole is. But, hey, he does Dear Leader's bidding, so who am I to complain? Yeah, that movie had it all. Just as Candace did. Perfect smile. Perfect figure. Perfect bubbly personality. Her one imperfection? She couldn't handle the constant anal sex. Drove her fucking insane. So fucking insane that she fucked herself to death up the ass with a plunger handle! Jesus H. That was a fucking mess. And another media bonanza.

"And just last month we premiered Randi's fourth feature, *Acid*

Test. And just last month, she plunged herself into an acid bath. Fucking everything was eaten away until her bathtub was nothing but pink and red goo. Damn shame. I really thought she had lasting power. Plus, I was hoping her next flick would be our latest snuff film. She was just too fucking mouthy to keep around. Ah well, there will be others. Hundreds if not thousands of other perky young ladies with stars in their eyes will do *anything* that they can to be the next big star. And the hits will just keep on comin'. And so will we, right boys?

"Yep, death after death after death. And hit after hit after hit. The viewing audience in this country is so fucking morbid and stupid. They've been so dulled by the violence of The Regime that *nothing* is shocking to them anymore. They just get titillated by watching the final performance of some hot piece right after she offs herself in some sensational way. Box office bonanzas, all of them.

"So anyway, our latest fallen angel knew all about this shit and she wasn't about to show up for our little premiere party. Until I sent her a picture of her sister and niece playing in a park and said 'I could shoot a bullet just as easily as I shot this picture. Be here at eight. Or else.' And well, here she is. Bleeding out all over our fucking film. Slit her thin, pale wrists. Killed herself just as her character did in this sappy fucking movie. Yeah, throw another bone to the Christian family crowd. Her character gets seduced by vermin and sullies her family's name. She has so much anguish that she commits suicide in the name of her lord. Dear Leader, of course. Yeah, it's a real lesson to stupid young bitches out there. Don't do business with (derogatory term omitted) and don't fuck (derogatory term omitted) or else you bring shame on your family, and your only salvation is self-sacrifice. I guess our little angel took this a bit too seriously, huh? Yeah, *Take My Hand* might be the most wholesome film we've produced. What a piece of shit. Makes me wanna gag. And if she thinks this little stunt is gonna save her precious family, then she has another thing coming. Have somebody put a bullet in those two little bitches, and they can all be reunited once again.

"The only mystery here is how did she know about all of this? She sure as fuck didn't speak to the dead, now, did she? Oh, who cares?

Probably a snitch and since we're owned by The Regime, all of our activities are protected. Protected? Hell, they're fucking encouraged! There won't be any investigation, and they'll all remain sad little girls with sad little endings. So, who gives a fuck? It doesn't matter *how* you knew, bitch. All of our little secrets are going to be buried with you. Well, right after we have some fun with your corpse. This gives us the perfect opportunity to produce that necrophilia project we've been wanting to do. Yeah, as the credits roll on your big screen debut, we'll each take turns with your pretty, cold body, heh, heh, heh. Then we'll dump your body back at your apartment. Let's get the film equipment ready. I want multiple angles for this. And get this piece of shit movie threaded into the projector. Who cares if there are some scenes that will be all red and bloody? It'll add to the atmosphere. And then, we'll pay our final respects to our fallen angel here. Good-bye, Angel Feathers."

Chapter 2

Avenging Angel

"Angel Feathers. What a stupid fucking name. I hated it when they gave it to me, and I hate it even more now. Sounds like a missionary stripper," Angel stated to herself as she peered down at her lifeless body that was surrounded by pompous, abusive men. "Yes, look at my still, dead body, motherfuckers. Look at what you made me do to myself. But my blood isn't enough now, is it? No, you're still going to go after my sister and niece. Shit, I shoulda known that reptiles like you wouldn't give me a loophole. Good thing I have another one. One that these assholes can't edit out."

Angel then heard whispering coming from behind her perch in the thick, white clouds. "Gee, this new chick seems kinda crazy. Who is she talkin' to?" "I dunno," another female voice replied. "You know how it is with newbies. There's an adjustment period. At least she had the good sense to just slash her wrists. I fucked myself up the ass with a plunger until I bled out. Not that it's an excuse, but I was having some issues back then."

"We *all* were having issues at the time of our death, Candace," a third voice replied. "We *all* were being humiliated and degraded and abused by these abhorrent men. All eleven of us, and now twelve. But we survived, now, didn't we? Well, at least our souls did. We're all up here together watching. Watching these awful men do awful things to yet another young starlet. Until she too, joins us. We may be in Enlightenment, but it is a living hell to just sit up here and watch. It's a living hell to not be able to bring these pricks to justice. We've all prayed for the power to intervene somehow. And all we get is silence. And eventually, a new cloud-mate."

Angel turned around and adjusted her eyes until she saw three female silhouettes through the dense clouds. She opened her full, pouty lips and said, "Yeah, well, *that* shit's about to change. Because *I'm* the answer to your prayers. *I'm* the one who you have been talking to and sharing your horrific stories with, um, Ginger, isn't it? Yeah, I recognize you from *Tomorrow's Sunset*. You were the first, weren't you? The first to take her life because of the horrendous treatment you were forced to endure. Are you in charge up here?"

"Well, I wouldn't say that I'm in *charge*," Ginger said with a chuckle as she stepped toward her latest friend. Her fiery red hair glistened from the surrounding celestial lights as she strutted like a super model on a fashion runway. "I'm just the most, um, experienced. Yes, I was the first to take my life because I couldn't stand the brutality any longer. Ran my car right into a tree. There was no pain. Just relief. And a sense of freedom. The chains of oppression had been lifted, and so was my soul. Right up to this cloud bank in the middle of the universe. A calm, soothing voice came out of this beam of light and told me that I was now safe. That I would never want again. And that I was to be the guide and advisor for those that they knew would soon follow my tragic path. I was all alone for a brief time until Violet arrived."

A second woman stepped forward and Angel gasped before gushing, "Oh wow. I can't believe I'm in the presence of Violet, the star of the *Amazonian Fury* trilogy. It is such an honor to meet you. You were so incredible in those movies. So powerful. You were my inspiration to be an actress. I wanted to play parts that were empowering to women, just as you were."

"Yeah, I was really fucking empowered. They kept me chained up in their basement until I went fuckin' nuts and scratched the fuck out of them every time they unchained me. So, I was deemed unmanageable and became the star of their first snuff film. Jesus, I can still feel the plastic bag around my face as I gasped for air. And I can still feel the *other* things those motherfuckers did to me too. And I'm sorry, Angel. I'm sorry that I was the inspiration for your choosing this path. I'm sorry that I had any involvement in your taking your own life."

"Oh, don't be," Angel replied through genuine laughter. "It's all good. I'll explain in a moment. But what happened to your hair and skin? You're all purple! I never would have recognized you!"

"Yeah, well," Violet replied while stroking her long, dark purple locks. "You see, while I was still alive, I read this really cool book called *Sin.D*. And well, the main character was a bad-assed bitch and was all purple and shit, so when I got up here and discovered that I could manipulate my appearance any way I wanted, I, um, well, I turned my hair and skin purple. It made me feel connected to that character. It made me feel a little less helpless as we watched more and more women fall prey to these bastards."

"Yeah, like me," the spiky-haired and tattooed Candace interjected. "Violet was the first friend that I made up here. I mean, *everybody* is super cool. All eleven of us. I don't know where the other eight are right now. Probably shopping. Those bitches love to shop. Anyway, we all have bonded. Probably because of our shared experiences. That's why The Keepers of Enlightenment grouped us all together. So we'd have others we could relate to. And Violet was the one that I could relate to the most. I mean, *all* of us are a bit wacky doodle, y'know? How can you *not* be after having your dreams raped out of you? But Violet and I were the two that were the most, um, *unhinged*, I guess you'd say. So, we really bonded. Plus, she's great to go to clubs with. She gets all kinds of attention with her purple skin. Yeah, we're all a bit crazy. Except for you. Outside of talking to yourself, you seem really calm. Almost like you know what's going to happen or something. And what was it you said about being the answer to our prayers? And why did you off yourself so soon? You weren't even raped or anything. You still thought your dreams were coming true."

"Ah yes, that," Angel answered while her sapphire-blue eyes

danced under her long, golden hair. "Well, see, um, hmmm. How do I explain this? Um, do you guys remember the other night when you were dreaming about having a conversation with somebody? Yes? Well, you see, the person you were talking to was me. I was interested in why every starlet that this studio signs ends up dead somehow. So, I thought I'd do a little investigating. And because all of us have come into contact with these men, *we* are connected. And I can, um, connect with those that I'm connected to. Don't ask me how. I just can. So, I came into each of your dreams and asked each of you what had happened to you. And you told me. And you cried. And *I* cried. Because it was the most horrendous, inhumane pile of shit that I had ever heard. And it had all been done to you by these thirteen men. Thirteen men who were about to do the same to me. My first plan was to just tell the studio head that I wasn't coming. But when he threatened my sister and niece, well, that calculation changed, and I knew what I had to do. There was no way out but to kill myself."

"But you had so many other options available to you," Ginger offered. "You could have warned your sister and niece. You could have taken them someplace safe. You could have gone to another part of the country. Why did you immediately jump to suicide? Now you have no way of protecting them. You are powerless up here."

"Well, there's a lot there to unpack, sister," Angel replied through her laughter. "Okay, first. Where could I possibly go in this country that would be safe? These motherfuckers are connected to The Regime. And there's no place to hide from The Regime's thugs. We'd eventually be found and then things would be even worse. And secondly, suicide's really not that big of a deal."

"What are you *talking* about?" a dismayed Violet asked. "Suicide is not that big of a deal? It is finality. It is the end of you. It is not okay to be in a situation where the only plausible escape is killing yourself. Suicide is not a big deal? I think that every person that has been so despondent that they've taken their lives, or tried to, would *very much* disagree with your flippant statement."

"Okay, okay, sorry," the back-tracking Angel replied. "I didn't mean to downplay suicide. You're right. It's one of the most awful things anyone can experience. It is absolutely horrendous to be so depressed and hopeless that you feel as though you have no other choice than suicide. And yes, it *is* a very big deal. It's just that, um, it really isn't that big of a deal for *me*."

The three other ladies stood with confused expressions upon their pretty faces as they waited for further explanation from this new, and very strange, arrival. "You see," Angel continued as her face blushed, "Um, well, this is like the fourth or, um, no it's the *fifth* time I've committed suicide. The first time was when I was six years old. You see, there was this supposed man of God who was getting kinda handsy with me and some of the other girls. So, after he had put my hands down his pants one day, I rushed home with tears in my eyes. Jesus, I remember how ashamed and humiliated that I felt. I just wanted to vomit. But instead, I laid down in a nice, comfy, warm bath, took my father's razor, and sliced my wrists open. I remember feeling so unburdened and free as my life drained out of me. Just before I passed, I uttered this phrase that my mother had just taught me.

"Oh, I forgot to mention that I come from a long line of gypsies who have the ability to connect with the spiritual realm and shit like that. Each member of my family can do different shit. Anyway, I said, 'Release me from my flesh so that I am free to take the flesh of those who would do me harm.' Yep, that's what I said. Same thing I said as I was dying over that film reel. Anyway, I was six years old, and I died. Oh man, my mom was so pissed! She took me out of the bathtub, dried me off, and watched over my lifeless body for three days. You see, it was my first time, and it took me a while to figure out what I was doing after I passed over. So, here I am, a six-year-old little girl, wandering around Enlightenment looking for a vengeful spirit or two to help me out. Because, um, that's *my* Gypsy thing. I can die by suicide, recite that phrase, then get vengeance upon assholes who hurt me in some way. It's pretty neat. Anyway, I was looking for a vengeful spirit to help me out, because I didn't know what the fuck I was doing and had no idea how to get my vengeance on Pastor CreepyAsFuck.

"And I found one! I found a vengeful spirit at a local ice cream shop. He is such a kind man. Bought me some Butter Ripple and listened to my story. He told me that I reminded him of his niece who lived on an Earth in a parallel universe or something, which I thought was sweet. Anyway, I told my story to my new spiritual friend, Uncle Joe, and he said, 'Why that motherfuckin' douchebag.' And before I knew it, I was looking down through the clouds and there was my new friend hovering over that twisted pastor. He whispered something into his ear and that, um, motherfuckin' douchebag, opened his Bible. And then the most amazing thing happened. Uncle Joe returned, put his arm around me and said, 'Now just watch *this* shit.' And I did. I watched. And I could see and feel everything that motherfuckin' douchebag was experiencing. Uncle Joe had made this asshole read Bible verse after Bible verse. And with each verse he read, he was inundated by the hurt and fear and humiliation of one of his victims. Verse after verse he read. And then he felt the anguish of victim after victim. All of that pain just kept piling up in that horrid man's rotting soul until he, um, well, he took a golden candle holder and plunged it down his own throat and choked himself to death with it. And Uncle Joe and I just laughed and laughed. Pretty cool, huh?

"Well, my mom didn't think so. After three days, I woke up in my bed and the first thing I saw was my mom scowling down at me with her arms folded. I tried to explain why I did it and what had happened. But did *that* help? Fuck no! I was *still* grounded for a month. No TV. No video games. No internet. Just school, dinner, and to my room to read the Gypsy Handbook of Ethics and Etiquette, 23rd Edition. Over and over for like, a bajillion times. That month sucked. But it was worth it. The new preacher wasn't a pedo or anything, so *that* was nice. Oh, and the new preacher's wife made waaaaaay better 'tato salad. That's really the only reason why Gypsies go to church. We steal a bunch of shit from the church picnics. And potlucks. And wedding receptions. And, well, you get the point.

"The second time I committed suicide was when I was twelve. This little boy was making fun of me and calling me names like 'Piggy' and shit, which really pissed me off. So, I once again laid in my bathtub, slit my wrists, said my little phrase and was whisked away to Enlightenment. But this was only my second time trying this and I still didn't know what I was doing, so I went looking for Uncle Joe. I looked all over Enlightenment, which is a big fuckin' place! Oh, I guess I don't have to tell *you* guys that. Anyway, I finally found him on one of the parallel Earths beating the fuck out of some guy. Man, Uncle Joe has such a great, warm smile when he's exacting justice on some mother-fuckin' douchebag. Anyway, after he was done, we returned to Enlightenment and I once again told him about my plight. But this time, Uncle Joe didn't think that death was appropriate. I mean, after all, the kid had only called me names. And this is when I learned my greatest lesson from Uncle Joe. The punishment must fit the crime. And this kid committed the crime of making fun of tons of other kids besides me. So, Uncle Joe showed me how *I* can interact with those who had slighted me so that I don't always have to come looking for him for help. It took several days' worth of lessons, but I finally got the knack of it. Just before I imposed my sentence on this little fucker, Uncle Joe whispered into my ear, 'Just remember. The punishment must fit the crime. Otherwise, the punishment may be inflicted upon you.' Then, he just put his arm around me as I made that kid into this big, fat, blobby fucker who farts every time he walks. To this day, he's known as Flabby Freddy Flatulants. Or 'Triple F' for short. He gets laughed at everywhere he goes. Never married. Hell, never even been on a date. He just works at home doing some sort of shit. Anyway, he really shouldn't have made fun of me.

"Now the third time I committed suicide was when I was sixteen. This boy who I had a *huge* crush on went to homecoming with some other little bitch and not me! So, a slit of the wrists, it is. But just as I was about to make his dick fall off, Uncle Joe found me and said that he understood how I felt but the boy hadn't really done anything wrong and if I do something to him, it would boomerang back at me. He didn't really have much to say when I told him that I didn't have a dick to fall off. Nonetheless, he talked me out of it. We had a good time eating ice cream and catching up though.

"Then the fourth time was right after I came to the movie capital of the world, about a year ago. I was all bright-eyed and just sure that I was destined to be a big star. I had the face, the killer bod, um, both literally *and* figuratively, the brains, and the talent. And, if I *did* become a big star, then maybe I'd be insulated from all the nasty shit The Regime was doing to normal people. Although I mainly just wanted to see my name up on a huge marquee in bright lights. Step one was to find an agent. And boy did I find one. He hooked me up with *this* studio, that piece of shit. But then, I left him after he demanded a bit more than a commission from me. I told him to fuck off, that I had my big break, and didn't need him anymore. He then tried to force himself onto me. I kneed him in the balls, ran home, and sliced my wrists open. Uncle Joe and I laughed and laughed once again when we watched his dick and balls fall off of him the next morning in the shower. Oh, and then he bled out. Man, watching the blood circle the drain reminded me so much of *Psycho*. But then his balls and wrinkled up dick clogged the drain and the moment was gone.

"And now, this is my *fifth* suicide and here I am. Except *this* time is different. These men are so *vile*, so *destructive*, so deplete of any *humanity*, that I wanted to do something *special* for them. And I wanted to invite my new friends to play along. So, what do ya say ladies? Do ya wanna see yourself in pictures? Again? Round up the other eight starlets and get your asses into makeup and wardrobe! Because these assholes are about to put the film on. And you do *not* want to miss your scene, heh, heh, heh."

Chapter 3

CASTING CALL

"Oh…my…fucking…*God!*" the ever-bubbly Skipper squealed to her shopping companions, Veronica and Ursula. "What, what is it?" the towering Ursula breathily asked. "Yeah, wazzup? Another shoe sale?" the disinterested brunette, Veronica, asked through her yawn. "You know, we don't really have to go shopping guys. I mean, we can pretty much just conjure up anything that we may ever need. Why waste our time wandering around aimlessly looking at a bunch of stuff that we could just make on our cloud? It's *really* cutting into my nap time."

"But, but," Skipper started to reply before gushing with excitement. "But it's *super fun* to go shopping! I can just as easily use my conjuring coins to buy new stuff than to make it myself! Just look at all of the wonderful things that are in the Cloud Nine Shopping Emporium! Did I *know* that I needed a foot massager before coming here? No! I *never* would have thought to conjure one! But here it is, in my bag! And it cost only 150 conjuring coins! This thing would have cost *at least* 200 conjuring coins if I had made it myself! You know they put the stuff on sale here to encourage us to shop so that they can keep the conjuring economy going."

"No, they don't," the ever-surly Veronica snapped back. "They encourage us to go shopping so that we have something to do. This is

Enlightenment. There is no need for an economy. They just offer us conjuring coins to go shopping or to conjure our own shit so that we'll get involved. It's their way of keeping us from isolating and to contribute to the prayers of the various planets in the various universes. It's just a reward for our participation in shit. And, I must admit, it works. If I didn't need to conjure a new hot tub for my deck, then I never would have responded to that prayer last month. So, I go down to Earth Quatro. Or was Earth Cinco? Oh, who cares? I go to whatever fucking Earth it was and give some motherfucker cancer. Just as his abused wife had been praying for. And for that, I collected a cool 1,000 conjuring coins. Enough for my hot tub and wine and groceries for a month. Once I need something else, I'll volunteer to answer another prayer. But why is it that we can't answer the prayers that we really want to? Why can't we go back to *our* Earth and answer the prayers to take care of those bastards that brutalized us?"

"Because," Ursula answered as she played with her beaded, dirty blonde hair. "Because those are *our* prayers. We can't answer our own prayers. We can only answer the prayers of others, and none of us prayed for anything before we killed ourselves. None of us believed there was anybody to pray to. So, we just blew our brains out, as our Skipper did. Or threw ourselves into a meat grinder as you did, Veronica. Or just take a tumble off a tall building, as I did. We didn't pray, so there was no savior. And there never will be. It seems as though those horrid men will keep torturing innocent, hopeful young women. They will not face justice. Until they die. Then they will face eternal justice. But how many women will be harmed before then? How many will feel the heavy weight of desperation and take their own lives, just as we all did. How many more must suffer before those bastards get to die of natural causes. It isn't fair. But there are no prayers to answer. Except our own. And we are powerless to answer those."

"But *that's* what's so exciting!" Skipper exclaimed as she bounced up and down while clapping causing her pig-tailed blonde hair to fly through the perfect seventy-two-degree breeze. "Our prayers *have* been answered! I just received an emergency text from Ginger! And you would have too if you'd conjure cell phones!" Ursula and Veronica looked at each other, shrugged and said in unison. "We're in Enlightenment. Why would we need cell phones?"

"Uh, for important stuff like taking pictures of the dinner you conjured and posting it and sharing it with your friends on all the other clouds, and getting 'Likes', *obviously*," Skipper immediately retorted. "And for exciting moments just like this! Check this out you two! This is what Ginger has said."

THIS IS A CASTING CALL FOR ALL ACTRESSES WHO HAVE FALLEN VICTIM TO DL PICTURES! We are thrilled to announce a great opportunity to see yourself on the silver screen once again! Our newly arrived producer, Angel Feathers, is offering all actresses who meet her criteria the chance of an after-lifetime! Are you an actress? Did you kill yourself because of mistreatment by DL Pictures? Do you have a headshot and resume? Would you enjoy acting in a scene while exacting painful revenge upon your oppressors? Then you too can play a part in her latest production! Come to Cloud Twenty-Three now! No audition necessary! You must get into wardrobe, make-up, and hair immediately! The show is about to start, and we do not want you to miss your scene. So, get here, now! Also, if anyone is near a bakery, could you pick me up some conjured glazed donuts? I'm out of conjuring coins. Thanks. See you soon, movie stars!

Ursula and Veronica stood silently with their mouths agape before being bombarded with the high-pitched shrieks of two women behind them. "Oh...My...*God*, you guys!" the black-haired, Betty Page-ish looking Claudia screamed in her high-pitched, cartoonish voice as she enveloped Skipper in a tight embrace. "Did you guys see the post? Isn't it exciting?"

"Yes, isn't this the most exciting thing, like, *ever!*" the curly-haired brunette Virgina parroted. "We're back! Back in the movies! Plus, since we're going back to Earth, we're obviously answering a prayer! And you know what *that* means! CHA-CHING! I'm going to be able to afford that pool I've been wanting to conjure! And then, I can get that pool boy that I've always wanted to fu…um…swim with."

"Oh…my…*God!*" Claudia squeaked back. "That is soooo true! I didn't think of that! I wonder if there's a contract or something. I really need to look that over and see just how many conjuring coins this part pays. *Jagged Lies* was a huge hit, and I think I have some negotiating power here. I have a really good head for business and…and… hey…Virginia. Could you help me straighten my head? I feel it starting to slide off. I really wish I hadn't decapitated myself with razor wire."

"Why don't you just conjure your head to completely heal like we've all done with *our* wounds?" Virginia asked. "Well," Claudia's shrill voice responded. "I've been meaning to, but every time I have enough conjuring coins to take care of it, I find something else that I simply can't live without! Like these shoes! Aren't they just fab?"

The other four ladies looked into one of Claudia's many shopping bags and let out an impressed, "Ooooo." "Okay, I'm really not into shopping," an amazed Veronica stated. "But where in the hell did you get those? Those might be the cutest fucking shoes that I've ever seen."

"Well, sorry toots," Claudia haughtily answered. "But these were specially conjured just for me. I knew I didn't have the skills to conjure such adorable pumps, so I had them special-conjured. And they cost me a pretty conjuring coin, let me tell ya. I mean, I can take care of my head *anytime.* How many opportunities will I have to get such a cute pair of shoes conjured?"

The other four ladies stood staring at Claudia in bewilderment until Ursula finally answered. "Um, actually, you'll have infinite opportunities. You're up here for all eternity. You can have those shoes, or anything else for that matter, any time you want them for all time. As long as you have enough conjuring coins."

"Huh, I guess you're right," the contemplating Claudia replied. "I hadn't thought of it like that. Maybe I should just bite the bullet and… oh. Sorry Skipper. I mean, maybe I should just take care of my head and get my luxury items later. Except, I need to conjure up a cabana first. My pool boy has requested to have someplace to change in before he cleans my pool."

"What?" a shocked Virginia yelled out. "You have a *pool*? And a *pool boy*? When in the hell did you conjure those?"

"Oh, last week," Claudia answered. "Or maybe it was last month. I don't really understand time up here. Anyway, it was recently. I was planning on getting my head fixed, but then I heard you talking about wanting a pool and a pool boy and I thought that would be pretty cool. So, I worked a little overtime, answered a couple of extra prayers, and conjured up my pool. And pool boy. And his big, long…"

"You bitch!" Virgina screamed as she lunged at Claudia and began pulling her straight, raven-black hair. "That was *my* idea! You stole *my* pool! You stole *my* pool boy! You stole *my* pool boys big…oh shit! I'm so sorry. I ripped your head off. Here, let me just fix that for you. I'm really sorry. I tend to overreact sometimes. Um, how's *that* feel? It's still a little crooked. Don't worry. I'll fix it. There. Perfect. Besties?"

Claudia tapped her left foot and folded her arms while glaring at Virginia. They stared at one another in cold silence for nearly a minute before Claudia flashed her wide smile, ran up to Virginia, and embraced her. "Yes, of course we're besties! I'm so sorry. I shouldn't have bragged. And you can come over to my pool anytime you want. And you can cum on my pool boy anytime you want too. But I'm sorry. You *can't* wear my shoes. Those are off limits. And that goes for *everybody*. Got it, bitches?"

The other four women quietly nodded in agreement. They knew Claudia to be one of the sweetest and most kind people they had ever met. But not when it came to her shoes. Everybody on Cloud Twenty-Three knew to *never* fuck with Claudia's shoes. Her pool boy? Sure, that was fine. But *never* her shoes.

"Heeeelllloooo Daaaawlings," the approaching Sophia stated in her drawn-out European accent. "Just what are you all standing around here doing? Have you not heard of our opportunity? We really must be getting back to our cloud. Oh, and please remember daaaaawlings. I get the large dressing room. I never know when I might feel a bit… randy. Isn't that right, daaaawling?"

The pink-haired and multiply pierced Randi looked into Sophia's brilliant tan eyes and said, "Oh, yes. We really do need the large dressing room. Because when Sophia feels a bit randy, well, that's my cue. Right Simone?"

A sullen, pretty Black young lady looked up into Randi's smiling, pierced face, nodded in agreement, and sunk her head. "Hey there, Simone," Ursula said softly. "It's so great to see you out and about. We haven't seen you for a while. Still not talking?" Simone vigorously shook her afro while continuing to stare at the ground.

"No, we still haven't been able to get her to talk," Randi responded while solemnly shaking her head. "She's conjured back her tongue. And eyes and ears. But she won't speak. Those bastards really did a number on her. Even in the most tranquil and safe world possible, she keeps to herself. She thinks it's safer that way. She was the only non-white actress that was ever cast by that fucked up studio. She shot her movie *Speak No Evil, Hear No Evil, See No Evil*. And she was a badass the entire time. She never put up with any of their shit. When those fuckers would call her a derogatory name, she would shoot right back. She was the very definition of an empowered woman. Until her screening. You guys think *we* went through a rough time? What happened to us is *nothing* compared to what they did to her. They loved watching women suffer. But this was a *Black* woman. She was exotic. A special treat for them. And they took their time with her doing all sorts of twisted shit. They told her that every time she screamed, it would get worse. And it did. Until she stopped scream-ing. They put headphones on her and blared her own screams into her ears until she went deaf. They made her watch the film of all the brutality that they had inflicted upon her. Over and over and over she watched the film of them doing the most heinous things to her. While listening to her own screaming. When she was finally released back to her cell, she took a jagged piece of stone that had fallen out of the wall and cut off her ears. Then she pulled out her tongue. And finally, she gouged each of her eyes out. She lay on that cold, stone floor and slowly bled out. Then, she came here. But she's never been the same. She'll *never* be the same. And I fear she may never speak again. We haven't shown her Virginia's text yet. We're not sure how she'll take it."

"Which is why, my daaaawlings, that our sweet Sophia is under *my* constant protection. I know there is a rumor going around that the three of us are involved in a bit of a three-way love affair. Such silly, catty chatter. My lovely Randi and I are, of course, intimately involved. But *not* our Simone. She has no interest in such things. She is merely our sweet, dear friend. A friend that we will protect at all costs. Now, I shall ask again. What are we all doing standing around? We have a movie to produce."

"Yeah, we'd better get shakin'!" Skipper exclaimed. "But before we do, Sophia, I just have to ask. I noticed you always wear a fur coat. And you have three more new ones in your bags. Why? It's always seventy-two degrees with no humidity here. Aren't you warm?"

"No, my dawwwwling," Sophia answered as she pulled her expensive sunglasses down upon her petite nose and stared intensely at Skipper. "I am *not* warm. *I* am *hot*. Hot as the burning sun. Because, daaawling. *I* am a *star*."

Simone looked up and tugged at Sophia's fur-adorned arm. "Yes, my daaaawling, what is it?" Simone pointed at Sophia's phone, looked up at her, and shrugged. "You want to know what we are about to do? Well, my daaaawling, it is something very special. But I am not sure that it is something that you need to be involved with. Or know about. Here, my daaawling. Let us get you back to your home where you feel safe, and I will tell you all about it. But please. Not here, daaawling. This is not the place for you to experience such memories."

Simone scowled at Sophia, stomped her foot, and pointed once against the phone. "I think we need to tell her," Randi advised. "Very well. Step back ladies. I never really know what might cause one of her episodes."

"No, we're fine," Ursula stated. "Yeah, we're here for her," echoed Virginia. "Anything that hurts her, hurts us too," Skipper agreed. "We are one with her," Veronica contributed. "Now and forever," Claudia squeaked in conclusion.

"Very well, then, daaaawlings," Sophia replied as she pulled out her phone. "Here daaawling. Just read this. This is what we have been speaking about." Simone began reading Ginger's casting call. The further she read, the wider her eyes grew. The further she read, the more sweat dripped from her ebony brow. The further she read, the more violently her body shook. The further she read, the more intense the storm in her mind became. Sophia tenderly placed her long forefinger under Simone's chin and lifted her eyes to greet her own. "And that, daaawling is what we are going to get ready for, What do you think about that?"

Simone looked away from her friend for a moment. Her mind was whirling with the sadistic sounds and images of her own torture. She felt as though she was once again drowning in a sea of pain and despair. She clenched her eyes shut and clapped her hands over her ears. Her seven friends encircled her and enveloped her shaking body in their warm embrace. Simone looked back up at the smiling, caring, beautiful faces of her friends. Her protectors. Her sisters.

She wiped sweat from her brow and smiled widely before opening her mouth and saying in a deep, determined voice, "What do I *think* about that? I'll tell you what I think. I think it's time we fucked up those White devils. Now, get me to my dressing room. I wanna look *fine* for this shit. And here is my rider. I want absolute privacy while I'm preparing for my part. I want twelve bottles of sparkling water. I want a fifth of whiskey. Canadian. And I want a box of Oreos. With all the white shit scraped out of 'em."

Everyone at the Cloud Nine Shopping Emporium jumped as they suddenly heard eight women burst out in joyous cheers and clapping and crying. The eight huddled women laughed and sobbed together until Simone broke their euphoric moment. "But just one question. Who the *fuck* is this honky bitch, Angel Feathers? What the fuck is she? A missionary stripper?"

CHAPTER 4

AND INTRODUCING, ANGEL FEATHERS

"Welcome ladies, welcome," the flame-red haired Ginger stated as she lovingly embraced each of the new arrivals to their cloud. "I trust that each of you have seen my rather exciting message. And I trust that each of you are ready to once again see your smiling faces flickering on the silver screen."

Her statement was greeted by an exuberant cheer by ten enthralled actresses. The smiling Ginger waved her hands for silence before continuing. "Yes ladies. This is the moment that we have all dreamed about since we were little girls. A moment when we could escape our humdrum lives and take on another one. Another face. Another hair style. Another personality. Another life that would be shown to millions upon millions of people across the globe. The moment when we would be greeted by red carpets and flashing cameras and autograph seekers. A moment when we would be seen as somebody special. Somebody important. Somebody with worth.

"As we all know, under The Regime, women were seen as nothing more than domestic servants and playthings and baby factories. We were stripped of any potential for higher education and fulfilling careers. We were stripped of any way of achieving a meaningful life. We were sentenced to a life of servitude, shackled to some man, or men. Making their meals. Cleaning up after them. Doting on them. Giving the obligatory blow job. That was the average woman's lot in life.

"But not the starlets. We watched them on our screens and dreamed of a life of glamour just like they had. We dreamed of having enough money to be self-sufficient. We dreamed of making our own choices of who we would be involved with. We dreamed of being acknowledged for our talent and individuality. Yes, we each had those dreams of fame and all the trappings that came along with it.

"But our dreams weren't purely narcissistic. We saw being a movie star as an escape. An escape from a life of somber servitude to one of respect and adoration by the masses. We were each discovered. We were each cast in big budget motion pictures. We each saw our dreams coming to fruition as we watched our movies for the first time in a private screening. A private screening with the thirteen men who had made our dreams a reality. Thirteen men who turned our dreams into living nightmares from the moment the credits rolled. They beat us. Humiliated us. Raped us. Degraded us. Repeatedly. Over and over, we were forced into performing the most deplorable acts. We had not escaped submissive doldrum. We had entered a sadistic hell. Our lives were not glamorous. They were destitute. They were hopeless. So hopeless that each one of us eventually reached our breaking point and took our own lives. These thirteen men had gone from being our dream makers into our sadistic captors.

"And each one of us prayed for justice to be served. As each one of us arrived on this very cloud in Enlightenment, we embraced. Our tears flowed from our mutual understanding of the cruelty we were forced to escape by committing the ultimate sacrifice. And our tears flowed as we watched young woman after young woman also fall prey to these maniacal perverts. We prayed to Enlightenment for it all to stop. We prayed to not allow yet another innocent woman be beaten and humiliated as we all had been. We prayed for justice against these horrific creatures. But our prayers were not answered. Our own prayers can *never* be answered. And so, we sat up in our cloud, and we watched and we wept and we prayed. And we dreamed once again.

We dreamed of our Earth becoming a place where women are given their due respect and station in society.

"Equal opportunities for education. Equal opportunities for careers. Equal opportunities for control over our own bodies. Equal opportunities for choosing who to love. Equal opportunities to be people who could hold their heads high as we walked down our streets brimming with pride and self-confidence. Equal opportunities to be equal to men. But as we watched from our cloud, we knew that our dreams were just that. Dreams. Just like our dreams of using fame to claim our independence. They were just that. Dreams. Dreams that turned into our own fiery pits of suffering. We watched and we prayed and day by day we lost hope. Hope that there would come a time for equality. Hope that women would be respected. And hope that there would ever be justice against these thirteen horrific men. Our hope was lost. So, we swam. We went shopping. We conjured new furniture for our homes. And we did our best to answer the prayers of others from some planet somewhere in the multiple universes. We have all resigned ourselves to a peaceful, yet largely unfulfilling existence. Not terribly unlike what we would have had on Earth. Our prayers would not be answered, and our dreams of equality and justice would never be realized.

"Until today. Today, another fallen angel has joined us. But this angel is different. *This* angel is a gypsy who has very special abilities. Just like us, this angel has killed herself. But she is different from us. Following her self-imposed death, this angel can return to Earth as a ghost. A very, very, frightening ghost who can impose her retribution on those that have wronged her. She has done it several times. And this time, she has targeted thirteen very evil men. Those same men who abused *us*. Each of us are connected to these thirteen men. And because of that, our latest arrival, our newest fallen angel, has the ability to invite us to play along with her. So, ladies, please join me in welcoming our latest fallen angel and the producer of your next motion picture. It is my great pleasure to introduce you to...Angel Feathers!"

Angel wiped an appreciative tear from her blue eye, straightened her white, flowing gown and stepped forward to address her congregation of sisters. "Thank you so much Ginger for that incredible introduction. And thank you ladies for the warm reception. It truly is an honor to be with each of you here tonight. You are all such incredible actresses, and I have seen each of you in your films. You are my inspiration. But I really need to clear something up. You see, my name *isn't* Angel Feathers. That was a horrible stage name that DL Studios came up with. It makes me sound like a missionary stripper or something. I fucking hate it."

Simone playfully jabbed Sophia in her ribs and whispered, "See? Toldja." "No, that isn't my name," Angel continued. "You see, my *real* name is…" She was suddenly interrupted by Claudia's high-pitched squeak. "So, tell us about these parts we're gonna be playing! And can I bring my pool boy to the set?" The rest of the women began clapping and chanting, "Show us the script! Show us the script! Show us the script!"

"Okay, okay," Angel answered through her chuckles. "Just unbind your panties for a second. I'll explain everything. But before I do, I just wanted to tell you that my name is…" She was interrupted once again, this time by Skipper. "What part will I have? Will I be powerful? And how am I gonna get on the screen? How is this gonna work? And how does any of this relate to those assholes on Earth? But, most importantly, what part will I have? Am I the lead? You know, with my girl-next-door looks, I really should be the lead. Why, I was absolutely *brilliant* in *Star Spangled Firing Squad* and…"

"Why in the hell should *you* play the lead?" Ursula roared as her dirty-blonde braided hair swayed. "Why, if this is a picture about retribution, then *I* should play the lead. Just look at me! I'm over six feet tall! I'm muscular! I could take my ghost hands and rip those fuckers heads off! And I do my own stunts! That's right! I did every stunt myself in *Blind Bondage*! No, if anybody here deserves to play the lead, it's definitely me! You can be my sidekick or kid sister or something. You sure as hell have the name for it, *Skipper*."

"Well, speaking of names," Angel attempted to interject before being interrupted once again. "Oh, daaawling," Sophia interjected.

"You are *all* fine actresses. But none of you has won a DL Studios FIFA Award for best acting like I have. Oh, how I wish I had been there that night to accept my award for my powerful performance in *The Black Tide*. It would have been *such* a grand speech in front of a global audience. Unfortunately, I was drowning in the ocean at that moment."

"Um," the lavender skinned Violet stated. "Yeah, I'm sure it *would* have been a great speech, Sophia. But you *do* realize that the FIFA Award for Best Actress isn't really a thing, right? It's just something that DL Studios made up in order to promote their own films and put asses in the seats. And, like, absolutely *nobody* watched those awards. Hell, they couldn't even get people to attend the ceremony at the Dear Leader Center for the Performing Arts. Remember when we were looking down and watching it? The front few rows of the theatre were filled with so-called dignitaries from the studio and The Regime. The back half and the balcony of the theatre were filled with cardboard cutouts of people. Seriously! They couldn't even find real people as seat-fillers! They had to use cardboard cutouts! And not only that, they used the same ones over and over! The camera scanned the "crowd", and every fifth cutout was that blond dude! And next to him, this red-headed chick. And next to her, some bald guy. And on and on, throughout the entire theatre it was the same five fucking cutouts! I guess it was better than all the empty theatre seats when Dear Leader's wife, or mistress, or whatever the fuck *that* thing is, made some bullshit documentary about herself. Remember that? It totally fucking bombed! Like, it was the worst fucking debut in the history of movies! And that's saying something. Anyway, all I'm saying is that the stupid FIFA Award for Best Actress isn't really a thing. Oh, and because of my exotic lavender skin, I should play the lead."

"You want fuckin' exotic?" Simone fired back. "*Any* of you could conjure up some purple fucking paint to slap on your pasty-white asses. *That's* not exotic. That's nothing but make-up. Now, *I'm* exotic. How many Black women do you see in the movies? I mean, that aren't being beaten, raped, and murdered. There are a lot of those. But Black women who have a real part in the film? Here's the answer you're struggling for. None. Absolutely fucking none. Which is why my performance in *Speak No Evil, Hear No Evil, See No Evil,* was so groundbreaking. The Regime's anti- diversity, equity, and inclusion program stripped Black folks and, well, pretty much all non-White folks from any parts in any films or TV shows. It was like we didn't even exist anymore. Well, except to be portrayed as lawless savages. There were plenty of *those* parts for us. But that was a really finite fucking career now, wasn't it? Because when the audience saw a Black person being shot in the film, they didn't realize that that person was *really* being shot! They had *no idea* that they were watching an actual snuff film! So fucked up, man. Anyway, I think that the lead should be exotic. And there's no fucking bitch here that's more exotic than me. So, move over bitches. It's time for Simone to shine."

"Okay, okay, ladies, I think we may have gotten a bit off track here," Angel said in an attempt to regain control of the group. She was immediately interrupted by Veronica. "You want to know who should play the lead in a film about retribution? Well, you're looking at her sisters! Who better to play the lead in a movie that's gonna be all bloody and shit than the heralded scream-queen star of *Meatgrinder Mayhem!*" The group fell into a confused silence, looked at each other, and shrugged.

"You know, *Meatgrinder Mayhem,*" an embarrassed Veronica continued. "Didn't any of you see it? It was *only* the highest-grossing horror film that year!" Veronica began seething as she watched her friends snickering and whispering to one another. "Oh, *I* get it. I was a scream queen who starred in a horror flick. So, I'm not *talented* enough to play the lead in any *other* type of movie, now, am I? Why, you petty, pigeon-holing bitches. Let me tell you all something! There are *tons* of great actresses who got their start in horror movies! Not only that, there are *tons* of great actresses who made a *living* being in horror movies! But they couldn't get a part outside of that genre because pigeon-holing assholes like *you* never gave them a chance! The same chance *you* were looking for when you arrived in that god-forsaken town with stars in your eyes. So, my being in a horror movie doesn't mean that I'm any less talented than you!

"And here's *another* thing! I'm sick of horror movies getting a bad rap. Is some of it junk? Sure. Just like every *other* fucking genre. But some of the most intricate societal examinations have come from horror movies. Or horror books, for that matter! Have any of you read the *Hanging Chads* series by Evan Clouse? No? Well, pretty much nobody *else* has either, but that's not the point. You should! That's some brilliant insight into human nature and the psychological effects of society's abuse. Oh, and there's shit tons of blood too. Just because a book or a film has gory kills doesn't make it any less important as a work of art in society! The murders are just the money shot to keep the viewer interested. The *real* story lies in the plot and the character development and the subtextual messaging that lies under its dark veneer. Fuckin' duh.

"Oh, and one *more* thing! Horror fans are like, the best fucking people in the world! They are sweet and respectful and are almost always animal lovers. They care about their fellow human beings because they have humanity. Yeah, horror fans, the same people who revel in watching all this twisted mayhem on the screen, are the most humane motherfuckers I've ever met. Just tell me, who would you rather spend a weekend with? A bunch of fake-blood-soaked horror fans whose biggest argument is who was the best Jason? Or a bunch of tight-assed Bible bangers who sit in the corner and whisper their holier-than-thou judgements on everybody in the room. While eating their tasteless fucking potato salad and ham sandwiches. Well, *I'll* take my respectful horror crowd over those self-righteous, bigoted, pervy religious fucks any day."

"As would I," Candace contributed. "Yeah, my movie, *Skin Tight, Up All Night* got protested by those assholes every night in every city. Do they protest children being gunned down in their schools? No. Do they protest The Regime's brutalizing citizens in the streets? No. Do they protest the crushing of people's civil rights? No. No, they protest a fucking movie about a teen-age runaway because it shows a little too much skin for their liking. Which, let's be honest. They *like* a little skin. In fact, they like a *lot* of fucking skin. Especially *children's* skin. You ever notice who it is that gets picked up for child sexual assault and kiddie porn? Is it a drag queen? Nope. Is it an immigrant? Nope.

Is it a horror fan? Nope. It is *almost always* some Bible-banging fuck who has passed his judgement on everybody around him while he's diddling his five-year-old daughter every night. *That's* who society needs to be afraid of! Not your run of the mill church-going types. Most of them are okay, I guess. But those that preach fire and brimstone from their towering pulpit and proclaim to know the word of God are narcissistic, twisted motherfuckers who think they're all-powerful and beyond the reach of society. *Those* are the motherfuckers we should be afraid of. *Those* are the motherfuckers to never leave your kids with. Anyway, my point is. I think that *I* should play the lead in Angel's production."

"I don't really care who plays the lead," Virgina contributed. "I just want to have a full bar in my dressing room. Just like I had on the set of *Know When to Say When*. Oh, and I'd also like a pool boy."

"Well, *I* care about who plays the lead!" Randi screamed. "I was incredible in *Acid Test*! I had the full range baby! I can do drama. I can do humor. I can do…"

"Drugs?" one of the women shouted out. Randi was infuriated as she heard her friends' immediate laughter. "No, not drugs," Randi haughtily replied. "That *wasn't* what I was going to say. Why? Anybody holding? What do you have? I used my last conjuring coins on some coke last night and I could really use a bump."

"Okay everybody, that's enough!" Angel screamed. "I want silence! Now! Time is short! Just look down there! They're cleaning the blood off of my body and putting me into a baby-doll dress. Fucking gross. Oh Jesus. When this is over and I return to my body, I'm going to have to clean so much cum off of my skin. And my hair and…okay. Not important right now! Please, ladies, please. Just be quiet for a moment and listen to me. The movie that I'm producing is a, um, compilation of sorts. Twelve different little stories. Twelve different little scenes. And twelve very different and very talented lead actresses. Yes, each of you will be starring in your very own little vignette. Now, here are your scripts. There's not much dialogue. It's mostly, um, action. Oh, and you'll probably want a shower after you finish your scene.

"Anyway, get into hair, make-up, and wardrobe. Be ready for when your scene is called. You have a very short window of opportunity to get into this film. If you miss your cue, then you miss your scene. And if you miss your scene, one of *these* motherfuckers gets to go free. And we don't want *that* now, do we ladies? Oh, and one final thing. Stop calling me Angel Feathers! My real name is…

CHAPTER 5

SHOWTIME

"Who in the *fuck* is Renata Miazga?" Pug Homleyman yelled out as he watched the opening credits of *Take My Hand*. "The fucking credits say, 'And Introducing, Renata Miazga'! Who in the hell is *that?*"

"Um, um," the Casting Director, Bob Lemmings, nervously responded. "I, I have no idea. This is *supposed* to say 'And Introducing, Angel Feathers'. Um, let me just look in my casting notes. Just one minute."

There was the sound of papers being searched while the soaring orchestra was playing on the film. Billowing white clouds basking in sunshine was being projected behind the opening credits as the lush, swelling orchestral arrangement played. "What the fuck? It keeps saying the same thing! It's like it's on a loop or something!" Pug yelled out. "Yeah, yeah, yeah, we've seen these fucking credits five times already! Executive Producer Ezekial Winthrop III. Always nice to use your money, Zeke. Directed by Justin Scallop. Assistant Director Kellen Richardson. You two are quite the pair, aren'tcha? You do *everything* together. I'm really looking forward to seeing you DP our little dead starlet. But be careful with her! She's as stiff as Dear Leader at a kiddie beauty pageant!

"Music Composed by Arpeggio Dante. Man, you really did

compose some sappy shit for *this* one, Peggy. Not sure how we're gonna get our dead Angel here to peg you after the film's over though. Maybe we can ball her hands up into a fist and someone can jam it up your ass for ya. I dunno. We'll figure it out. Costume Designer, Phillip Phillips. Huh. We're gonna have the same problem with you, PP. We can't force a corpse into pissing on you, and I know you can't cum until she does. Fuck. Maybe we'll all just piss in a soda cup then pour it on your face while you're eating her cold snatch. Let that be a lesson boys! When the world gives you lemons, piss in a cup and pour it over your pervy friend's face!

"Written by James Proctor. What book did you rip off *this* time to come up with *this* script, James? Doesn't matter. We've got lawyers and the dumbass authors don't. We can steal whatever the fuck we want and there's nothing they can do about it. Yeah, you're a pretty sad excuse for a writer. Sure, you can string together some words to come up with a well-formed sentence, but you don't have an original thought in your fucking head! That's alright. Neither does the audience. They just gobble up the same fucking stories with the same fucking characters who act out the same fucking tropes over and over and over. Less is more, right James? The less originality you have, the more shit you sell! But try to be original tonight, wouldja? Every time we have one of our gangbangs, all you do is copy whoever fucked her before you. Someone just plugged her ass? Well, there goes James's cock up her ass. Somebody just bit one of her nipples off? James bites her *other* nipple off. Somebody just whipped the shit out of her? James comes along and has to whip her harder. It's really fucking boring, man. We're doing a corpse tonight. Try to think of something original to do with it, wouldja?

"And here it is *again*! Edited by Kyle Splicer! You did a real bang-up job on *this* one, Kyle! Why did you edit the opening credits to keep running, over and over? See? Once again, we have the Director of Photography, Sam Shutter! This really was some of your best work, Sam. Damn, how you got shots of the sun coming through her white nightgown to provide just a hint of sexual titillation in this moral puke fest. Yeah, you definitely gave those hypocritical Christians something to go home and jerk off to.

"Production Design, Jake Johnson. You really did a good job on this film, Jake. You had to construct a whole town that looked pure and wholesome 'cause there aren't any of those fuckin' places left! Yeah, Dear Leader has seen to it that what used to be quaint little peaceful farm communities are now filled with polluted air, toxic streams, rotting buildings, and depressed peasants who work on their former family farms under the agricultural oligarchs. What a bunch of dumb fucks. They actually *voted* for this shit. You know. When voting was still a thing. Anyway, nice job on the set.

"Ah, and now our cast. And starring Crash Collins and Lance Thruster. This is so fuckin' rich. These stupid fucking Christians are going to watch a supposedly wholesome family film that stars two of the biggest, and I do mean *biggest*, gay porn stars to ever blow their wad on camera. And well, on pretty much everything else too. Jesus, can you two shoot a stream of jizz. It's almost artful the way you can splatter anything within ten feet of you. It really is a talent, boys, heh, heh, heh. I cast you two in this one on purpose just to fuck with the holy rollers. Plus, we want to keep our little club together, now don't we boys?

"And there it is again! And Introducing Renata Miazga! And look! It's just frozen there now! The clouds are still moving and the music's still playing, but her name is just sitting there! Were you fucking drunk when you edited this shit, Kyle? And where is *Angel's* name?" Pug wrapped his arm around the stiffening, made-up corpse that was sitting in the red velour theatre seat next to him and said softly, "Yeah, I'm really sorry about this baby. You wanted to see your name on the silver screen didn't you? Don't worry baby, we'll fix this before it's released in the theatres. And you'll thank me by spreading those stiff, blue legs of yours, now, won't you?"

"Um, actually," Bob Lemmings commented. "She *is* seeing her name on the silver screen. I found the audition notes. Renata Miazga is Angel's real name. No wonder why we changed it. That name isn't memorable at all."

"No, *that* name fuckin' sucks," Pug snorted. "I remember now when she first came into her audition. A pretty, innocent face. Long, blonde hair with a slight natural curl. Perfect tits and an ass you could bounce a quarter off of. And those fuckin' legs. Jesus Christ baby, you were hot. I mean, you're pretty fucking cold *now*, but your body is still fucking hot. And what a stupid fuckin' name! Renata Miazga! That's not the name of a starlet. That's the name of a Hungarian bag lady or some shit. So, we changed it. We knew we were going to use you for our line of religious family flicks. We knew you looked like the wholesome girl next door that every mother wanted as a daughter-in-law, and every man wanted to fuck. And Angel Feathers was born. Kinda made you sound like a missionary stripper. Which was the whole point. Watch this little bitch, fellas! Here's a girl you pray with on a Sunday morning, then take home, bend over, and fuck that lily-white ass! It was fucking brilliant. But why is her *real* name on this, and why is it just frozen there on the screen? We've been watching the same fucking credits for fifteen minutes! I've heard of filler, but this is fucking ridiculous!"

The men stared at the screen in silence as the sun shone upon Renata's name causing it to glow in a brilliant white. They then gasped as the name turned to a dark red. "Wow, *that's* weird," Pug stated. "How is it that her blood only stained her *name* on this portion of the film? The whole frame should have turned red. And is that a laugh track I'm hearing? Listen, boys. Do you hear it? Does anybody else hear that woman's laughter? This shit had better not be on the other prints or by God I'm gonna…oh, wait. Finally. The movie's starting. And there she is. Our little Angel in the prime of her short life. Let's just sit back, relax, and watch *Take My Hand* starring our deceased little Angel. Hey, Peggy. Pass me the popcorn. No, not the pretzel sticks. I know what you do with that shit. Just the popcorn."

The swooning orchestra continued to play as the opening shot in the movie showed Renata's character putting damp garments on a clothesline. The morning sun shined through her pure white dress, revealing her shapely silhouette. Her glistening blonde hair swayed in the breeze, mimicking the motion of the golden wheat in the background. From a distance, you could hear a woman's voice calling out a name. "Chastity! Chastity, dear! Finish your laundry and come in for breakfast! Your eggs are getting cold!"

"I'll be right there, Momma!" Renata's character, Chasity, yelled back in her youthful voice. She grasped the gold crucifix that was hanging from her neck, looked up to the wispy clouds in the sky, and thoughtfully said, "Thank you, Lord, for blessing me with my family. I am so lucky to have been born to such a loving pair of parents. My only desire is to serve them, Lord. Oh, and you too, of course! But if I could ask for just one favor Lord. Could you please tell my brother, Chad, to stop looking at those nature magazines? I fear that the pictures of those naked savage women may be giving him impure thoughts, Lord. Thank you. Coming Momma!"

Chastity whistled and skipped toward her two-story Victorian pure-white home. She opened the gate on the freshly painted picket fence and continued to skip into her kitchen which was bathing in the Lord's sunlight. "Good morning, Momma!" She said before pecking her father's cheek and saying, "And good morning, Poppa!"

"Oh, fuck, man," Crash Collins said as he watched the movie. "This was the first scene I shot with her. I got so fucking hard when she kissed me on the cheek." "I know what you mean," Lance Thruster replied. "Every scene I was in with her, all I could think about was how much I wanted to fuck my "sister". Well, and my *daddy*, heh, heh, heh. I can't wait until the Christians watch this shit. They'll all be raving about how holy and inspirational it is. Meanwhile, we'll have memories of fucking the lead actress's corpse."

"Good morning, pumpkin," Chastity's father greeted. "And just what good deeds does my lovely daughter have planned for today?" "Oh, Poppa, I'm *so* glad you asked," Chastity enthusiastically answered. "Well, after I finish the laundry, I shall do my Bible study. You and Momma are so right. Young women can learn all that they need to from the scriptures. I think that these women who are marching to get access to higher education are just silly. Why, all we need to know is how to read and write so that we may read our Lord's message and write loving poems and stories about his love for us. And we learn that by the sixth grade. Oh, how I feel those women are just evil for wanting to learn more so that they can steal jobs away from our men. Don't they understand that men have been placed upon our Earth to provide and women are here to support them? Don't they understand that women's minds are too cluttered and we are too emotionally fragile to do anything but tend to our mates and households and children? I simply don't understand it, Poppa."

"Well, *I* do," Chastity's mother stated after getting an approving nod from her husband. "I understand those women quite well. I went to school with a number of them until I dropped out and committed my life to worshipping our Lord, Dear Leader. And supporting my husband. Those women are evil, Chastity. They are whores. They think of nothing but themselves and take opportunities away from their men. And speaking of men, these whores will lie with any man who crosses their path. They are godless creatures, Chastity, who do not deserve our respect."

"Your mother is quite right," her father replied. "They are trash. They use their bodies for the most godless activities. Then, they want to abort one of God's children. They actually believe that they have dominion over their own bodies. You know you are in the presence of a demon, Chastity, when they say that their body does not belong to God. Or to our Lord, Dear Leader."

"Yes," Chasity stated after thoroughly chewing and swallowing a bite of scrambled eggs. "You are so right. Only a demon would deny God's providence over their body. Only a demon would not believe in the sanctity of the life that is growing inside of them. And because of their sins, they must be punished. They must bring that precious life into the world and find a way to support it without expecting handouts from our most generous regime. They must suffer and their child must suffer so that they both have the opportunity to become pious. Thank you, Momma. Thank you, Poppa. Thank you for your love and teachings."

"So, what shall you do following your Bible study?" her father inquired further. "You mustn't have idle hands, for that is where the devil lurks." "Oh, how I know," Chasity responded. "Sitting around with nothing to do can lead to all sorts of sinful thoughts, Poppa. That is why I will then retrieve the fresh eggs from the chicken coop and take them into town to sell them. Dear Leader has blessed us so with high prices for eggs. There is a shop in the restricted side of town that I thought I might try. I have heard that they do not have many staples there, and I thought I might get a better price for our eggs."

Chastity's father looked sternly at his daughter's bright face and said in a deep voice, "No, Chastity. No. You are *never* to go to the restricted side of town. There is a reason why they are surrounded by checkpoints and electric gates. The most evil vermin reside there, Chastity. The (obligatory term omitted) and the (obligatory term omitted) and the (obligatory term omitted) live there. They will rape you, Chastity. They will murder you. They are nothing but savage cockroaches who will tear you apart. Dear Leader has been wise to keep them away from us, the rightful citizens of our nation. It is for our safety and protection. And it is for *your* safety and protection, Chastity, that I forbid you from *ever* going to the restricted side of town. Do you understand?"

"Yes, Poppa, I understand about most of them, I think," Chastity replied while her cheeks glowed in an embarrassed rose hue. "I certainly understand about those who look differently from us. The dark-skinned ones. I understand that one's skin reflects the purity of one's soul. That is why Dear Leader is keeping the dark-skinned ones away from us. Because they have no souls. But Poppa, I do not under-stand why there are some there that look like *us*. What have *they* done to be placed amongst the soulless?"

"They are placed there, my daughter," her father answered, "Because, although they may *look* like us, they are not *like* us. They are tricksters who impersonate those with a soul. But they are just as soulless as the other creatures that reside there. They are soulless because they do not believe in the divinity of our lord and savior. Be careful around them. They may look and speak like you and I, but they are not. The moment you show them the slightest bit of human-ity, they will steal the shirt right off of your back. They will take every penny from your wallet. They will pluck the gold fillings from your mouth. They do not worship our Lord. They worship money. They worship things. And I will not have them eating my eggs. Is that clear?"

"Of course, Poppa," Chastity answered while wearing a beaming smile upon her pure white face. "I believe that I will begin my Bible study *this instant*. All of this talk of demons has made me yearn for the word of our Lord. Thank you for a lovely breakfast, Momma. And thank you for your wisdom, Poppa." Chastity pranced up the stairs with the sun shining through her sheer white gown.

"Jesus, you can nearly see her pubes in this shot," Pug exclaimed. "Really nice lighting and camera work there, Sam. Oh shit! A nipple! I just saw a nipple! Oh fuck, those pervy fuckin' Christians are gonna eat this shit up."

Chastity raced into her room, lovingly picked her Bible up from her nightstand, and sat at the edge of her bed with perfect posture. She opened the book as the camera slowly zoomed into her tranquil face.

"Is it getting cold in here?" Pug answered as he buttoned his suit.

Chastity's brilliant blue eyes looked directly into the camera.

"What the hell is that clicking sound?" Pug asked. "It sounds like all the theatre doors are locking."

Chastity's moist, red lips curled upward into a knowing smile as the film turned blood red.

"Aw shit, this must be one of the sections that this bitch bled all over," Pug lamented. "Huh, I kinda like it though. Gives it kind of an evil look. Doesn't work for this holier-than-thou piece of shit, but for a horror movie? It's not a bad idea. Somebody want to check the temperature? And the doors?"

Chastity opened her pouty lips and said in a dark voice, "Oh, you *really* don't need the temperature to be raised. Believe me, gentlemen, you will be getting plenty warm soon enough."

"What the hell?" James blurted out. "That wasn't in my script. Or in anything that I've ever read. There's no way I could have ripped off that line. What in the hell is she talking about?"

He was interrupted by Chastity's booming voice blaring out of the theatre's surround-sound speakers. "Good evening, gentlemen. It is a pleasure to be with you tonight. I am speaking to you as my character in my movie, Chastity. You, of course, know me by the name that you gave me, Angel Feathers. But that *isn't* my *real* name. My *real* name is Renata Miazga. That was the name my parents gave me when I was born, and I *cherish* my name. This specific name was given to me because my parents knew of my special abilities. You see, Renata means to be reborn. And as you gentleman can clearly see, I *have* been reborn. Reborn to be with you tonight on this most special evening. And my last name, Miazga, means to pulp or crush. I think that *that* will become clear to you as well as our evening proceeds. You see, I have the special ability to be reborn if I recite a certain little phrase following my suicide. Yes, I can be reborn then visit those who have, um, let's just say *mistreated* me. So, I have been reborn to be with you tonight, gentlemen. And it is most certainly my greatest pleasure.

"And you gentlemen *really* don't need the doors to be opened," Renata continued as the entire theatre was bathed in the deep red hue of the film. "You don't want to go *anywhere*. Surely, you wouldn't want to miss some of the *edits* that I've made to your movie, would you? They really *are* to die for. And it will be such a *special experience* for you. Yes, all thirteen of you. I am going to give each and every one of you the same opportunity that you gave me. The opportunity to see yourself on the silver screen. Yes, each and every one of you will play a little part in my movie. And I have cast some *amazing* actresses to be your co-stars. I think you just may recognize them. Now, gentlemen, just sit back and relax until you are called to play your part in your special scene. Oh, and you may want to get some more popcorn. It *may* just be your last meal, heh, heh, heh."

Chapter 6

Pointless Resistance

"I don't know what the hell is going on, but I'm getting out of here," Ezekial Winthrop III stated as he got up from his theater seat and rushed up the carpeted aisle towards the front exit. He grabbed the handle and immediately screamed in anguish as 150,000 volts of electricity shot into his fingers and coursed through his body. He collapsed on the gaudy carpet sobbing in a puddle of his own urine.

"Now, now, Mister Winthrop," Renata's smiling, blood-red image said from the movie screen. "Don't you know that it's rude to leave in the middle of a movie? Why, just look at how you've disturbed the other patrons. And look at the mess you've made on the floor. Such a shame. A grown man soiling himself. Please, Mister Winthrop. Just go back to your seat and relax. Leaving the theatre through that exit is quite impossible as you've just learned. Besides, why would you want to leave? This movie is going to be quite electrifying."

"Oh, fuck this!" Lance Thruster yelled at the screen. "I'm getting the fuck out of here!" He rushed to the front side of the theatre towards the emergency exit. He placed his hands upon the metal door's push bar and began screaming. The entire theatre was filled with a sizzling sound and the scent of burning flesh as his hands were being cooked upon the door. He ripped his hands from the bar, leaving strips of frying skin popping and snapping upon it. He looked down at his scorched hands, hung his head, and solemnly proceeded back to his theatre seat.

"Oh, Lance," Renata's image chided. "You are quite the ham, aren't you? You certainly smell like one at the moment. Did you know that I had a huge crush on you? Your firm body with bulging muscles. Your sculpted facial features covered in the perfect amount of stubble. And that ass! Damn, baby, I bet you could bounce a quarter off of that thing."

"S-stop t-talking a-a-about me l-l-like a p-piece of m-m-meat," The sobbing Lance stated while looking at his medium-rare cooked hands. "Oh, right," Renata countered. "Yes, you certainly wouldn't want to be objectified, would you? You wouldn't want to be judged just based upon your looks, right? Of course not. You are so much more than that. Your brains. Your acting talent. Your, um, oh, who the fuck are we kidding? The only reason you were able to get into major motion pictures was because you had a video of you fucking some married producer up the ass and you blackmailed him, right? Other than that, you couldn't act your way out of a paper bag. And you're dumber than a fucking rock. Not as *hard* as a fucking rock though, right? I've heard that half the time they had to bring in a stunt cock to plow some guy's ass in your gay porn films because you weren't able to get it up. Not for *regular* sex, anyway. No, you couldn't get it up for *that*. But put a whip in your hand, or some chains, and you were ready to go, right stud? Yeah, you needed violence. And blood. And pain. You needed to see your conquest suffer. Then you could fuck anything that moved regardless of gender. If they were in pain and they had a hole, you could fill it. You fucking sadistic perv."

"Hey!" James Proctor yelled out as his head and greasy brown hair shook with anger. "This is a Christian movie! Watch your language! I didn't write any of those fowl words to be in this!"

"Oh James," Renata said through her chuckles. "You *really* don't understand what's going on here, do you? This isn't your script anymore. I've made a few changes. And you and I both know that if the book that you ripped off for this script had contained profanity, you would have used it. Even more, right? Because you always have to one-up the original author. You have built your entire career by stealing other people's ideas and trying to outdo them. You're a fucking hack. But look at you getting all outspoken and shit. I'm proud of you. I remember reading an opinion article of yours in the early days of The Regime. You called people who spoke out against their tyranny to be "pointless". Is it pointless to raise your voice to protest against the abduction of innocent people? Against breaking into people's homes and dragging them into the cold? To place them in concentration camps? To beat and murder people in the streets? You call raising your voice against those atrocities pointless? I call it *patriotic*. What's *pointless* is burying your head in the sand and becoming just another sycophantic lemming to The Regime. Just keep your head down and march to whatever beat those brutal fucks are playing. *That* is what is pointless. And what is *also* pointless is trying to leave this theatre. There is no way out. For *any* of you. Just be submissive and quietly comply. You should be used to that, James. Now sit the fuck down. We'll get to you in due course.

"The film!" Sam Shutter shouted. "I've got to get to the film!" He rushed to the back of the theatre and opened a side door. Renata chuckled as she heard his clomping footsteps ascend the stairs into the projection booth. Her laughing increased as she heard him taking a hammer to the projector. The cavernous, blood-red chamber was filled with evil laughter and the banging from the projection booth. After five minutes of futility, Sam re-entered the theatre with his head hung and took his seat. "I don't know what's happening," he said with panic in his voice. "I beat the hell out of that thing with a huge hammer. And it had no impact. There's this weird black smog that's enveloping it. Protecting it somehow. The hammer never made contact. It can't be destroyed."

"No, it *can't*," Renata agreed. "It *cannot* be destroyed. And neither can *we*. And by we, I mean women. You can restrict our rights. Subjugate us. Beat us. Rape us. Even kill us. But you cannot destroy us. You cannot destroy our pride. Our fortitude. Our dignity. We shall continue to hold our heads high and march. And yell. And protest. And do whatever we need to do until we are recognized as equals. Equals? Fuck, we're so much better than you ball-ess pussies. There will come a day when the gentler sex will be mostly in charge. And believe me, gentlemen, we won't be known as gentler any longer. We will do to *you* what you have done to *us*. When we want to breed, we'll use you as our fuck toys. When we want to eat, you shall prepare it for us. When our homes are dirty, you shall clean them. You will do our gardening. And laundry. And be our low life subservient in our offices. We will berate you. Humiliate you. Dehumanize you. Not all men, mind you. Evolved men will rule alongside us as equals. Just as they've been fighting alongside us all this time. But *you* misogynistic motherfuckers? After you provide no further benefit to us, we shall castrate you, throw you in the corner of a damp, cold cell, and laugh while watching you bleed out. We will destroy you and every other rapist, pedophile motherfucker out there. That is what your sentence should have always been, and one day, we shall make that justice a reality. And it will be quite easy because you are nothing but sniveling, pussy bullies. We will destroy *you*. But you can never destroy *us*. Or our projector. Or our film. We are impervious to you. Our collective strength is immortal. Your flaccid bigotry is finite. And it is soon coming to an end, gentlemen."

"No, it isn't, you stupid bitch," Pug Homleyman snarled through his fat, blistered lips. "Nothing is coming to an end, or haven't you noticed? Haven't you noticed all the women who are no longer in the workplace because they're home cooking our dinners and changing snotty kids' diapers, the way they were intended to? Haven't you noticed that there are no women in voting lines? Haven't you noticed that there are no women on the streets after dark unless accompanied by their man?"

His voice lowered and grew darker as he continued. "Haven't you noticed the amount of pregnant women who throw themselves down the stairs? Or impale themselves with a coat hanger and bleed out in some alley? Haven't you noticed all the fucking women who are now silent unless spoken to? All the women who have taken their own lives? Haven't you noticed your *own fucking body* with its wrists slit sitting next to me? All dolled up, and ready for action? Yeah, that's right bitch. We're going to fuck your corpse. Over and over. And I don't know how you're able to do this shit. I don't know what kind of fucked-up voodoo is happening. But I *do* know that I'm going to enjoy cumming in your dead fucking mouth even more with you watching. And I'm going to enjoy doing the same thing to the *next* starlet that we recruit. And the next one. And the next. Until they too are so beaten down and hopeless that they off themselves. We're the pussies? We're not the ones killing ourselves. And you say we can't destroy you? Well, let's just test that theory out, shall we? Come on, fellas. Let's tear down that fucking screen."

"Wait, what are you doing?" Renata asked in a quivering, frightened voice as thirteen enraged men climbed the three-foot stage and approached the crimson screen. "No, no, you can't," she pleaded. "This was so perfect. I had it all planned out. You can't do this to me! Not again!"

The men began laughing hysterically as they all grasped a piece of the taught screen and began pulling it down. Sweat flew from their brows as they tugged at the screen while their lead actress wept and cried out for mercy. They high fived and cheered and reveled in their cruelty as she screamed out for them to stop.

"You're killing me!" Renata yelled out in anguish. "You're killing me all over again! You weren't supposed to be able to do this! Stop! Please stop! I'll be dead forever! Please, I'll do anything!"

Her cries went ignored as the screen came tumbling down and the frenzied men mercilessly ripped it apart. Shards of the nylon and polyester screen were picked up by the frigid gales coming out of the blasting air conditioning vents and flew around the theatre in cyclonic waves. "Are you still with us bitch?" Pug yelled out as his frenetic eyes scanned the morbidly silent room. "Are you still here? Are you ready to watch a *real* show? Are you ready to watch us decimate your cold fucking corpse? I really fucking hope you're here to see this. Because we are going fuck your body every way imaginable until it falls apart in our hands. We're going to fuck it to shreds, you no-talent little twat! Get her body boys and lay it on what's left of the screen!"

The other twelve men emitted Cro-Magnon grunts of lust and retribution as they approached Renata's stiff, blue body. The dim house lights suddenly went out, and the men began tripping over one another in the darkness. They stood in silence and shivered as their eyes attempted to adjust to the blackness that enveloped them. They were alone in a senseless cavern. There was nothing to see. Nothing to hear. Nothing to feel but each other's frantically searching arms. The entire theatre had become a cold, dark, silent tomb.

Until the soft, evil laughter began again. Then, the sound of the projector starting back up. And finally, a light squeak as a replacement screen slowly descended from the rafters. The theatre was cast in a dark red glow as Renata's angelic face appeared to them again from another world. She stopped her light chuckles, opened her perfect lips and said, "So, what did you think, gentlemen? What did you think of my performance? Was that some award winning, bad-ass acting or *what*? Come on now. Be honest. You really thought you were destroying me, didn't you? Sending me to my final resting place. Ripping my soul apart. My pleas were pretty convincing, don't you think?

"Yeah, I know. You won't admit it. Pseudo-macho fuckers like you *never* admit to being duped. But I knew. I knew that my performance moved you. It moved you into a frenzy of cruelty. The more I plead for your mercy, the crueler you became. And that's what all of this is all about, isn't it gentlemen? Cruelty. You don't behave in this sadistic way for money. Hell, it's not even for power and influence. It's all just for cruelty. You get off on watching others suffer. Especially women and children. You are so small that the only way you can have any self-esteem is to beat down others. Each time your whips draw another stream of blood, you feel strong. Every time you cause tears to fall from a child's eyes, you feel powerful. Every time you rape and beat the life out of a woman, you feel omnipotent. Well, you are *not* omnipotent. You are impotent. You are disgusting. You are inhumane.

You truly are sadistic devils. And tonight gentlemen, you are going to face your final judgement."

"How, how are you doing this?" a distraught Pug asked of the empowered image on the screen. "How is this possible? You're fucking dead! Your body is right here! It is lifeless! How are you doing this?"

"Typical fucking man," Renata scoffed. "You motherfuckers never listen to us, do you? Okay, one more time. And listen this time, because I'm not going to explain this again. I'm a fucking gypsy that comes from a long line of powerful gypsies. I have the ability to exact revenge on those who have mistreated me if I recite some words while I'm dying from suicide. That's what I did earlier tonight. I got all dressed up, came here early, took the film off the projector, laid it on the floor, slit my fucking wrists, said my little spell, and fucking died. I went to Enlightenment, found some other actresses that died because of your wickedness, and now we're here for our bloody retribution. Fucking duh. Do I need to paint you a fucking picture? Yes, I suppose I do. Men have to be shown before they believe. They have to have their noses rubbed in it before they stop shitting on their own floor. Yes, I shall paint you a picture.

"A lot of pictures in fact. A lot of little, tiny pictures that will fly by frame by frame through that projector. And you will watch those little pictures. Well, until it is time for your scene. Then I'm going to make each of you a fucking star. Got it now? So, can we just stop this futile silliness and get back to the movie? Just stop trying to leave and destroy the projector or the screen or whatever. Oh, and don't try to call anyone. Your cell phones are quite useless at the moment. It is futile. As I said before. Just sit there and be submissive. It will be much more pleasurable. Well, for me, at least. You thirteen are fucked no matter *what* you do. I do need to thank you, however. All of your scrambling about aimlessly has bought us some time to get ready. You know. Hair. Make-up. Wardrobe. Learning our lines. That shit takes time and this production has been thrown together a bit hastily. So, thank you, gentlemen. Thank you for allowing us the time to prepare.

"Now let's just get on with the show. Just sit there and watch my character introspectively reading her Bible for a few minutes. I need to go and check on your first co-star. And please. Stop with your silly protests. It really is pointless to resist."

CHAPTER 7

———

AND OUR FIRST CONTESTANT IS...

The screen turned from dark red to the film's original vibrant array of colors as the camera pulled back to show Chastity sitting on her bed in her sheer, white gown. She was clutching the gold cross pendant that hung from her neck and wore a reverential expression upon her youthful face. She smiled slightly as her gleaming blue eyes scanned passages in her golden, 'Dear Leader Edition' Bible. The keen observer could see the words 'Made in China' on the back cover, just underneath Dear Leader's arrogant, pugnacious face that was looking down at a bowing, subservient Jesus Christ who was washing his grotesque feet.

"Oh, how I love my Bible studies," Chastity softly stated. "With each passage that I read, I feel more connected to our Lord. With every holy scripture, I long to sit at his feet, just as Jesus is doing on the back cover. I have heard of our Lord inviting young girls to his divine mansion to be blessed by him. Oh, how I dream of being touched by the hand of my Lord. How I dream of being blessed by him. Everything that he does comes from the caring that he has in his heart for us. He wants to protect us and cradle us in his love. That is why his scriptures mandate the extermination of the evil ones. This one might be one of my favorite scriptures."

Ye, and I hereby DECREE that the Godless VERMIN that SOIL our land will be ROUNDED UP and kept away from MY PEOPLE! Everybody who acts against your FAVORITE DEAR LEADER will be put in CHAINS! The PIGGIE WHORE REPORTERS who ask stupid questions of me! The scum who march in OUR STREETS! The RAPISTS and MURDERERS who came from some other shit-hole place! The CORRUPT and VERY LOW IQ politicians who try to Block me from giving YOU your GOLDEN AGE! ALL will be punished for not giving ME, your FAVORITE DEAR LEADER, the RESPECT I so rightfully DESERVE! THANK YOU FOR YOUR ATTENTION TO THIS MATTER! DL

"You are welcome, my Lord," Chastity softly said to her opened Bible. She lifted it to her pink lips and gave the text a light kiss. "I will *always* pay attention to what you have to say. For *your* word is the word of God. It says so in this next scripture."

Ye, or something, EVERYBODY needs to BOW to ME, your FAVORITE DEAR LEADER! I am THE WORD OF god. You are to PRAISE ME and PAY TRIBUTE TO ME! Fathers will work for ME! Mothers will give their daughters to ME! And if they're HOT you don't have to pay TAXES! PROBABLY! THANK YOU FOR YOUR ATTENTION TO THIS MATTER! DL

"How I wish my parents would have given me to my Lord," Chastity dreamily stated as she closed her book and stared out her window at the brilliance of her Lord's creation. "Just look at all he has given us. Our flat planet is the perfect distance from the sun. And because of that we have warmth and air to breathe and water to drink. We have animals to eat. He has made our world beautiful by planting trees and bushes and flowers. I pray that he will plant something in *me* someday. But I'm nothing more than a simple farm girl. He doesn't even know I exist. But he loves me. I can feel his love with every rain drop that falls on my tender skin and with every breeze that flows through my golden hair."

There was a light rap on Chasity's bedroom door. "Why, who could *that* be?" Chasity asked herself as she floated past her walls that were adorned by cheap, knock-off prints of Dear Leader in gladiator uniforms. She approached the door and said, "Yes, who is it? Is that you Momma? Poppa? It had better not be you, Chad! I love you because you are my brother, but you cannot come in here and look at my laundry again."

"It's not your mother," a woman's kind voice replied from behind the closed door. "Nor is it your father. Or your pervy fucking brother. Open the door, Chasity. I'm your new friend, Ginger." "Oh! Ginger!" Chastity excitedly exclaimed as she threw the door open. "Oh, how I was wondering when you might pay me a visit!" The image on the movie screen was suddenly awash in a deep crimson as Ginger entered.

Thirteen shivering men who were sitting in the theatre gasped in unison upon seeing the change in color. All they could do was watch and wonder what this occurrence may hold for them. Whatever it might be, they all knew that it wouldn't be good.

"Um, well," the red-headed and floral dressed Ginger replied as she entered the scene. "You kinda *knew* when I'd show up. That was my cue. See? Look at the script. You say, 'with every breeze that flows through my golden hair.' Then, I'm supposed to knock on the door."

"Yeah, yeah, I know," Renata whispered in response. "I'm improvising. Okay, let's just get on with the scene." "Yeah, alright," Ginger agreed. "So, Chastity, what are you doing in here all alone?" Chastity picked up her golden Bible from her bed, hugged it, smiled, and threw it across the room.

"Reading *this* stupid fucking thing," Renata answered through a slight laugh. "Oh, my fucking God. What a piece of *trash* that book is. It's just a rehash of all of his stupid fucking social media posts from the past several years. Except, he thought it would make it sound holy if he put 'Ye' at the beginning of each one. This shit just amazes me. I kinda get how he was able to con the low-information voters. They don't pay attention to anything except their immediate gratification. As long as they're entertained, they're content. And the bigots were, of course, already in his corner. He was their champion that allowed them to come out of the closet and shit on everybody that wasn't white. And straight. And male. But his *real* accomplishment was in winning over the supposedly religious people. He convinced them to trade in their old 'Jesus Is Love' cult for his 'Let's Fuck Everybody Over So I Can Get Rich and Blown By Teenage Girls' cult. And now that his Bible is the only official religious text allowed in this knuckle-dragging country, his bullshit posts are *scripture*! His addle-minded rambling is now seen as the word of God by these numb nuts! How fucked up is *that*?

"You know, Ginger, I have to tell you something. Oh, and I should tell those assholes who are watching us right now. Hey, turn and wave to our audience." Ginger faced the thirteen men in the audience, smiled, and waved at them. The confused men looked at one another and cautiously smiled and waved back.

"Holy shit!" Ginger exclaimed. "You really have all thirteen of them in here! This is so cool." "Yeah, it totally is," the laughing Renata agreed. "Anyway, what I wanted to tell you is that right after I shot this scene, I vomited. I ran into the bathroom and puked my guts out. Even though I was acting and playing a part, I couldn't stomach saying how I wanted Dear Leader to plant something in me. I mean, Jesus fucking Christ! How far up the 'Ew' meter is *that*? I've heard that motherfucker has a shrimp for a penis, he shits himself all the time, and he smells like raw sewage fucking a skunk! No wonder he has to rape to get laid. No one would *willingly* fuck that slimy little prick.

"Anyway, this was the first scene I shot, and I remember thinking to myself, 'Renata. What the fuck have you gotten yourself into?' I mean, the plot is nothing more than insane propaganda and the script is fucking laughable. But then, I thought, 'When will you ever get another chance? This is your big break. After this, you'll lobby for a part in some other type of movie. Maybe an action flick or spy thriller or something. In the meantime, you will be the darling of the Christian community. You will have your fan base. You will have your name in lights.'"

"Yeah, fame is a seductive bitch, alright," Ginger replied. "And *this* movie is absolute garbage. Not that mine was art or anything, but at least *Tomorrow's Sunset* wasn't just poorly written propaganda intended to indoctrinate the masses. It was, um, slightly *better* written propaganda intended to indoctrinate the masses. But that's only because the book that James Proctor ripped off was a better book. But the book used for *Take My Hand*? Absolute garbage. Anyway, I was hoping to borrow your dad's car so we could go for a spin."

Renata slipped back into character for a moment and said, "Oh, no, Ginger. I love you and everything, but women aren't allowed to drive in our household. Why, we are just too ditzy to be able to operate such a complex piece of machinery. And emotional. Why, what would happen if somebody cuts us off? We'll probably break down in tears and lose control and crash into a tree."

"Yep, that's the plan," Ginger said as she and Renata began laughing together. "You know what?" Renata said. "You're right. Fuck it. Let's take dad's car. And I think that we should have a male companion accompany us. You know, to keep us safe."

"Now, *that* is a great idea!" Ginger exclaimed. The camera zoomed into a close-up of Ginger's auburn eyes as she turned to the audience and began scanning their concerned faces. "But just who should it be? Oh, *I* know. Jake Johnson. The production designer. Oh Jake, won't you please play a little part in our movie?"

Jake began shaking as Ginger's lithe form walked toward the camera. She smiled and stood at the edge of the screen. She then took one more step forward and her physical body entered the theatre. The thirteen men gasped and ran towards the back exit. Ezekial Winthrop III placed his hands on the door handle and received another 150,000 volts through his body. Y'know. Because he isn't terribly bright.

Ginger cackled with glee as she approached the shaking, huddled mass of testosterone. She looked Jake Johnson in his tearful eyes and said, "Come along now, Jake. We're just going to go for a little ride.

Don't worry. It will be fun. You know how good I am at handing an automobile."

"I-It's like she's really here!" Jake exclaimed as his hand was embraced by Ginger's. "I can feel her hand! And it's warm! Like she's really alive! And, I-I can't stop myself from following her! It's like I have no control over my body!" he was yelling out as Ginger led him to the front of the theater and up the short set of stairs to the stage. "I-I-I know I shouldn't go with her, but I can't do anything about it! It's like she has control over me! It's like she's…"

Ginger and Jake's deep red images were suddenly being projected onto the screen. "Jesus Christ," Pug muttered in a shaking voice. "They're taking us into the movie. They can actually take us into the fucking movie."

"Hey giiiiiirl!" Renata squealed as Ginger and Jake approached the black sedan that she was standing near. "So, here's my dad's car. I mean, not *my* dad's car, of course. *My* dad drove corvettes and shit. He was so fucking cool. Took me to concerts and political rallies when I was a little girl. Always the first person to lend a hand to anyone in need. Organized community watch groups. Never spoke ill of anyone. Well, anyone who didn't deserve it. Yeah, he was my real-life hero. Until The Regime marched him into a re-education camp. Shortly after, we were told that he fell into a wall. Which somehow caused several contusions, bleeding in his brain, and lacerations all over his face. The fucking attack dogs of the Regime murdered my dad. And for that, and so much other shit, there will *never* be forgiveness. Just bloody fucking revenge. But I've gotten off script. Heeeey giiiirl. So, here's my dad's car. It's completely middle-of-the-road and boring and shit, but you and your boyfriend can take it for a spin if you want."

Ginger began laughing and said, "Oh, this isn't my boyfriend. This is Jake Johnson. He is, um, I mean *was* a production designer for Dear Leader Studios." "Oh, wow," Renata replied as she faked being genuinely impressed. "I know, right?" Ginger continued. "Pretty big deal to work for such an influential studio, right Jake?"

Jake stood there shaking as he tried to force his mouth open to respond. All that came out were pathetic muffles. "Oh shit, sorry, sorry," Ginger said through her laughter. "I forgot. I'm in control of Jake's body. He can't talk unless I release him and, well, *that* shit's not happening. But yeah, Jake was a big deal at the studio. He is, um, I mean *was*, a masterful production designer. He's responsible for building this entire town for your movie, Renata. And so many more. Jungle sets. Spaceships. Pirate's coves. Dingy urban neighborhoods. Yep, he could design it all.

"But your *specialty* was *dungeons*, wasn't it Jake? Yeah, cold, dark dungeons. With chains on the walls. And whips and racks and all sorts of twisted shit that you and your twelve friends would use to torture all of us starlets. I can still feel the cold steel of the shackles that you designed biting into my wrists. I can still feel the blood dripping down my back after being whipped by you or one of those other fucking degenerates. Yeah, you were a master production designer. Your talent was on full display when you built that chamber of horrors. And when you tinkered with the car that I was supposed to drive for my follow-up film. Yeah, you little fuck. I knew. I knew that my next movie would be my last. Heard you talking to Pug about how you rigged the brakes so that I would crash for real in the final chase scene. I knew. And I knew that there was no way out. Well, except for one. So, I decided to do it myself and deny you assholes the filming of that final dramatic scene. But what's the point of me droning on and on about this when we have such a lovely day to go for a ride, right?"

"You bet!" Renata replied as she flipped the keys to Ginger. Who immediately dropped them. Because she catches like a…um…never mind. "Fuck. I never *was* very athletic and, um, shit where did they go? Oh, here they are. Behind the back bumper thingy. Okay! Let's go! Now, just take my hand and I'll lead you to the front seat. There you go. Nice and comfy? Huh. No seat belts in this prop car? Doesn't matter. We won't need them anyway. And it doesn't matter that this thing doesn't have an engine either. Why, we're going to experience the magic that is motion picture special effects! Okay, see ya back in the clouds, Renata!"

"Okay! Byeeeeee!" Renata yelled after them as the black sedan roared out of the gravel driveway that was lined with quaint petunias. "Oh, shit! For a prop car, this thing really moves!" Ginger screamed over the hum of the "engine". "Shit, zero to sixty in like, ten seconds! But that isn't fast enough, now, is it? Wanna go faster?" Ginger looked over at Jake's sweating face as he vigorously shook his head and let out a muffled scream of terror.

"Yes? No?" Ginger inquired further while wearing an enthralled smile upon her pretty face. "Come on, man! Spit it out! Okay, I'm going to take your muffled screams of terror and head shaking as a 'Yes'. Okay? Let's floor this fucker!"

Ginger stomped on the accelerator thingy and the sedan immediately increased its speed from sixty. To seventy. To eighty-five. To one-hundred-twenty. "Oh shit, this is fun!" the thrilled Ginger screamed out. "Wow! These blood-red trees are nothing but a blur. Whoa! Fucking racoon in the road! Missed him. But I think the hubcap thingy just fell off. Hey! How are you doing over there, Jake? Are you having fun? Are you having as much fun as I was having on the night that I drove on this exact same road at this exact same speed on the night of my death? Are you feeling what I felt? Are you feeling the sheer panic? Are you filled with regret over decisions that you have made in your life? Are you filled with depression? Hopelessness? Yeah, you are. I can see it in your frantic face. You want so desperately to find an escape, but you can't. You're trapped in a living hell of your own creation, and you're filled with nothing but spine-chilling terror. Just like I was. Until I was driving on this very road at this very speed that night. I closed my eyes, smiled, and let all of my pain go. And now, I'm going to give that relief to you."

"Oh fuck, that was so much fun, ladies!" Ginger announced as her soul returned to her cloud. "I'm telling you, that Renata is the real deal. Her acting is top shelf. You just gotta watch for her improvising. She tends to do that a lot, so you gotta stay focused and look for an opportunity to get the scene back on script. Maybe she should have done stand-up or something. She would have done well on a sketch comedy show. You know. Until The Regime outlawed them. And check *this* shit out!

"Oh, my fucking God! His face is *completely* buried in that tree! He doesn't even look human. Just a big ball of gooey, slimy red putty! And his eyes are popped out! And his spine is twisted in like, twelve different directions! And his legs are crushed against his neck! Oh shit, that *was* fun. Okay, Renata's telling me to get the next actress ready. And that would be, uuuummm, Violet! Your scene is next! Are you ready?"

Violet lifted her purple-skinned face and glared at Ginger for a moment before snarling, "I was re-*born* fucking ready."

Chapter 8

Don't Get Pissy With Me!

Twelve men gasped in horror as their former colleague's mangled frame reappeared in his theatre seat. They solemnly stared at his unrecognizable face, crushed torso, and twisted limbs while the movie screen turned from dark red to its original colors as *Take My Hand* resumed. They shook their heads with resignation, brushed away popcorn and licorice remnants from their red velour seats, and settled in to await the next scene in this dastardly story.

Chastity closed her Dear Leader Edition of the Bible, smiled broadly and said, "That was one of the most inspiring readings of my lord's scriptures yet. How I wish that I could spend my entire day reading his holy words. But, c'mon Chastity. Time to get up. Those eggs aren't going to collect and sell themselves. She bounced down the stairs, pecked her mother on her cheek, and said, "I've completed my morning's Bible study mother. I'm now off to collect our eggs."

"Very good, dear," her mother replied as she washed the breakfast dishes in an overly sudsy kitchen sink. Her mother's made-up, youthful face had thick white suds dripping off of it. As did her light blue house gown that strained against her voluptuous breasts.

"I gotta hand it to you, Phillip," Pug stated. "That was some great costume design. Even though we're trapped in this dungeon of a theatre, this shot still makes me hard. Goddam, look at those suds dripping off of her like she's been covered in cum. Great camera angle too. Those fucking Christians, man. If this film ever makes it into the theatres, this is going to be a cash bonanza. There's nothing those holy rollers love more than titillation with their Bible-banging bullshit. Bang the Bible during the day and go home and bang the bishop at night. Or something else. You ever notice how it's always the self-righteous, White, Christians who get caught with the kiddie porn and fucking their kids? Almost always. It's either them, or the rich and powerful, like Dear Leader. But the genius of Dear Leader was that he was able to convince millions of really stupid fucking people that it was everybody *but* those groups. Yeah, it was always the immigrants, or the transsexuals, right? Of course, it never fucking was. Millions of people rose up against a made-up pedophilia cabal. They were more than willing to believe this conspiracy theory bullshit as long as it was the *other* team that was being accused. But once they were told that it was actually *their* guy who was running a pedophile cabal? Fuckin' crickets. They're as incapable of acknowledging when they're wrong as Dear Leader. He truly does represent those fucking morons. And us, of course.

"And *we* won't admit to being wrong either. We have earned *everything* that we have built and achieved. I don't care what these dead bitches say. Only the strong will survive. They're fucking dead. We're still alive. And we're going to continue to be alive. Jake's death came as a surprise. We didn't know what was happening and weren't prepared. But now we know. Now we can fight back. He said he could feel Ginger's hand. It was like she was alive. That means the women have a physical form when they come into the theatre. There's just one of them and twelve of us. We're going to tackle the next bitch that comes through that screen and beat her to a pulp until she's fucking dead. Again. Then we'll do the same with each one of them until they turn this fucking movie off and unlock the doors. The meek can inherit wherever they're coming from. The rich and powerful shall inherit the Earth. Now let's just watch our little Angel here and wait. As soon as that screen turns red, it's gonna be fucking showtime."

"But Chastity," her mother continued. "Just remember. Only sell them to the shops owned by our glorious oligarchs. They are an extension of Dear Leader and therefore an extension of God. Do not be tempted by filthy money that may be offered in the restricted area. Money is the root of all evil, after all. And our oligarchs will provide just enough for us. Just enough to put a solid roof over our heads and food upon our tables. It is through their wisdom that they provide us with just enough money for our survival. By keeping us from wealth, they are protecting us from the hellish pitfalls of greed. They are wise and they are kind. Unlike those Godless vermin who live in squalor in the restricted area. They know no love or kindness. It is all about them. All they want is more money and power so that they take over the world. And then, do you know what they will do? They will place us all in chains and make us their servants. They will brutalize us, Chastity. And that is why we only sell our eggs to our glorious oligarchs. They will never exploit us like the evil ones would do. Selling *them* just one egg could lead to the downfall of the pious, my darling. Do you understand?"

"Why *of course* I do, momma," Chastity sincerely answered. "You and poppa are right. Their skin is as dark as their souls. But Dear Leader's love is so great, it extends even to them. He could have them vanquished from the Earth. But does he? No. He allows them to continue living in their sinful ways. And he prays that one day they will see his light. I just don't understand Momma. Why can't they see his love and kindness?"

"There are some in this world who are nothing more than beasts, Chastity," her mother answered while wiping a thick glob of suds from her pouty, glossed lips. "They are not capable of understanding. They are not capable of opening their hearts to Dear Leader's love. Because they *have* no hearts. No souls. They are animals, Chastity. Beasts. And if it weren't for the graciousness of Dear Leader, they would indeed be exterminated. Now, go collect our eggs then go to the car. I will have Chad drive you to market. Women are far too emotional to be able to drive."

"Oh, don't I know it!" Chastity agreed through a light laughter.

"Why, I wouldn't know the first thing to do behind the wheel of a car! I would get all confused and step on the wrong pedal then start crying and probably crash poppa's sedan! I see other women driving and I pray for them. I pray that they one day will understand that we women are better off being cared for by our men. We are much safer that way. As is the world. Okay, I'm off for our eggs! Bye, Momma!"

Chasity's lithe frame was bathed in brilliant sunlight as she skipped towards the quaint chicken coop. "Good morning chickens! What treasures do you have for me today?" she excitedly squealed as she entered the clucking confinement. "Oh my! The oligarch market will certainly be pleased today! Just look at this bounty of eggs! Now, don't look at me like that. I know you want to keep them, but this is how we feed our family. So, just stop your clucking this instant you naughty little birds."

Chastity exited the chicken coop with a basket full of fresh eggs. She shielded her eyes from the glaring sun as she peered up at the gorgeous blue sky. "Glory be," she said. "What a perfect day in our midwestern town. Before Dear Leader, this town would be covered in ice and snow in January. But now? A perfect seventy-six degrees. And when we need to be protected from the sun, the plumes of SMOG from the oligarch's majestic factories fill the skies with their glory. Yes, the Smoke Made Of God enters our lungs and forces us to cough out the demons that are inside. Bless the factories. Bless the Oligarchs. And bless Dear Leader for this most perfect January day.

"Yes, bless it all," Chastity continued as her voice deepened and the screen faded into a dark red. She turned to her audience and said, "Bless the greedy for poisoning us. Bless them for wiping out entire portions of coastline throughout the globe. Bless the melting arctic caps that have caused the sea levels to rise and drown all in its path. Bless the historic tornados and hurricanes that kill thousands every year. Bless the wildfires that run rampant through the brush and destroy homes and wildlife and people while Dear Leader watches and fiddles. Bless the cancer that he and his evil sycophants have caused through poisoning our air and water. Bless his destruction of all life on this planet.

"But what do *you* assholes care? As long as you can make your really fucked up movies and have your little playthings, all is right with the world, right? Do you believe this shit that you put on the screen? Do you actually believe this poorly written, bullshit propaganda? No. Of course you don't. You *know* what you are all doing to this planet. You *know* the cruelty you are inflicting. And you get off on it. Just like you get off on abusing innocent women.

"Which reminds me! It's time for our next co-star! Gentlemen, it is my great pleasure to re-introduce you to the star of the *Amazonian Fury* series, Violet!" A tall, lean, lavender-skinned woman came into the frame and hugged Renata. "Thanks so much for this opportunity, Renata. It is an honor to be in your movie," Violet stated.

"Oh, no, the pleasure is all *mine*," Renata gushed in response. "You were so wonderful in those movies. So strong and powerful. You were like a force of nature. And now, you are here in *my* movie. Are you ready? Are you ready to once again be that force of nature that was so inspiring to so many?"

"You *bet* I am," Violet sneered. She flashed a wicked smile as she turned to her anxious audience and began surveying their trembling faces. "And just who will be my co-star in this scene? Let me just double-check the script here. I wouldn't want to make a mistake in casting. Ah, yes. Here it is. Phillip Phillips. The costume designer. Yes, you certainly constructed some nice costumes for *me*, now, *didn't* you? That was a helluva straight jacket you kept me in. It was chained to the stone wall and every time I resisted, it would squeeze me just a little bit more until I could barely breathe. Come, Phillip. Won't you join me?"

Violet stepped forward and emerged out of the blazing red screen. She floated down the three stairs to the theatre carpet and extended her hand to the quivering Phillip. "Now!" Pug yelled out. Twelve men jumped out of their seats and pounced upon Violet's body. They bombarded her purple face with their flailing fists until her body stopped struggling.

"What the fuck?" Pug exclaimed as he watched Violet's purple body disintegrate into a pile of lavender ashes. There was suddenly the soft, evil laughter of a solitary woman. The men looked up and saw Violet floating above them. "Silly, silly men. Did you think that we would allow ourselves to be beaten by you again? Did you think that we would appear to you in a physical form that could be injured in any way? Of course we wouldn't. We have suffered enough at your hands. And that suffering will *never* be experienced by any of us ever again. Ever. But *your* suffering has just begun. Just ask your former friend, Jake. Wow. He looks like a bag of flesh that's been put through a trash compactor. That's a tough act to follow there, Phillip. Ginger did a helluva job on him. But why don't we give it a try?"

She floated to the floor, and her warm hand took his. "Ew," she said as she grasped his clammy hand. "You're fuckin' gross and sweaty. Well, that's understandable, I suppose. You *are* about to die." The transfixed Phillip allowed himself to be led by Violet back into the crimson movie screen. Violet smiled, snapped her fingers, and Chastity's farm was replaced by a moist, dark dungeon.

"Here, we are. Let's just try *this* on for size," Violet whispered as she began placing a filthy, blood-covered straight-jacket around his stiff frame. "Oh, you want to fight back so badly, don't you? You want to resist. You want to run back into the safety of the theatre. But you can't. We have control over you. You will move when I allow you to move. But don't worry. That will be coming quite soon. Now that you're all trussed up, we'll just drag you over to the chains on the wall. Ooooooo. How does *that* feel? Does it hurt your head every time I drag you over a jagged stone? I remember, it certainly hurt mine. I remember you laughing at me as blood dripped down my blonde hair. Seeing my beautiful hair like that was quite traumatizing to me. So much so that, when I died, I changed it to purple. Do you like it? Do you like my purple hair and skin? Of course you do. I know how much you enjoy causing a woman's skin to turn purple. And black. And blue. There we are nice and chained up. And now, I will release you from my control. You may speak and move around as much as you would like. In fact, I encourage it."

"L-listen, Violet," the panicked Phillip Phillips blurted out. "Please. You don't have to do this. None of you have to do this. A-a-and none of this was my fault! It was all Pug and the others! I was just following orders!"

"Oh, sweetie, you are pathetic, aren't you?" Violet responded. "You were just following orders? And just how well did that argument work out for the Nazis placed on trial at Nuremberg? Not great, right? And it won't work in *my* court either. Wanna try again?"

"Okay, okay," Phillip yelled out. "You're right. You were always right. Right about everything. Right to fight back against us. But I've learned my lesson! I'm really sorry! I'm a changed man! Please just give me the chance to prove it to you and ohhhh! The straitjacket is too tight. It's constricting around me."

"Well yeah, duh. That's how you designed it remember?" Violet answered as though she were speaking to a toddler. "Don't you remember tying me up in this thing then shocking me with a cattle prod to force me to move? Like *this*?" Violet placed a cattle prod to Phillip's gaunt-looking neck and shot 5,000 volts into his body. He screamed out as his body involuntarily flailed against the stone wall. "S-s-stop it! Please!" he pleaded. "The more I move, the more it tightens! I can barely b-b-breathe!"

"Ah yes, breathing," Violet casually replied. "Quite the luxury. But you remember now, don't you? Do you also remember my nails? My long, sharp nails that I would slice you with every time you released me from the straight jacket? Here. Let me remind you." Violet slashed her claws across his yellowish cheeks. Blood flowed down his sweaty face and onto the straight jacket while Violet laughed at the carnage. She slashed him again. And again. And again, while he shrieked in agony. "Wow. You're really a bleeder," Violet said while peering at his lacerated face. "And maybe I should get a manicure. That last swipe nearly took off your nose. Look at it, just hanging there above your sliced lips. But enough about your face. Let's get back to breathing, shall we?

"Yes, I guess I was quite a handful for you boys. I fought you with everything that I had any time I had a free hand. The moment you freed me; I slashed the fuck out of you all. I guess you could say I was a bit high maintenance. So, you put a plastic bag over my head and raped me while I fought for my life. You fucked me while I gasped for air. The last thing that I remember was your arrogant smile while you pissed on my dying face. But that's why they call you P.P., now isn't it? You get off on piss. Pissing on others. And, well, being pissed *on*. You really are a fucking perv. So, I have some good news for you here, P.P. I'm going to give you one last real-life fantasy."

Violet chuckled as she pulled a plastic bag out of thin air. "Now, let's just put this over your head and…um…nope. The opening goes here and now just tighten it around your scrawny neck and there we are! You see? Not so bad. There's an opening at the very top to let air in. Of course, that opening could be used to let *other* things in too. Say, do you know if there's a lady's room around here somewhere? I've *really* got to piss. No? Well, what to do, what to do. I *really* need a receptacle to piss in. Hey! I know! Your nickname just gave me a great idea!"

Violet's toned body elevated until she was hovering directly over Phillip's head. She spread her legs under her angelic gown and lowered herself until her crotch was just above the bag's opening. She then began pissing. "Oh shit, I really needed that," she said breathily as her golden urine poured into the top of the bag. "Oh yeah. I really shouldn't have drank all that lemonade. This might take a while."

Urine poured over Phillip's head and began filling the bag. As he screamed and flailed, the straitjacket became increasingly tighter. His screaming intensified as the urine reached his bottom, bloodied lip. The screams became gurgles as the warm, yellow waves rested just under his lacerated nose. He thrashed his head vigorously as Violet continued to urinate on him until his hair was floating in the sticky refuse. He desperately began inhaling and swallowing as much urine as he could take in, but he was unable to keep up with Violet's cascading waterfall of piss. The air in his lungs was being squeezed out of him by the straitjacket and drowned by Violet's pungent fluids.

Violet floated back to the floor and sealed the full bag. Phillip's head looked like a dead puffer fish floating in a filthy tank. She stared into Phillip's panicked, dying eyes. She then looked down at his groin. "Jesus Christ you're a freak! What the fuck is wrong with you? Here you are *dying*, and the piss is *still* turning you on! Look at that fucking boner! Whatever. I've got to go now. Our scene is over. Take your final bow, asshole." She stared back through the screen at the eleven remaining men in the theatre while wearing a wicked smile and said, "But *you* boys still have scenes coming up. Don't worry about learning your lines. All of this shit is just being made up as we go along anyway. And we're having a helluva fun time doing it, heh, heh, heh."

CHAPTER 9

WHAT ABOUT BOB?

"Jesus Christ! Now the whole place smells like piss!" Pug yelled out as Phillip Phillip's straightjacketed, urine-soaked body appeared in his theatre seat chair. "This is fucking ridiculous! Somebody help me move these bodies. Maybe we have to sit here and wait to be plucked off one by one, but we don't have to look at *this* shit. Kyle, help me move Phillip. We'll just pick him up and put him in the back row."

The studio's Chief Editor, Kyle Splicer, dutifully jumped to Pug's side. The two men took in a deep breath, held it, and placed their hands under Phillip's saturated armpits. They began to lift and their hands slid through the corpse's flesh. "What the hell?" Pug yelled out. "Grab his wrists. We'll lift him that way." The men grabbed Phillip's wrists and pulled. Their hands slid through his as though he were comprised of a thick goo. They stared in amazement as they watched the putty-like wrists reattach themselves to the stiff arms of the corpse. A chill then ran down the spines of eleven men as they heard a maniacal laugh coming from the surround sound system. They turned to the dark red screen and saw Renata's gleeful face.

"Now, now, boys," Renata said in a scolding tone. "We won't have any of *that*. We won't have you hiding the bodies of your deceased friends away. No, you need to look at them. You need to smell them.

Every moment that you are here, you need to be confronted by the consequences of your actions. They are responsible for their own demise, just as you are all responsible for yours. And *you* are all responsible for *each other's* deaths. None of you could have inflicted these atrocities on your own. You needed a demented band of brothers to make this happen. It is quite the little co-dependent community you have there. Which is a bit ironic. When we think of community, our mind always goes to neighbors helping neighbors, right? Shoveling the driveway for the old lady across the street. Letting someone's kids stay at your place during a family emergency. Bringing a casserole to welcome a new arrival. Or, just hosting a cook-out. The thought of community always makes us think of the positive aspects of what it means to be human. And maybe that's part of our problem. Maybe the decent people in the world are blinded to the possibility that *some* communities *aren't* helpful. Aren't caring. Aren't humane.

"Maybe we are blinded to the possibility that *some* communities are pure fucking evil. The kindness in our hearts and our naïve belief in our *own* sense of community leaves us unprepared for the formation and rise of a community of sadists. Our minds cannot wrap themselves around the possibility of the brutal violence that permeates through some individuals. And we cannot fathom that those warped individuals will find others who believe in the same torturous, macabre worldview as they. But they *do* exist. And they find others. And others. Until they form their community that is built upon hatred.

"The kind-hearted are attending birthday parties for their neighbor's kids and checking on their well-being and sending flowers to funerals. They are organizing funds to pay for a stranger's surgery. They are holding the door open for a person in a wheelchair. They are helping a person up who has fallen. Because that is their community, and they are protective of it and all who reside within it.

"Just as the sadists are protective of theirs. While the kind-hearted are *helping* those within their community, the treacherous are building communities to tear it all down. Communities to keep people sick by denying them health care. Communities to keep people ignorant by indoctrinating them with bullshit propaganda through the controlled education systems and state-run media. Communities designed to cruelly divide people into an 'us' and a 'them' so that they can swoop in and conquer us all. And why? So they can enrich themselves through their gruesome acts with treasure and power. These are communities made up of soulless demons who care about only one thing. Their own self-survival and enrichment. Their gluttonous lust for money and power and sex. And no matter how much they attain, it is never enough. They are never satiated. They must fuck people over and over and over. Because that is who they are. They get off on seeing others suffer. Be beaten. Raped. Emotionally tortured. Murdered. They love every moment of it.

"*You* love every moment of it. Each one of you in your little community of sadists gets off on cruelty. In your case, it's raping and abusing women to the point that they are so beaten down and hopeless that they take their own lives. Oh, how powerful you feel when that happens. What big men you think you are. And the rest of us are ensnared in your little traps of horror because we cannot begin to believe that anybody could be so demented. We cannot believe that an entire community could exist that was formed for the soul purpose of the destruction of humanity. So, we throw our innocent cookouts and are shocked when the storm troopers crash through our back-yard gates and beat us and kidnap us and rape us and murder us. We are taken off-guard because our minds are incapable of comprehending the threat that is slowly building around us. We do not see the dark shadow of another type of community that is forming to enslave us.

"Sooooo, *that* shit's gotta stop, don'tcha think? When this age of cruelty ends, and trust me boys, it *will* come to an end. It *always* does. And when *this* particular age lets out its final gasp, we must learn from it. As a kind-hearted community, we must learn about all of the possibilities of human nature. We must admit to ourselves that not every person is redeemable. We must acknowledge that some people are truly pure evil. We must learn how to recognize them and ostracize them and prevent them, through any and all possible means, from forming *their* communities of hatred and violence. We must hunt them down, castrate them, and never allow them to breed. We must imprison them and watch them, and their dark souls, wither away into nothingness. Some might say that we will then become just like the evil ones. That our souls will be tainted if we resort to the same cruel tactics as them. I disagree, boys. For starters, fuck the sadists. They started this shit, so I have no problem with fighting fire with fire. If their only care in the world is their self-preservation, then we will become *more* hostile, *more* cruel, *more* extreme, and *more* threatening and drive their little pussy asses into the shadows. Until we have the opportunity to find them. Then we're back to the whole castration, imprisonment thing.

"And what we would be doing would not be out of cruelty. There is no such thing as being cruel to a demon. No, we would be doing it out of love. For the love of our fellow human beings and peaceful communities and supportive societies we would be rooting out the evil. We would root it out and destroy it before it gets the opportunity to do the same to us. This is an ever-lasting, existential battle. It isn't about politics. It isn't about ideology. This is about basic good versus basic evil. This is about people caring about others more than themselves versus people who care only for themselves and delight in making others suffer. If you laugh when a child cries, you are evil. When you look forward to chaining a woman up and raping her, you are evil. When your heart beats faster because of the thrill you get when you watch someone bleed from the lashes you have inflicted, you are evil. Um, sometimes. There are qualifiers to that *last* one like, who is bleeding out? Did they deserve it and so on. Not *all* of this shit is absolute, so don't be so fucking judg-ey.

"Anyway, where was I? Oh yes, it is out of love that we pull the thorny weeds from our gardens so that our beautiful flowers may thrive. We yank them out and deprive the weeds of nutrients in the soil and water and they lay there and get all brown and dried out and die. So that the flowers may live. So that their beauty may thrive. Healthy communities uplift. Toxic communities destroy. It is up to each of us to decide which community we want to belong to. And the lengths we are willing to go to preserve and uplift humanity. Yeah, that seems like a good place to stop. Anyway, my point is, boys, you can't move the bodies. They'll just slide through your grip and then regenerate. And how can we make them do that? Because we're vengeful angels and that's just something we can do. Don't know why. It's like angel magic or some shit, so don't question it. Okay, but enough of my silly rambling. I need to go check on our next actress. In the meantime, please enjoy this scene from *Take My Hand*. This part is really fucked up. I can't believe this was produced for a Christian audience. Actually, I kinda can. There are a helluva lot of holy rollers out there who turn out to be incestuous pricks. Okay, let's roll the film."

Renata's red face disappeared and faded into the brilliant colors of a scenic landscape. Chastity came bounding from the chicken coop with her basket of eggs and approached the sedan where her brother, Chad, was waiting. "Jeez, it's about time," Chad snarled. "Oh, don't be such a grumpy Gus," Chastity playfully replied. "Come on. Let's go to town and sell our eggs." The pair started driving down the pristine gravel driveway and turned onto a paved road.

"Hey! What are you doing, Chad?" Chastity yelled out as the camera zoomed in on Chad's right hand casually going up Chastity's lily-white thigh. She took his hand and threw it off of her leg while saying, "I have told you before, Chad. We aren't to do that. It is bad. Now keep your hands to yourself."

"I wasn't going to do anything," Chad replied. "I just wanted to see your underpants. That's all." "Yeah, I *bet* that's all you wanted to do," Chastity responded while folding her arms in disgust. "I bet you wanted to do something gross. And you're my brother, which makes it even *more* gross. Just drive me to town and keep your hands to yourself."

"I thought you said you loved Dear Leader," Chad replied as his eyes darted back and forth between the road and Chastity's crotch that was barely covered by her sheer, white gown. "Well, of course I do!" Chastity yelled back. "What does *that* have to do with anything?"

"Well," the manipulative Chad answered. "For somebody who says

she loves Dear Leader, you sure don't follow his teachings very well."
"Um, what do you mean?" Chasity asked while beginning to blush in
embarrassment. "Well, if somebody *truly* loved Dear Leader then she
would know this scripture. And I quote from the Dear Leader Edition
of the Bible,

*Ye, WHITE MEN will be allowed ANY AND ALL JOBS that they Want! I,
your Favorite DEAR LEADER, has just Declared that DEI is DEAD! WOKE
is DEAD! Our Great Country is even GREATER because WHITE MEN will
not be discriminated against by LOW IQ DEI HIRES! And our Wonderful
Women will Support their MEN in ANY AND ALL Ways they Need!
WIVES will support HUSBANDS! SISTERS will Support BROTHERS!
DAUGHTERS will Support FATHERS! Our NATION will be GREAT
AGAIN! THANK YOU FOR YOUR ATTENTION TO THIS
MATTER! DL*

"Yeah, I know that scripture," a confused Chastity said. "What does
that have to do with anything?" "Well," Chad began explaining as a
slight trail of drool formed at the corner of his lips. "Our Lord said
that women, which is *you*, must support men, which is *me*, in any way
that we need. He said wives must support husbands. Well, just how do
you think wives support husbands? They support husbands by letting
them see their underpants. And maybe inside their underpants. And
then maybe letting them put something inside of them, right?"

"Well, I suppose, but," Chastity began responding before being cut
off by her lascivious brother. "So, if that is how *wives* support
husbands, then that is how *sisters* are supposed to support *brothers*. It is
right there in the scripture. Dear Leader loves us, right? And he wants
us to spread *his* love through loving *each other*. So, if you truly love
Dear Leader, then you will abide by this scripture and support and
love your brother."

"Huh, I never thought of it that way," Chastity replied. "I just
thought I was supposed to do your laundry and clean your room and

stuff. But that makes perfect sense. Momma supports Poppa that way. So, it just makes sense that a sister should support her brother that way. And I do love Dear Leader so. Pull over, Chad. I want to show you how much I love you. And Dear Leader. And I'll start by showing you my underpants." Chastity began pulling up the hem of her white dress as the camera zoomed in. The screen turned dark red and instead of Chastity's panties, there was the smiling face of Sophia.

"Oh, daaawlings," she said as her body emerged from the movie screen. "That truly is quite disturbing. Especially the way it was edited. Just look at how long you held that shot on her underwear. Quite trashy. Not becoming at all for an actress of Renata's talents. Nor mine. I won an award, after all, for my captivating performance in *The Black Tide*. Do you gentlemen remember? Perhaps I shall jog your memories of how a true star can perform. But every breathtaking performance is dependent upon proper editing. The perfect cut here and another one there makes all the difference in a scene. Isn't that right, Kyle Splicer? Take my hand, daaawling. And let us make magic together."

Kyle involuntarily took Sophia's ring-adorned hand and silently followed her into the dark red movie screen where they appeared on the deck of a fishing boat. "Did you know that I just adore fishing, daaawling?" she asked of the trembling Kyle. "I just love the smell of the salt air and the sounds of the black waves lapping alongside the boat. And I love placing the bait in the water. It is amazing to me the huge creatures that you can catch with just a little bit of bait. Would you like to go fishing with me, daaawling? But of course, you would. You would just looove to be my bait, wouldn't you? But there is far too much of you. You will scare off the fish. I do believe that this will require some editing."

Sophia pulled out a large, serrated knife and smiled at Kyle as he struggled to free himself from her spell of immobility. "Now, now," Sophia scolded. "Don't move. I know that it pains you to leave things on the editing room floor, but sometimes less is more. Sometimes it is necessary for us to eliminate that which is extraneous garbage so that the work of art may thrive. Sometimes we must rid ourselves of the bad in order for the good to survive. That is true in film. It is true in our society. And daaawling, it is *certainly* true when preparing bait."

Kyle let out a blood-curdling scream as Sophia sawed through his right wrist. The emancipated hand fell off the side of the boat and splashed into the ocean. "Yes, good," Sophia praised. "Scream for me. It is what this scene requires. The scream represents the pain you are experiencing, certainly. But it also represents your powerlessness. You cannot move, because I shall not allow it. And you shall not bleed, because we need this scene to be played out for a while. Plus, I do not wish to stain my new dress. Why, it cost me thirty-five conjuring coins, daawling. But I *will* allow you to scream. Oh yes, daaawling. Scream for me."

Sophia's grisly request was granted while she sawed his entire right arm off with the knife. She grunted and sweated as the serrated teeth went back and forth through his skin. Then muscle and tendon. Then bone. Then tendon and muscle again until the back layer of skin gave way and his bloodless arm followed its hand into the raging waves.

"Oh, my daaawling, you do scream well," she said while pushing him onto the floor of the deck. Salty red waves washed over his face as she positioned her lanky body over his left leg. "Just one more little edit, and I believe we will be ready to catch some fish." She lifted the knife and plunged it into Kyle's upper thigh. The sound system filled the theatre with Kyle's high-pitched shrieks as Sophia cut. And cut. And cut. Until the leg was severed from his body.

Kyle sobbed while Sophia lifted him up to the side of the boat. Lightning crashed in the distance as the violent red waves turned darker. "Yes, I do believe that we have performed the perfect number of edits. It is the perfect scene. Just long enough for the audience to understand what is happening, but not so long as to be tedious. I mean, I could have cut off your other arm and leg, but what impact would that have had. It would have made this entire scene quite boring. Why, perhaps the audience would leave before we reach our climax. And here it is.

"The perfect ending to the perfect scene. *My* perfect ending was chaining myself and jumping into the ocean. My lungs filled with water, and I plummeted into the punishingly cold ocean. I remember sobbing while feeling free for the first time in a long time. Free from your torment and abuse. Free from the pain. I welcomed that watery grave on that evening. And now daaawling, your watery grave will welcome *you.*"

Sophia let out a deep chuckle as she casually pushed Kyle over the side of the boat. Her chuckle became a maniacal laugh as she watched him struggle to stay above the pounding waves with only his right leg and left arm. He gasped for air as his remaining limbs flailed in the violent surf. The last thing his dying eyes saw before succumbing to the pull of his oceanic grave was Sophia pulling a cigarette from a gold case, placing it into her full, red lips, and casually lighting it.

She exhaled a long plume of smoke as she leaned against the side of the boat. A demure smile came across her face as the storm cleared and the brilliant stars of the night sky sparkled down upon her. She watched as his moonlit corpse came floating to the top of the sea and said, "Yes, daaawling. Very nice performance. And very nice editing. You made me a star tonight, Kyle. Or should I now call you 'Bob'?"

CHAPTER 10

———

GYPSY HEART

"Nice speech about community, daaawling," Sophia said to Renata as the figurative baton was being passed between the pair on their cloud in Enlightenment. "Hey, thanks," Renata replied. "And I'm sure you'll have a great scene too. Break a leg."

"Ooooh daaawling," Sophia answered while primping her hair one final time and taking a drag off of her cigarette. "I'm going to not just *break* a leg. I'm going to saw one off. And an arm. Then watch that pathetic worm flail around in the dark, cold ocean until he drowns. It should be quite dramatic. And violent, heh, heh, heh. Yes, this shall be my greatest performance. Although, acting is so much easier when you can personally relate to your character. And I most certainly can relate to mine."

"Yeah, it's going to be cool," Renata responded. "Well, take your time with him. I need a few minutes to collect my thoughts. They're watching the scene between Chastity and her pervy brother. Then you're on. I'm just going to go into my dressing room for a while and decompress. And thanks for the compliment about what I said about community. It means a lot."

An exhausted Renata walked through the misty clouds and entered her dressing room. She sat in front of her make-up mirror and stared into her own piercing blue eyes. "Yes, community," she said quietly to herself. "Community has always been quite important to me. Important to my entire family." Tears began forming in her blue eyes as she began thinking about the origins of the Family Miazga. She continued to stare at her own face in the mirror while reciting her family's history to herself.

"Community was important to us from the very inception of my family. Our family's history has been traced back to the early 1700's in Poland. The very first recorded Miazga woman was said to be a strange sort. She kept to herself in a shack in the woods. Except for one night each month. On the night of a full moon, she would enter the small nearby village and patronize a local pub. It was said that she was intoxicatingly beautiful with long, blonde hair and electric blue eyes. Well, maybe they didn't describe it as 'electric' back then, but that's what my mother told me when I was a child. In fact, my mother told me that I look *exactly* like the one existing portrait of my ancestor. I don't know if that is true. I've only seen a glimpse of it. It was destroyed in the…I don't want to think about that.

"She would go to this pub and drink and laugh. Because of her beauty, she had plenty of boozed-up suitors. She would smile and dance with each of them. Then she would make her choice. And it is said that her choice was always some unscrupulous businessman or politician or somebody of that ilk. She would take that man to the local cemetery where they would make love under the glow of a full moon. It didn't matter what season it was. Whether it was hot or freezing, they would fuck over the exact same grave. Whose grave? Who knows. Every month she would have a new suitor and every month she would have a new sexual conquest. She would then go home and wipe something on her belly that she had been cooking up in a large kettle. She would say a few words. And this next part is quite unbelievable. If I couldn't commit suicide, exact revenge on my enemies, then return to my body, I'd never believe this shit. But it is said that twenty-eight days later, she would give birth to a new child.

And it is said that as she was pushing her new infant out from its womb, the father of that child would die. He would have a massive heart attack or something and just keel over.

"This went on for a year. Every month she would fuck some asshole from the bar. Every month she would give birth to a new kid. And every month the sperm donor would die. It didn't take long for the village people to figure out that something was very wrong. They were already superstitious as fuck. Hell, most of them hung garlic above their doors to ward off vampires. So, it wasn't a great leap for them to accuse somebody of witchcraft. And, well, in *this* case they were probably right. So, they got all pissed off and went to her hut with their torches and pitchforks. They barred the exits, set the hut on fire, and laughed as they heard her tortured screams. But all they heard was *her* screams. Not the children's. In fact, the remains of the twelve children were never recovered from the ashes. The townsfolk figured she had sacrificed them or eaten them or some shit. But that *isn't* what happened. No, not at all. As that village would find out twenty-three years later.

"Twenty-three years to the day that my ancestor was burned alive, a traveling carnival of gypsies arrived in the village. The people in the village were thrilled to have this vibrant menagerie arrive in their town. They wore multi-colored slacks and gowns and scarves and gaudy jewelry. They played string and wood and percussive instruments. They danced and sang with the locals. They displayed genuine love for the locals. And the locals loved them in return. They loved their exuberance and care-free demeanor. They loved their music and dancing and broad smiles. They helped the gypsies erect a large tent in the middle of the town and took their seats waiting to be enthralled. And enthralled they were.

"The gypsies performed all sorts of acts for the amusement of the townspeople. There were magic tricks and juggling and puppetry. There was music and sword swallowing and fire eating. And there was a grand finale. A large, black carriage that was being drawn by four large, black horses entered the center of the tent. The awestruck audience looked on with great anticipation as they awaited the thrilling conclusion to the festivities. The carriage doors creaked open.

"And twelve colorfully garbed people emerged. There were six young men and six young women. All of them had pale skin, blonde hair and bright blue eyes. They all looked to be in their early twenties. Which they were. They were all between twenty-two and twenty-three years old. The audience applauded and cheered their arrival. They laughed and clapped while they awaited the final act from these twelve attractive young people. The laughing and clapping ended when they heard the growls.

"The young men began foaming at the mouth and growling. Hair began to sprout out of their skin, and their bodies began to contort and grow. The laughing and clapping changed to shrieks of terror as the young werewolves pounced upon the unsuspecting audience members. They slashed and bit and tore through the flesh of the villagers. Those that tried to escape found themselves being pulled back by an unseen force. The six young women's eyes were glowing as their raised arms were emitting some sort of gravitational pull that grabbed the villagers and threw them back into the gnashing teeth of their brothers. But none of them were killed by them. At least not at that moment.

"Once all of the villagers had been subdued, the gypsies rounded up all of the unharmed children and took them to safety. The screaming and bloodied adults were dragged into the local pub. The six young women's eyes glowed once again as they placed an impenetrable lock around the dry wooden structure. Their eyes turned from bright blue to blood red. And the structure went up in flames. The entire population of adults in that town were burned alive. And the gypsies claimed the village as their own. From that point on, it has been called many things. But in hushed tones, all of the locals know it as the Township of Miazga.

"No one knows exactly how my ancestor's children were placed with the gypsies. Perhaps she had a premonition of things to come and hid them away right after each was born. Maybe she just had some shit to do one night and asked the gypsies to babysit. Who the hell knows? But my mother was convinced that our original ancestor sacrificed herself to protect her lineage so that the Family Miazga may ascend to great influence.

"Whatever the reason was, those twelve children lived on. And man, were they fucking little hellions. The men drank and sang and spread their seed with any woman who would spread for *them*. And the young women were *just* as active in *their* seduction of suitors. And they had a fuck-ton of kids! And grandkids!

"Because each child in each generation was just as lustfully full of life as the previous. If not more so. And each child that was produced by a new mate had different abilities. Some turned out to be werewolves, sure. And some, of course, turned out to have some force field thing ability. But as their genetics merged with others, their abilities changed. They evolved. So that each Miazga child that was brought into this world was as unique as a snowflake. None were identical in their supernatural abilities. But they were identical in never committing to one mate. For well over three hundred years not one Miazga has ever been married. Not one has ever changed their name. And there were thousands of them.

"There *were* thousands of them. Until they met a force that even *they* could not overcome. The gypsies in Poland were one of the first groups to be targeted by the invading Nazi regime. They were rounded up and killed by firing squads and gas chambers and all that horrific shit that they were doing. And, well, what *their* ideological ancestors are doing today. But those Nazis weren't just about military might. They had an understanding of the supernatural. It has been said that several members of the Miazga lineage actually helped the Nazis in identifying people with special abilities and showed them how to neutralize their powers. We do not know for sure. All that we know is that our entire family was rounded up and murdered alongside all of the unfortunate others. And we know that in the Township of Miazga, there is a cemetery that houses the final resting places of my family. A cemetery that is vibrant and colorful. There are flowers and trees and bushes. Even in the wintertime, it is always the most beautiful location in the town.

"Except for a corner in the very back of the cemetery. There are three graves there with no inscriptions whatsoever on the headstones. No names. No dates. No identities. But they must be Miazga if they are buried there. But unlike the rest of the cemetery, this location is dark and barren. Nothing will grow there. Birds will not sit on the headstones. Squirrels won't go anywhere near it. Nor will any human visitor. Three graves that have been excommunicated by every living creature on this Earth. That is the punishment for traitors to the Miazga name. Well, and probably an eternity in the fiery pits of hell, but *that's* not special. Hell, that's something that the simpleton fuck-wads in The Regime will find out soon enough.

"Yes, my entire family was wiped off the face of the earth. Well, all except for one. My grandmother. She was smuggled out of Europe and landed in New York. From there, she made her way to rural Nebraska where she met a young man. A nasty young man who raped her, resulting in a pregnancy. My grandmother died while giving birth to my mother. And as my mother was screaming out her very first cries into the chaos that is this world, the young man died too. He had a sudden heart attack while helping his father bale hay. What comes around, goes around, I guess.

"My mother was taken in by a very pious family. She was raised to be subservient to her elders. Especially them. She was used as a maid and a farmhand. She was essentially their slave. Until she ran away as a teenager and went to Omaha. She went there with nothing but the dress on her back. And one small portrait. And two books. The Gypsy Handbook of Ethics and Etiquette, 23rd Edition. And another book that is said to be written in blood. A book that tells the history of her family. The Family Miazga. My mother lived a quiet, solitary life. She worked in mundane jobs. She could have been so much more. Achieved such great things. But she was frightened. She was fright-ened of her family's history and frightened of the abilities that she possessed. She was frightened to have children and carry on the legacy that she viewed as a curse.

"But love happens, right? She fell in love. And although she didn't marry the man, she did bear his child. A girl. My older sister. When nothing bad happened, she thought 'what the hell'? She continued her clandestine relationship with this man. She told me that he loved her and his daughter from afar. He would visit frequently, but due to his standing in the community, and his being married to a wealthy heiress, the affair would be kept secret. And two years later, she gave birth once again. To me.

"My older sister never had any interest in the family history, nor did it seem she possessed any special abilities. And that was perfectly fine by my mother. She was thrilled that the Miazga curse may have finally been broken. Her relief was short-lived, because upon *my* birth, my mother once again felt that the Miazga name and our associated abilities were a curse. Because as I was being delivered, my *real* father, my mother's one true love, had a heart attack and died. He was not my dad. I never knew him. My mother met another man shortly after my birth and married him. She called him her security blanket. He was comforting for her. Plus, it didn't hurt that he was shooting blanks, so another pregnancy was out of the question. My sister and I adored him. He was my hero. He was my dad. And he was murdered by the fucking Regime.

"So, my sister would be shielded from learning about her ancestry. I, on the other hand, was not. From my earliest years, I was always attracted to the supernatural. The paranormal. The macabre. I delighted in watching gruesome movies. I loved to read stories about witchcraft and ghosts and sinister characters getting their bloody comeuppance. And I loved to read a certain book that my mother had placed on her nightstand beneath a certain portrait.

"My mother caught me reading it when I was five years old. Jesus, I can still remember all of the color in her face being flushed away when she saw me. She grabbed the book out of my hand and locked it and the portrait away in her closet. She told me to ignore everything that I had seen. That it was for my protection that I not know of such things. But I couldn't ignore it. I had questions. Lots of them. And my mother, may Enlightenment bless her soul, understood that I would be in constant turmoil if she did not guide me through my family's history. So, she sat with me each night while my sister was playing with her fashion dolls or some shit. She went page by page through the book. She told me that I looked like a youthful, but almost identical version of the original Miazga in the portrait. She also told me that I had a similar anti-authority, fuck-you attitude as she. Seriously. Her words. My mother was the sweetest soul that I have ever met. But fuck, could she talk like a fuckin' sailor. I'm glad I didn't inherit *that* shit.

"As we were looking through the book one night when I was six, she asked me to flip through the pages. Were there any particular phrases or excerpts that stood out to me. I flipped through until I stopped on page twenty-three. On that page there was an incantation and an explanation of what that incantation can do for one who has the ability to access it. I remember the glowing words on the page pounding in my brain until it was imbedded there. 'Yes, this one,' I had said to her. She looked at the passage, turned ashen white, and took the book from me. She tried taking me to church. And, well, *that* shit didn't work. Besides, we just went to church to steal shit anyway. As much as my mother tried to disregard her past, she could never get the gypsy out of her. And she knew that *I* was connected to it and always would be. So, she tried to teach me about the power of the passage and how it connects me with vengeful spirits in Enlightenment. I now understood my nature. I understood my calling. And I understood that nobody was going to fuck with me.

"My mother held that same ashen expression when I woke up after being dead for three days. As did my dad. I was only six, but I felt such a rage in my heart after that pedo priest tried to fondle me. I went into the bathroom and saw my *real* father's razor lying on the sink. After all those years since his passing, and despite her marrying another man, my mother had never disturbed it. It had always been there. And my six-year-old mind now understood why. My *real* father's razor was to be used for my demise. And my salvation.

"A year later, my dad was ushered out of our home and into a re-education camp. Soon after, we were informed of his supposed accident and subsequent death. Only a few weeks later, my mother died. Our house burned down with my mother in it while my sister and I were at school. No one knows how it started. It was ruled accidental, but I think that's bullshit. It happened right after my sister and I were "borrowing" some cupcakes from the church potluck. There was a woman there who looked down at us. Once she saw our faces, she gasped. She then looked at my mother with an evil expression. We were quickly whisked away and we never went to church again. Because that woman was the wife of my real father. She looked at us and she saw *him* in our young faces. And she knew. She's rich, well-connected, and vengeful as fuck. I just know she had my mother murdered. But I can't prove it. And if I'm wrong, and I try that slit and slash shit, it'll come back on me. And Uncle Joe will be pissed. But if I can ever prove that shit, I'm going to roast hot dogs over that bitch's burning corpse.

"After my mother died, my sister and I were sent to separate foster homes. She ended up being adopted by hers. I, um, kept running away from mine. But hey, I muddled through. Emancipated myself at sixteen, came to Hollywood a couple years later to be a star, and here we are. And as different as my sister and I are, I love her so. And her daughter. Well, *especially* her daughter. She has that same twinkle in her eye as I did at that age. The Miazga curse may have passed over my sister, but it sure as hell is firmly implanted in her daughter. She's gonna be a fuckin' hellion. And I'm going to be by her side to guide her.

"Wow. I haven't thought about this shit for so long. My family. My sordid, fucked-up, special family. But talking about this helps. Thanks for listening, Angel." Renata began chuckling as she made faces at herself in the make-up mirror. She then responded to herself in a deeper, cartoonish voice, "You're welcome, Renata. You can talk to me anytime."

"And me as well," Ginger said from behind her. Renata jumped out of her seat and grasped at her heart. "Oh, Jesus Christ Ginger! I didn't know you were there! Wear a fucking bell or something, wouldja?"

The laughing Ginger said, "I'm so sorry. But you were so caught up with bearing your soul to yourself and your story was so riveting that

I didn't want to interrupt you. Anyway, Sophia's just about done with her scene. Are you ready?"

"Yeah, yeah, just a sec," Renata said in a hurried voice as she turned back to the make-up mirror. "Let me just fix my face. I wanna look my best for when I, you know, fuck up these asshole's faces. And make sure Virgina's ready. She has a lot of booze to conjure for her scene. Yeah, this is gonna be a gas."

Chapter 11

Mixology

"And then there were ten," Renata coldly stated to her trembling audience as what was left of Kyle Splicer's soggy body appeared in his theatre seat. "We're about a quarter of the way through the feature, and I'm just curious. How are you enjoying my film? Are you captivated by it? Is there enough action? Aren't you just sitting on the edge of your seat in anticipation of who our next victim will be? Please. Give me your thoughts. I have a thick skin. I can take it. And it's not like kissing my ass is going to help you, so let's have it."

"It's a piece of shit," Pug Homleyman gruffly responded. "You wanted to know what I think? Well, I think it's a piece of shit. What's the point? It's just scene after scene of some chick murdering some guy. There's no real plot or story here. Hell, there's hardly any character development. This is nothing more than political rage torture porn."

"Fuck yeah, it is," the laughing Renata responded as her face glowed dark red. "That's *exactly* what it is. It's providing a service. My film is doing what every victim of horrendous abuse fantasizes about. Identify your abuser. Unmask him for the disgusting piece of shit that he is. Get him in a vulnerable situation. Then fuck him up. Give him a taste of his own merciless medicine. Let *him* feel what *you* felt as he was abusing you. Make him scream for mercy just as he made you do. Laugh at him while he dies, just as he laughed at you. Treat him like the insignificant worm that he is. You all made us feel insignificant. We were nothing more than props in your twisted fucking fantasies to be discarded when you got bored with us. Well, we *aren't* insignificant. We are real human beings with real lives and real aspirations. To you, we were nothing more than a hole to stick your pathetic cocks into. Well, turnabout is fair play, gentlemen. To us, you are nothing more than a revenge fantasy. And we're going to play this shit to the hilt.

"So yeah, political rage torture porn has a nice ring to it. It should be the tagline of this fucking movie. Sure as hell better than the tagline for *Take My Hand*. What was it again? Oh yeah. This is so laughably bad. 'Join Dear Leader in his Golden World of Patriotism. Godliness. Sacrifice.' Fuck that! What a bunch of propaganda bullshit! It still blows my mind that anyone fell for his shit, let alone tens of millions of people. Seriously, just how self-absorbed are these people? Or are they just that fucking dumb? They carried his banners and marched and bought all of his fucking cheaply made merchandise because he made them believe he was their champion. How? How could they believe that? In what bizzarro universe does a narcissistic megalomaniac who has a history of fucking over *every single person* he has ever come into contact with become a champion for anybody but himself? What a bunch of gullible fucking morons!

"All he has done since coming into power is strip the populace of their rights and economic prosperity and dignity. And he has turned on all the of White men who are exactly like him. Yep, they voted for this shit and now they can barely afford to put food on the table. Health care is a luxury. The education system and libraries and media have all been gutted so that people are even *more* fucking stupid and dependent upon The Regime for their survival. Family farms? The oligarchs own them. Small downtown businesses? The oligarchs own them. Natural resources? The oligarchs own them. The Regime have given the rich, White oligarchs everything in this society and everybody else are nothing more than plebes who are supposed to pay tribute to Dear Leader for the meager crumbs that they are left with.

"Which is why he has you produce shitty movies like *this*, right? It's all a part of the same drip, drip, drip of propaganda. The same assault on our ability to process information and see anything other than what The Regime wants us to see. It's mind-control disguised as entertainment. Yeah, yeah, yeah. I know you've heard all of this shit from me before. But that's how propaganda works. This is why The Regime repeats the same bullshit lies day after day, week after week, month after month, year after year. It's that constant drip, drip, drip of bullshit that causes people's eyes to glaze over until they are nothing more than mindless zombie servants of The Regime.

"And that is why *I* repeat the same themes over and over. I'm trying to get people to *open* their eyes. Open their eyes so that they can see how they are being lied to. Used. Manipulated. Open their eyes to the fact that The Regime cares for nothing except absolute power and wealth for themselves. Open their eyes to see how ridiculous and futile and counterproductive their hatred towards others is. Open their eyes to so that they can recognize what is toxic and what is humane. And *I* understand just as the propagandists understand that you can't accomplish that with one passing comment. In order for the message to be absorbed by the collective consciousness, it must be repeated over and over and over. Until cracks begin to form and they begin to question their own beliefs. Until they can identify the actions that are being taken by the powerful to suppress and control them. Until they realize that their freedoms are being stripped away and they are now viewed as nothing more than subservient cattle. It has taken decades of toxic lies being repeated over and over to instill this insecurity and hatred. And it will take decades of *many* voices speaking of true freedom and humanity to turn that around. I am only *one* of those voices. And not a terribly important one, at that. But I will use my voice to repeat my message of humanity and earned retribution until I am no longer able to speak.

"Which will be a while, boys. So, you might as well just settle in and enjoy the rest of the film. Mine and this godforsaken pile of dung that you assholes produced. How anyone could find *this* shit entertaining is beyond me. I was literally embarrassed when I first read the script. But being a working actress is better than being a starving one, right? I remember how excited I was when I first met the casting director, Bob Lemmings. Even though he was this fragile, boney-looking motherfucker with a bad greasy comb-over, I knew the influence he had. I knew he was the chief talent scout and casting director for DL Studios. And he was so nice to me. He told me how talented I was and that I would be perfect for this part. He even admitted that this movie was absolute drivel that had been ripped off by their head writer, but that it was a major role in a major movie that would lead to more substantial parts. And I took that bait. Hook, line, and sinker. He, of course, didn't tell me what horrors you were all planning on putting me through in order to land those other parts, now did you, Bob? But water under the bridge, I suppose. Thanks for your feedback, Pug. I can honestly say that I could give absolutely zero fucks about your opinion of my work. Well, gotta go and see if our next actress is ready. While you're waiting, please enjoy this next scene from *Take My Hand*. Well, 'enjoy' is a bit strong. Please *tolerate* this next scene. See ya soon, boys."

Chastity pulled on the damp hem of her dress that was covered in her brother's patriotic seed and sticking to her thighs. "I just knew that Chad was wiser than I. How could I not have seen that every time he was looking at my underpants that he was doing it out of the love that he had for me and for Dear Leader? I feel so ashamed to have doubted him. He and Poppa and Dear Leader are right. We women have been put upon this Earth for the glorious purpose of serving our men. And that is what I will do from now on. Without question. But first, I must sell my eggs. And here we are. The best egg market in town. But what is that behind the barbed wire fence in the restricted area? Oh my. Just look at that dress in that store being run by brown people. It is *beautiful*. And the one that I am wearing is soiled by Chad's divine seed. Oh, how I wish I had a dress that pretty. But my eggs won't fetch enough money for it. Unless...what is that sign across the street?"

Chastity sauntered toward the rusty fence that was surrounded by masked, armed men. "Excuse me, kind sir," she said to one of the imposing masked men. "Thank you for your service to Dear Leader and to our country. I think it is just wonderful how you are separating the brown-skinned ones from us children of God. But I see a sign over there at that ugly little store that says 'Buying Eggs For the Best Prices'. May I please enter so that I may inquire about selling my eggs?"

"Sure you can, sweetheart," the man said. "I don't know why you'd want to do business with those (derogatory term omitted), but hey. It's your life. You better just understand that those (derogatory term omitted) bastards will screw you out of every penny if you let them get their hooks into you. That's all they care about. Money. And I've heard they can turn into cockroaches at night, too. Yep, they may have the same colored skin as us, but they are not like us. They are servants of the devil. They are not the servants of our lord, Dear Leader. Do you still want to go over there?"

"Um, well, yes, I would," Chastity replied. "I certainly understand how nasty those people are, but they pay higher prices for eggs and just across the street is a shop with the prettiest dress. Don't you think it would look nice on me?"

"Yeah, yeah it would," the armed guard lasciviously said. "But you better be careful in *that* shop too. It's run by the brown skinned. And you know what *they're* like don't you? All they think about is sex. They make you listen to their pounding rhythms until you get carried away and start dancing and gyrating and before you know it, they're raping you and then you're stuck with a screaming brown kid."

"Well, I will certainly be careful, sir. Thank you for the warning," Chastity replied. "But I believe I would still like to go over there. Just to look around, if that is okay with you." The guard's eyes roamed Chastity's tone figure before saying, "Yeah, alright. I'll let you through. But there's a toll you have to pay."

"A toll?" Chastity screamed out. "Oh, darn. I haven't money to pay a toll. I guess I'll just have to sell my eggs on this side of the fence. But thank you anyway, kind sir."

"Okay, wait, wait, wait," the guard blurted out. "Listen, uh, I'd really like to see you in that dress. So, uh, maybe there's something that you can do to pay the toll." "Well, what would *that* be?" Chastity inquired. "Um," the guard began answering, "well, you see, the toll is paid for patriotic reasons. It is money that keeps these fences up and keeps you and your family safe. But, um, I *also* keep your family safe, right? But I can't do that without your support. So, if we could just go behind this shed over here and you could use your pretty little mouth to, um, *support* me. Then I can consider the toll to have been paid, and I can let you through."

"Why, it would be my absolute honor to support you, sir!" Chastity squealed. Three minutes later the guard emerged from behind the shed while zipping his pants. Chastity followed wearing a big smile on her face while wiping her mouth. "Thank you so much sir for allowing me to support you and Dear Leader's mission," Chastity stated while walking toward the barbed-wire gate. "Will I be required to pay another toll to get back in?" The guard appeared to smile under his mask and breathily said, "Oh yeah. Yeah. You'll need to pay another toll. You know. To support me so that I can keep your family safe."

"Okeedokee!" Chastity exclaimed. "I'll be back in just a little while! And thank you, kind sir, for your service. And for allowing *me* to service *you*."

The screen turned dark red and Chastity's pure face faded into that of the brunette, curly-haired Virginia. "Like, what's up, guys?" she gleefully asked as the camera zoomed out revealing her body that was barely covered in a polka-dot bikini. "Do you guys, like, remember that pool party scene from my movie *Know When to Say When?* You know, like, the scene where all those men got me drunk, then had their way with me? I remember being so, like, nervous, before that scene. But Bob, you were so helpful. You made me a drink to calm my nerves. Then, all those *other* actors made me drinks. And before I knew it, I was, like, totally sloshed! And those men weren't acting, were they? Nope. They really did get me drunk, and they really did have their way with me. On camera. For the whole world to see.

"And I was too hammered to even know what was happening. Until the next day. I was, like, totally devastated. I couldn't believe what you had done to me. I felt used. I felt ashamed. I felt, like, completely hopeless. I was hungover, disillusioned, and depressed. So, I made myself one last cocktail. With a special ingredient in it. So, do you remember that scene? I'm sure you do. But, like, I really didn't like how that scene ended. You know, with the gang rape and all. So, Renata thought it would be a good idea to shoot that scene over. But with a different ending."

"Who in the fuck is Renata?" Pug asked his assistant director. "Angel," Kellen responded. "Renata is Angel's real name." "Oh, right," Pug replied as he shrugged.

"So, I need a co-star for this scene," Virgina continued. "And Bob, I think it should be you. You were the one who fixed me a drink to get me ready for my scene. So, I'd like to return the favor and make *you* a drink to relax you for *your* scene. Like, take my hand, Bob. Let's go to a swingin' pool party."

The film faded into a brilliant red, sunny day by a pool. The majestic waves lapped the side of the pool as Bob's frozen body sat in a lounge chair. From the far end of the pool, a shirtless, muscular man who was fishing leaves from the water winked suggestively at the enthralled Virgina. "Oh, don't mind him, Bob," Virginia stated as she stood behind the bar cart. "That's just, like, Claudia's pool boy. She let me borrow him for this scene. You see, I, like, haven't had enough conjuring coins to make my *own* pool boy, but Claudia is such a sweetheart that she told me she'd share. And believe you me, I plan on doing just that. I mean, just *look* at him! Hubba, hubba, right Bob?

"Anyway, he won't bother our fun. Oh man, you are really white, Bob! You're gonna get, like, all sunburned! Here, let me help you with that." Virgina took a tube of sunscreen and squirted a glob on Bob's quivering face. The white goo dripped down Bob's face and onto his plain white shirt. "Oh man!" Virginia squealed. "Does *that* bring back memories! Your face looks a lot like *mine* after my gang rape scene! Kinda makes you feel silly, doesn't it Bob? Oh, hey, hey. You're all shaky and shit. There's no reason to be frightened. Just ignore the camera and go with it. Here, let me fix you something to calm your nerves. Are you a gin man? Whiskey? Vodka? Oh, it doesn't matter. How about I make you my special cocktail? Hmmmm. What sounds good?

"Ooooo, this anti-freeze is a pretty green color. How about a shot of that? And then one part arsenic. Yum. Now one part cyanide. Mmmmm. And just a splash of sweet and sour mix. Top it off with a poison ivy leaf, and there we have it! My signature cocktail! The Tiki Tonic! Alright, now let's have a sip. Come on Bob, open your mouth. Oh right. You can't. I have you, like, paralyzed. What to do, what to do? Oh! I know! I'll use this funnel that we use to put gasoline in our lawn mower. Yep, we have to cut our own grass in Enlightenment, Bob. Don't ask. Okay now we'll just jam this funnel down your throat like this. Yep, kinda makes you gag, doesn't it? Now you know how *I* felt. I mean, like, most of those guys weren't much to write home about, but Jesus fucking Christ! That *one* dude was slinging an anaconda! I nearly threw up!

"And now, here comes your drink. There we go. Yes, good boy. You'll be nice and relaxed in no time. In fact, you'll be dead to the world. Oh, I bet that's really warm going down your throat, now, isn't it? Oh, your eyes are getting teary. And really fuckin' red. You can feel my drink eating away at you, can't you? All of those yummy ingredients burning through your throat and organs. Wow, that's some really bloody frothy shit coming out of your mouth, Bob. Eeeew. It's all bubbly. Oh wow! Are those pieces of your organs coming out, Bob? Is my cocktail causing your organs to break apart then get puked up? Yeah, I bet that's what's happening. I shoulda warned ya. I like my drinks with a bit of a kick. Oh shit, Bob. You have blood spurting out of your pants leg. Is blood coming out of your ass and dick? Yup. Your ball sack must have just exploded, 'cause there goes your testacies into the...oh shit! Right into the pool! Gross! Good thing I have a pool boy. I bet *he* knows what to do with a set of balls, am I right, Bob? Huh. Jeez, Bob. I'm really sorry. I don't think the sunscreen is going to work on *this*. I mean, like, your entire face is starting to crack open and, oh cool! Your skin is, like, totally slipping right off your skull!

And you're still alive to feel it all! Now is that one mean drink or what, Bob?

"Oh, hey baby? Turn up this song wouldja? I just *love* those Latin beats. Makes me all hot and shit. Yeah, yeah, yeah. Dance around for me baby. I'll be joining you in just a sec. Okay, Bob. This has been fun and everything, but I'm kinda bored with you and I kinda wanna have some fun with the pool boy. So, wouldja just, like, you know. Die? I mean, you don't even have a face now. Just a bloody skull with two eyes poking out and....ow! Fuck! Your eye just popped out and hit me in the forehead! Well, make that one eye and...ow! Goddammit. I've got to get out of the splash zone. Am I right, Bob? Bob? You still there? Okay, Bob. I'm sorry, but I think you've had a bit too much to drink. I'm gonna have to cut you off and send you on your way."

Virgina was joined by the pool boy. The pair wrapped their arms around one another while standing directly behind the bloodied and decimated corpse of Bob. His greasy scalp was sliding down the side of his exposed skull while his entrails oozed out of his ruptured abdomen. "Oh, Bob!" Virgina shouted through her laughter. "You really are a good time at pool parties. You, like, really let it all hang out!" Virgina and her pool boy smiled as they stared directly into the camera. Virginia then said, "And let that be a lesson to *all* of you out there. There's nothing wrong with imbibing a little bit. But moderation is the key. Always know when to say when. Otherwise, you might end up like Bob here. You know. Skinless with your organs and shit bursting out of your body. And no eyes. Or balls. Bad shit like that. So, watch how much you drink. Good-Byeeeee!" The scene faded as the smiling pair waved at their dismayed audience from in front of a glorious crimson sunset.

CHAPTER 12

UNCLE JOE, THE ICE CREAM MAN

"Why, *there's* my little Renata!" Uncle Joe exclaimed as he arrived on the actresses' cloud in Enlightenment. "My little birdies told me that you had returned, but I just couldn't believe them. Why would my Renata not come to visit me?"

"Oh, Uncle Joe, I'm so sorry!" Renata replied as she firmly embraced the hulk of a spirit that was Uncle Joe. Although standing only a little over six feet, he appeared to her to be a giant. Balding head. Broad shoulders. Tree trunks for legs. And that smile. That ever-present smile that beamed down upon her every time they had met. Their first meeting was when she was six years old. She was but a child who had no idea how to wield her powers. And then, she met Uncle Joe who took her for ice cream at the Cloud Nine Shopping Emporium. He explained just how powerful she was and exactly how to harness those abilities to go back to Earth in spiritual form and exact her revenge upon those who had wronged her. He gave her a demonstration. And she delighted in every moment of it. Renata proved to be an apt pupil.

Her next encounter with Uncle Joe was when she was twelve. Only this time, the lesson that he taught was restraint. He had told her, 'The punishment must fit the crime'. So, she didn't kill that little bully who used to call her names. She simply turned him into a blob of ridicule. Her third encounter was quite disappointing. Her sixteen-year-old broken heart left Enlightenment unfulfilled after Uncle Joe had told her that being ignored by her schoolgirl crush was not grounds for death. Or *any* form of reprisal for that matter. In fact, he had told her that if she wielded her power against an innocent, that the reprisal would boomerang back upon her. She left Enlightenment with a shattered heart. And a belly full of Butter Ripple ice cream.

And just last year, Renata saw Uncle Joe once again. This time, the pair hugged and laughed as they watched her former agent's balls and phallus fall off in the shower. As she looked into his brilliant blue eyes, his parting words from that day rang in her ears. "Always remember, Renata. You will *always* have a home here in the clouds with me and the other spirits. But not yet. Now is not your time. I truly love our visits, but you must return to your true home on *your* Earth now. You have much to accomplish, my young friend. Much indeed. I have seen it. Well, actually, *I* haven't seen it. I was told by The Four Horsemen of the Apocalypse what your fate will be. Then they started playing cowboys and cowgirls while riding around on their Shetland ponies. Because, um, well, The Four Horsemen are ten-year-old children. No shit. I'm not fucking with you on that. Anyway, back to my main point. What the horsemen told me was that you and another shall save humankind on your Earth one day. In fact, that day is soon approaching. And I may be tough, but I'm not one to question those all-powerful little tikes. So, return home now. I pray to The Keepers of Enlightenment that we will never again have to meet under such grave circumstances. But if we ever do, I will have a stool waiting for you next to me at the ice cream shop."

Yes, Uncle Joe always held that brilliant smile upon his kind face. He would smile when he was a mortal upon his Earth while beating a neighborhood bully. Or wife beater. Or any other form of degenerate who dared to oppress those he cared about. On his Earth, Uncle Joe was known as the neighborhood fixer. If you had a broken pipe, you could call Uncle Joe. If your car was stuck in the snow, Uncle Joe would be there. If you needed transportation to the store, Uncle Joe's shuttle was at your service. And if you had a husband who regaled in turning your face black and blue, Uncle Joe was there too. There were many occasions that torturous wails could be heard in a quaint neighborhood in Madison, Wisconsin. And the joyous sounds of many parties that were thrown soon after.

He smiled as he completed his contract work for an international hit-man agency based in Brooklyn. Although he was reluctant to join, he had been coerced into joining Murder, Inc. Coerced by the brutal beating of his beloved wife, Blair. The couple lost their child that day. On that day, Blair's beaten body could no longer sustain the special life that it had carried. Uncle Joe did not smile on that day. Nor did he smile on the day that his best friend set him up to be murdered. But his smile returned as he looked down from Enlightenment and watched his beloved niece follow in his footsteps. And he smiled as she joined him in Enlightenment and the pair were once again united to rid the demonic scourge known as Vetis from their Earth.

And he smiled every time he saw his favorite pupil, Renata. "I'm so sorry, Uncle Joe," Renata said to him. "I had every intention of coming to see you, but my latest, um, project, is a bit time sensitive. You see, this movie production company that is run by the evil Regime abuses young actresses so brutally that they eventually have no hope and take their own lives. And they intended to do the same to me during the screening of my debut film. So, I thought it would be really fuckin' cool to give these other actresses the opportunity of an after-lifetime. See those dudes down there?"

Uncle Joe peered down from the clouds, through the theatre screen, and found nine terrified men quivering in their theatre seats. And four mangled corpses. "Yeah, I see 'em," Uncle Joe answered. "They look like a bunch of motherfuckin' douchebags."

"Oh, they *are*, Uncle Joe! They *are*!" Renata squealed in response through her laughter. "They do absolutely unspeakable things to innocent women. Which shouldn't be surprising. They are members of The Regime on my Earth. And from the top down, these men are known for their brutality. Men, women, children. Doesn't matter. They abduct innocent people off the streets. Send them to torture camps. Rape them. Torture them. Murder them. Just for their own enjoyment. They do it just because they can. They are disgusting. They are, as you said, motherfuckin' douchebags. And they must be stopped. And I don't know how to stop them *all*, but I sure as hell can enjoy watching *these* fine actresses beat the living fuck out of them. Or drown them. Or poison them. Or whatever they want to do with their special scene in the movie.

"Which reminds me, Hey! Is Claudia about ready? Her scene is up right after this little snippet from my film, *Take My Hand*. Oh! Uncle Joe! Would you like to watch it with us? I mean, the movie itself is absolute garbage. The script was stolen from a pukey book by some unimaginative hack and the entire thing is nothing but propaganda for The Regime. It's overtly misogynistic, xenophobic, and racist while spouting supposed Christian values. You know. Not unlike a whole lot of fuckin' churches down there. Those hypocritical Christian bastards will eat this shit up. So, its absolute trash, but I'm really proud of my performance in it. Would you like to stay and watch? This next scene is only a few minutes long and then, well, *heh, heh, heh.* Then one of our lovely actresses will get to star in her very own revenge torture scene. And one of *those* motherfuckin' douchebags will be her co-star. For a while. Until the motherfucker is dead."

"This is really amazing, Renata. I'm so proud of you," Uncle Joe gushed as he pulled a pillowy seat up next to her and conjured a bag of popcorn. "Hey! How did you do that?" Renata asked. "What? This?" Uncle Joe replied as he laughed. "Oh, this shit is nothing. Only uses two conjuring coins. And I've got tons of them. You have no idea how much you can earn up here by answering people's prayers on one of the Earths. Or other planets that exist throughout the endless parallel universes. You answer a prayer; you get paid in conjuring coins. You should come by the house sometime. I just conjured an incredible addition. It's a day room that leads out to a pine deck with a built-in hot tub. Now, I must admit, that cost me a pretty conjuring coin, but it was so worth it. Me and my beloved wife Blair soak in the hot tub while the eternal stars shine down upon us. We drink a little wine, then we, um, oh. Never mind. You shouldn't be listening to this. My point is, conjuring up some popcorn doesn't cost much. This is like, a millionth of an answered prayer or something."

Renata's face displayed half shock and half amusement. "Oh my God!" She yelled out. "Are you telling me that spirits up here fuck?"

Before an embarrassed Uncle Joe could respond, Virginia's voice appeared from behind them. "Uh, yeah. Like, duh. What in the hell do you think I want a pool boy for? I don't even have a pool! I just want a super cute plaything to, um, clean my pool, heh, heh, heh."

"Listen, don't we have a movie to watch?" Uncle Joe asked in an attempt to change the subject. He waved his hands and a box of conjured candy appeared between them. "Here. Want some chocolate covered nuts? Or red licorice? How about gumballs?"

Renata laughed in response, laid her blonde head upon Uncle Joe's broad shoulder and said, "I'm fine for the moment, Uncle Joe. Let's just watch my scene. But maybe some ice cream would be good?"

Chastity entered the restricted area and nearly twisted an ankle in a huge pothole in the pavement. She looked down in disgust and said, "Oh dear lord. Why don't they fix their streets? Why do they live in such squalor? I nearly fell and broke my eggs. And without my eggs, I can't afford to buy that pretty dress in that shop's window. Dear Leader is right. As is Poppa and Momma. These creatures truly are animals. But they pay top dollar for eggs, so away we go."

Chastity visibly shuddered as she opened the squeaky door to a dingy grocery store. The dilapidated wooden shelves were covered in flaking paint and held dusty cans of soups and vegetables. Each floorboard creaked as she cautiously made her way to the front counter. She clutched her eggs to her breast and cleared her throat to attract the attention of the storekeeper.

"Why, hello there young lady, how may I help you?" the storekeeper said in an evil sneer as he turned to face her. He had greasy hair that appeared to be pasted to his head and an overly exaggerated long nose. He wore a black cap on top of his head and his greasy hair curled down the side of his pale face. His teeth were dark yellow and rotting. Chastity recoiled from the stench of his breath before answering.

"Yes, um, hello there," she answered in a shaky voice while her blue eyes darted down to look at her feet. "Oh, dear lord!" She exclaimed as dozens of cockroaches began climbing her tone, white calves.

"Oh, don't mind *them*, my dear," the storekeeper said through a devious snicker. "That is just some members of my family coming to say hello to you. They are quite excited. We don't get many visitors from the unrestricted area. Now, what brings you into my fine establishment?"

Chastity vigorously shook her legs, causing the roaches to go flying before saying, "Um, yes. I have come to sell my eggs. Your sign says that you pay top dollar for them and I would like to inquire as to what you would pay for these."

"Yes, yes, we do *indeed* pay top dollar for eggs," the storekeeper replied as his dead eyes sparkled with greed. "Top dollar indeed. And these are quite fine specimens. They would be perfect for frying or using in a sacrifice ritual."

"Using in a *what*?" Chastity nervously asked. "Oh, but I joke, my dear," the storekeeper snorted. "Just checking to see if you were paying attention. Your eggs are quite, um, peeeerfect. Yes, they look quite delicious. And for *these* eggs, I would pay you this amount." He pulled a wad of bills from an old cigar box and presented it to Chastity.

"Oh my!" Chastity exclaimed with joy. "Why this is *way* more than the oligarch's shops will pay! Although, I have been told that the oligarch's money comes from pure and honest means and that *your* money comes from doing evil. Is that true, mister?"

"Why, who told you such a thing?" the storekeeper replied while recoiling from the counter and clutching his heart. "Why, nothing could be further from the truth, my dear. Every penny that we collect has been earned by us through, um, hard work. Yes, that's it! We work hard for our money and would never lie to get it. Or steal. Or take advantage of our neighbor's good will until they trust us implicitly and, over time, hand all of their money over to us. And their jewelry. And worldly possessions, heh, heh, heh. We would *never* form media and entertainment empires to indoctrinate the ignorant into buying our wares or installing us as the ultimate world power. We would *never* do such things, my dear. As I said, we earn every penny through our hard work."

Chastity heard the tittering of a group of cockroaches before saying, "Whew. Well, that's a relief. I wouldn't want to go against Dear Leader's preachings by selling my eggs for money of ill-repute. So, yes. I accept your offer. You may have my eggs for the price you have given me."

"Eggggggsellent," the storekeeper said while reaching for his newly purchased eggs. "Yes, this is quite wonderful, my dear. You come back anytime. I will always have money for your eggs. And anything else that you may wish to sell me. I will always pay you top dollar. As will my family."

Chastity shrieked as thousands of snickering cockroaches came scurrying out of the floorboards, off of the shelves, and out of cracks in the walls. Thousands more poured upon her head from the ceiling as she fought to brush them off of her quivering body. She screamed once again and ran out of the shop and back into the garbage-filled asphalt of the restricted area.

"Pity," the shopkeeper said as his disgusting insect family climbed over his face and body. "She didn't drop the money. The pure ones usually drop the money. Ah well. We can always print more, now can't we, my lovelies?"

"Jesus fucking Christ, Renata!" Uncle Joe yelled out. "This shit is really fucking antisemitic!"

"Yeah, I told you it was absolute trash," Renata answered while wiping ice cream from her chin. "This is the shit that The Regime spreads on my Earth. Pretty disgusting, huh?" "I'll say," Uncle Joe replied. "And people *believe* this shit?" "Oh, you'd be surprised," Renata answered.

The smile faded from Uncle Joe's face for the first time since his reunion with his young friend. He stroked his square chin and said in a remorseful voice, "You know what? No, I'm *not* surprised. I've seen a lot of shit in my lifetime. And after-lifetime. And *nothing* about human nature surprises me anymore. There are tons of really good people in these worlds. People who would give you their last piece of bread or take the shirts right off of their back to keep you warm. Tons of them. They are loving, peaceful beings. And that is the problem. They're *too* peaceful. *Too* loving. *Too* trusting.

"Because there are tons of *other* people too. Soulless, evil people who will exploit you and use you in the most horrific ways just for their own amusement. And there are tons *more* people who are more than willing to discard their so-called faith and sense of ethics for the promise of money or power. They are seduced by the evil ones and allow them to rot their souls. I've seen it firsthand many times over. And the evil ones will run right over the pure. Because the pure cannot fathom that anybody could be so evil. They try to compromise with them. Reason with them. Until it's too late. They finally realize that true evil *does* exist in the hearts of some when they feel the knife in their back. I'm sorry, Renata. I didn't mean to spoil the moment. Let's get back to your movie."

"Chastity!" her brother Chad yelled out as he grabbed her elbow. "Where have you been? I've been looking all over for you! What are you doing in the Restricted Area?"

"I just sold my eggs, Chad!" Chastity squealed with excitement. "Just look at how much money I got for them!"

"Wow, that is really good," Chad replied. "But you got it from the thieves, Chastity! You know we're not to do business with them! What are we going to tell Poppa and Momma?"

"Oh, please don't tell them, Chad!" Chastity pleaded. "Pleeeease? I'll do *anything* you want. Please? If you support me, then, um, I'll support *you*. Again."

Chad's eyes lasciviously roamed over his sister's taught body before saying, "Well, okay. But just this once. Come on. We'd better get back to our people in the unrestricted area. Let's get away from these vermin."

"Okay, but I have just one stop left to make first," Chastity replied as she watched a muscular tan boy arranging a pretty dress in the shop across the street. "Just go to the car. I promise, I won't be long."

The movie screen turned dark red and Claudia's smirking face glared down at her captive, trembling audience.

"Wow, that was a really cool effect," Uncle Joe stated. Renata giggled and said, "Oh yeah, you need to stay for this next scene. The fun's *really* about to start."

"But that character's name is Chad?" Uncle Joe inquired. "Is he one of the douchebags in the audience?"

"Oh yeah," Renata answered. "The actor's name is Lance. Lance Thruster. But he's not going to be in the movie for a while. Why? Is there something special about the name, 'Chad?'

Uncle Joe let out a belly laugh and said while wiping tears of glee from his eyes, "Yeah. You could say so. Hey! I have an idea! Would it possible for me to invite my niece to watch the scene that this Chad is going to be in? She rules Perdition on the far side of Enlightenment, so it'll take me a while to get her. Would it be okay to bring her here for that scene? She *really* has a thing for 'Chads.'"

CHAPTER 13

ASS TO MOUTH

"Why, hello guys!" Claudia enthusiastically squeaked to her quivering audience. Nine men stared at the young actress who was wearing a diabolical smile on the crimson screen. Nine men began trembling uncontrollably. Despite the chilly temperatures in the theatre, nine men began sweating through their suits as they wondered which of them would be the next victim of this macabre haram of retribution.

"Do ya like how I look?" Claudia continued. "I got myself all dolled up for ya! Just how ya like me! Do you like my black bangs? And my skin-tight black mini dress? Really does wonders for my tits, don'tcha think? And my legs! See how long and tone they are? And way down on my cute little feet are my newest black pumps. Do ya like them? These cost me quite the pretty conjuring coin, let me tell ya. I bought these on Cloud Nine. Oh, you don't know about that do ya?

"See, Cloud Nine Shopping Emporium is where all the spirits go to shop. It's a wonderful commercial strip mall with all sorts of stuff. You need a new purse? Cloud Nine. A new dress? Cloud Nine. How about a wok? Yep, you guessed it fellas! Cloud Nine. Shopping, dining, dancing. It's a one stop pleasure palace conveniently located right off of the Saint Olga Expressway in the middle of Enlightenment. They have everything that you may ever want. You really should check it out once you get there.

"Um, well, *actually*, you probably won't get that chance, will you? I mean, I'm kinda thinkin' you gents might be going to a place a bit, um, *warmer*. Why, I'm betting that Kyle, Bob, Phillip, and Jake are roasting their chestnuts over an open fire even as we speak." Claudia's eyes sparkled as she looked around the theatre and found the four mangled corpses of the co-stars of the four previous scenes. "Wow. My fellow actresses sure did a number on *you* four, now didn't they? I know you can't answer me, but I'm just *dying* to know what the Dark Lord is doing to you right now. I'm gonna have to apply for a visa and take a tour of that place sometime. Did you gents know you can do that? Yep, you can take tours of hell. Tourism is a *total* cash cow for Satan. Spirits from Enlightenment spend tons of conjuring coins just to go and check it out. Oh, and see what has happened to their deceased enemies. Me and the other ladies have been talkin' and we're thinkin' about going on a road trip to hell just to visit you gents after this is all over. And try the wings. I've heard they have the *hottest* wings in the *entire* universe at this joint called 'Just Wingin' It'. Kinda sounds like how this author writes his books, but I digress.

"Actually, it isn't so much of a *road* trip as it is a portal through the interconnected galactical realms trip. But that takes too long to say, so road trip it is! Would you like that? Would you like for us to come and visit? Would you like us to watch your eternal damnation? Why, sure ya would! Everybody loves a visitor! Even when you're getting repeatedly fucked up the ass by a flaming pitchfork! Am I right? You boys should know about *that*, right? You sure as hell put some hot shit up *my* ass, now didn'tcha?

"But why dwell on that? Let's just let bygones be bygones, alright? Good. Now, back to my main point. How do you like my new black pumps? Pretty, aren't they? Oh, they look red to you, don't they? Yeah. Renata's blood is all over this piece of film that's going through the projector, so I look totally red. *Blood* red, heh, heh, heh."

"Who the fuck is Renata?" Pug whispered to Ezekiel who just shrugged in response. "Oh, Jesus Christ!" Arpeggio Dante yelled out.

"How many times do you have to be told this? Renata is Angel's *real* name! Angel Feathers! Who plays Chastity in our shitty movie! I know the same character has three different names in this book, but it *really* isn't that fucking difficult."

"No, it really isn't," Claudia agreed as her voice darkened. "It isn't difficult at all. Renata Miazga went to tinsel town to become a star. She was discovered by *you* jerks. You changed her name to Angel Feathers. Then cast her in this sad excuse for a film where her character's name was Chastity. Everybody got it? Good. Anyway, I'm glad you spoke up there, mister music composer."

Chastity began strutting toward the movie screen. Once she got to the red edge, she lifted her right foot and pointed it out of the screen and toward her audience. "See? My shoes are black. As is my dress. And hair. But my face is pale white. Here. Let me show you." She took one more step and Claudia's full-color body emerged into the bathing light of the projector. "Neat trick, huh?" She said mischievously.

"Now, as I was saying, I need a new playmate. You see, Virgina took my pool boy back to Enlightenment after her scene and, um, well...let's just say he's gonna be spent for a while. So, I need somebody new. And since we've been talkin' about being fucked up the ass, I think I know just who my perfect co-star will be. Who in this room loves fucking women up the ass with all sorts of foreign objects, hmmmm? And who loves forcing women to peg *him*? Why, if it isn't our very own music composer, Arpeggio Dante! Or, as you fellas call him, Peggy. Right? So, take my hand, Peggy. Let's make some beautiful music together."

Arpeggio began uncontrollably sobbing and pleading with the vengeful actress. "P-P-P-lease. No. Please s-stop. I p-p-promise to never do a-anything bad a-a-again." Claudia looked down at the shriveled man with disgust and said in her cartoonish, high-pitched voice, "Well, isn't *this* just pathetic. What did you tell *me* Peggy? What did you tell me the night that you kept putting hot pokers up my ass? What did you tell me as I screamed out in pain for you to stop? Oh, I remember. Just shut up bitch and take it. Yeah, *that's* what you told me. So, I guess I have the same message for *you*. Take my hand. Follow me into the screen. And shut up you bitch and take it."

Arpeggio fought to keep control over his body, but he could not prevent his sweaty hand from reaching up into Claudia's cool palm. And he could not stop himself from following her into the blazing red movie screen. All he could do was submissively comply. And weep for his torturous fate.

The red screen depicted a still-weeping, bound, and completely nude Arpeggio draped over a wood table. His head hung solemnly from the head of the table as Claudia spread his hairy legs.

"Ah, there we are," Claudia gleefully stated. "All ready for entry. You see, Peggy, I'm gonna make your dream come true. You like being fucked up the ass? So be it. I'm gonna conjure up a nice, big, metal, jagged strap-on dildo. I'm gonna put it on, spread your ass, and put it up you until your internal organs explode. But first, I gotta conjure up this thing. Let me just look up the price on my 'All Things Conjuring' app.

"Let's see here. How many conjuring coins will this cost me? Only three? Hell! That's a bargain! Alright, I'm not the best at this, so stop yer whimpering and shut the fuck up. I need to concentrate." Claudia closed her eyes and extended her open hand. Her brow furrowed as beads of sweat dripped off of it. She could feel something being manifested in her hand. She opened her eyes while wearing a delighted smile and looked at her creation.

"What the fuck?" She yelled out as she looked at a flaccid, pink rubber, three-inch phallus. "What in the hell am I supposed to do with *this*? Shit. *This* won't cause any damage. What a waste of three conjuring coins. Okay, shut the fuck up, Peggy. Let me try again."

The useless member disappeared from her hand as she once again closed her eyes and focused on her morbid task. Her slender fingers began stretching out so that they could hold the large object that was beginning to be conjured. She smiled once again as she opened her eyes. "Oh, fuck," she said with frustration as she peered into the green eyes of a grey, whiskered ball of fur. "LucyFur! How in the hell did *you* get here from your Earth? I wanted a deadly strap-on to fuck up this pussy and…oh, shit. I think I know what I did wrong. I ended up conjuring a deadly pussy cat. See? This is why I just go shopping at Cloud Nine. I suck at this. I suppose I could *order* a deadly, metal strap-on dildo, but the shipping costs will kill me. Plus, it'll take forever to get here. The delivery spirits are on strike, and I don't want to use the scabs. Okay, well, LucyFur, I'm really happy to see you, but you need to go back to Arima on *your* Earth, okay? You don't belong on this one. Bye kitty! Have fun ripping the throats out of fascists on your planet!"

Claudia watched as LucyFur disintegrated back into the cosmos, then said, "Well, fuck. What's a girl to do?" A hand holding a large black dildo emerged from stage right. "What?" Claudia asked the hand. "What did you say? I can't hear you. Speak up." "I said!" an irritated Sophia yelled out in her thick European accent from off-stage, "Use this!" "Oh, I'm sorry, Sophia, but that just won't work. I need something metal and jagged so that it will tear his insides up when I fuck him with it. Thanks for the offer though." The hand holding the black dildo quietly disappeared from the screen while Claudia stroked her red chin in contemplation.

"Would you *please* stop your whining? I'm trying to think here," Claudia said sternly to the sobbing Arpeggio. "Alright, Claudia, just think. This scene is totally fucked up. I'm totally off script now. Besides, this author already had a scene like this in *Satan's Shopkeeper*. I need something original. Wait a minute!" She stared out of the movie screen at her audience. "Why did you assholes sign me, anyway? It was because of my great improvisational skills, right? I mean, that's how I was discovered. Several of you dicks saw me at the improv theatre. And I must admit, I am good at it. Just throw out a word. Anyone. Come on, don't be shy."

The remaining eight men sat with confused expressions on their faces as they stared at Claudia's eager expression. Her expression then changed. Her sweet, innocent face contorted into a twisted demented demon as she screamed out in a deep gravelly voice, "I said give me a fucking word!" "Um, bathtub!" Pug yelled out from the theatre.

Claudia's face changed back and she smiled. "Okay, okay, bathtub," she said as she began feverishly pacing around the screen. "Okay, just give me a sec. Bathtub. Yeah, that's really good. Okay, here it goes." She sat down on the floor and began pretending to wash herself. She pretended to wash her feet. Then her hair. Then shave her legs. The scene dragged on for an eternity while the bored audience looked on.

"This isn't why we cast her," Pug whispered to Ezekiel. "We cast her because she has nice tits. She fuckin' sucks as improv."

"Okay and scene!" a giggling Claudia yelled out as she bounced back up onto her black pumps. "Oh, this is fun! I haven't done this in ages! Give me another one!" "Pomegranate," one of the men yelled at the screen. "Um, I don't really know what that is," Claudia replied. "Give me something else." "Cat!" another man yelled out. "Booooring!" Claudia replied. "That's too easy. Come on, fellas! Challenge me!"

"Razor wire," somebody yelled out before trying to take back his suggestion. "I shouldn't have said that. Oh shit, sorry Peggy. I mean, um, bathtub! No, you already did that. How about full moon? Yeah, do full moon. That'll be great!"

"No, no, no," Claudia stated. "Let's go with your first suggestion. Razor wire. Yeah, I like that. I like that a lot. I liked it the night of the screening of my film, *Jagged Lies*. I liked it after all of you forced me to do such horrific things. The torture. The rape. And, quite frankly, the downright disrespect that you showed me. And I really liked it after Peggy here made me sing."

She turned toward the sniveling Arpeggio and began approaching him. "Do you remember your singing lessons from that night, Peggy? Do you? Do you remember violating my ass with that hot poker over and over and telling me to sing higher? That I was off-key and needed to be punished? That I was too flat? Then too sharp? And every time I didn't hit the right note, you plunged that hot poker up me again, didn't you? Of course, there *was* no right note. I could have sung like an angel, and you still would have tortured me. And now, I *am* an angel. Of sorts, I suppose. And now, perhaps *you* should be taught some lessons.

"Yes, razor wire. I enjoyed it that night when I went home and found some in the garage. My entire world was shattered. My psyche was fried. I felt trapped. Hopeless. Imprisoned by a life of sadistic servitude. And my ass hurt like a motherfucker! I stared at that roll of razor wire and felt hope. I had found an escape from the hell that you men had put me through. I must admit, I sliced my hands up pretty good as I fashioned it into a noose and hung it from a ceiling beam. But it didn't matter. I didn't feel a thing. After what you had done to me, I no longer felt pain. And I was certainly not afraid to die. Death was not something to be afraid of. Death was my salvation. How fucked up is that?

"How fucked up is it that you twisted fuckers beat and raped and oppressed me so much that I actually welcomed death? I welcomed it as I was hanging there gasping for my last breath. And I welcomed it as I felt gravity cause the razor wire to slide through my neck until my headless body collapsed on the floor. I could have gotten rid of this scar on my neck. It would have been easy to do. But I wear it. It will always be a part of me to remind me that pure evil exists in these worlds. I wear my scar with pride. Not pride for committing suicide. But pride for what I will now do to any sadistic fucker that crosses my path. And here we are. You, Peggy, are a sadistic fucker. And you just happen to be in my path. And I just happen to have a lifetime supply of razor wire at my disposal. Look at my hand. Nothing there, right? And abracadabra! See? Razor wire. Oh, I can conjure *this* shit up in my dreams. And speaking of dreams, I do believe it is time for you to go nighty-night."

Claudia's mini dress clung to her thighs as she straddled the panicked Arpeggio's hairy back. She began giggling as she threaded the razor wire between the lips of his mouth. Her giggling turned into a maniacal laugh as she tightened her grip on the wire. Arpeggio uttered panicked pleas as he could feel the sharp edge of the razor wire stinging the edges of his mouth. She leaned forward and whispered into his ear, "Now, sing for me bitch." His high-pitched screams echoed off of the red walls of the theatre as Claudia pulled the razor wire back and forth through his tender cheek flesh. Blood poured from his face and her palms while the wire sliced through his cheeks. Then his jaw bones. His body violently convulsed as the wire ferociously cut through the top half of his head. And then, his body was still.

Claudia wiped her brow with her bloody hand and looked down at her work. "Whew! I guess I don't have to saw it all the way off. This fucker's dead. And check *this* out!" She gleefully began pulling his hair causing the top third of his head to open wide, then shut. Open and shut. Open and shut. Blood flew about the room while Claudia giggled at the gruesome sight. "This is really cool! He looks like a really fucked up *Pac-Man* or somethin'!" She climbed off of Arpeggio's stiffening body and stared at her aghast audience. "And scene! See? I toldja I was really good at improv! Thanks for the suggestion! Okay, Peggy. Back to your seat with you. Thanks for making beautiful music with me. And thank you for being such a lovely audience. I hope you enjoyed my performance. And now, back to my cloud in Enlightenment. But don't you gentlemen worry. The show isn't over. Hell, *this* shit hasn't even begun yet, heh, heh, heh. Isn't that right, Renata?"

CHAPTER 14

RICO SUAVE

"Oh, you are so right, Claudia," Renata answered as she entered the scene. She waved her hand and the nearly headless corpse of Arpeggio Dante disappeared from the wood table and manifested in a theatre seat. "Yes, we have more work to do. Five down. Eight to go. Are you getting bored gentlemen? Is it tedious for you to watch your colleagues die in scene after scene? Well, don't worry. We'll do our best to keep you glued to your seats. Each of our remaining actresses have all sorts of wonderful ideas. They'll each be along to give you their pitch. But in the meantime, why don't we watch another scene from my debut? Enjoy it while you can. Because I believe that this will be the *only* viewing of *Take My Hand*. And I know for *certain* that it will be *your* last viewing of *anything*. So, good-bye gentlemen. For the moment. I need to go check on our next actress. Simone is so excited to be speaking again after she cut out her own tongue. And I bet she'll have quite a lot to say to you."

The screen faded from dark red to brilliant white and Chastity once again appeared through the projector's lens. She watched her brother Chad trudge back through the security gate that separated the restricted area from the chosen ones while brushing her flowing blonde hair from her delicate, smiling face. Her attention then turned to the dress shop across the street. She began skipping around the deep, water-filled potholes in the pavement while suspicious and sunken eyes of emaciated people peered through the windows of local homes and shops.

"Oh, just look at them," Chastity said to herself while looking around at her surveyors. "Those, poor, poor people. The dark-skinned ones. And the non-believing White ones. And all of the other non-believers. I feel so sorry for them. They live in squalor. They barely have enough money to eat. Why, they only earn a meager living because of the grace that we chosen ones show them from time to time. Like me, selling my eggs. That horrible man now has eggs to sell, and I have enough money for my new dress. I hope. Don't these people understand that they don't have to live this way?

"Don't they understand that all they need to do is to accept Dear Leader as their lord and savior? That all they have to do is worship at his feet? That even if they are dark-skinned, that his love for them will provide them with opportunities for a decent life working in the fields and mines? Why don't they just open their hearts to his love? Oh, I guess I know why. It's just like Poppa says. The vermin don't *have* hearts. They are rats who have doomed themselves to live in the trash of their own making. But still, it makes me sad. Just like this boy who works in this dress shop.

"He certainly *looks* friendly enough. He has such a sweet, innocent brown face. And broad shoulders. And muscular arms. And such an incredibly tight...no! Oh, Dear Leader! It's just as Poppa has told me. The brown boys can put a spell on us White girls. They use their devilish smiles and muscular bodies to entice us into doing things with them. Impure things. And then, we are burdened by their babies. But they are half-breed babies, so they aren't to be kept. We chosen ones all believe in the sanctity of life. No woman should *ever* get rid of a child that she is carrying. It is going against Dear Leader. It is going against God. Unless you are carrying a brown child. No, they will grow up to be soulless takers just like their fathers and must be elimi-nated. So says Poppa. And so says Dear Leader. I'm so thankful for

Poppa's guidance. Otherwise, I'm afraid I could be tempted by the evil charm of one of these boys."

Chastity entered the dark dress shop and immediately went to a beaten mannequin in the window. Her blue eyes widened as she felt the fine silk of the blue and yellow dress in her lithe fingers. Her jaw dropped in amazement as she looked at the price tag. "Why, I do believe I *can* afford this. And have extra to take home to Momma," she said to herself in a quiet excitement.

"May I help you, beautiful?" a young man's voice came from behind her. Chastity turned around and gasped as her deep blues eyes met those of the young Hispanic man. He was standing five feet behind her wearing a tight, black T-shirt and tight blue jeans that left little to the imagination. His arms were covered with tattoos of what Chastity had been told were gang symbols. *My what beautiful tattoos,* Chastity thought to herself as her eyes scanned the young man's brawny arms. *That one is a woman's name. Poppa always said that they would hide their gang affiliation that way and tell you that it is the name of their mother. But it isn't. It is code for their gang of drug runners. And that one is of a beloved animated mouse. But it isn't really. Poppa says that they use cartoon characters to mislead us. And that one, on his bicep. His big, tight, bulging bicep. Um, that one is of flowers. But it probably means that those are flowers that will be on your grave if you cross these vermin. I must be careful with this boy. I must just buy my dress and get home. And I mustn't look him in his...*

"Hey, you in a trance or something?" the young man said as his placed his index finger under Chastity's chin and lifted her head. Chastity fell into the boys sparking mahogany eyes and immediately blushed. "I said, can I help you? Beautiful?"

"Um, why yes," Chastity blurted out while remaining fixated on the young man's handsome face. "Um, I was just wondering about this dress. You see, I was standing on the corner, and I saw it in the window, and I thought it was just beautiful and I thought that I would just inquire about it. But I must know. Was this purchased by drug money? Because I cannot wear anything that has come from poisoning our youth who are the future of our great country."

The young man chuckled while delicately stroking Chastity's pale, bare shoulder. "Drug money? Why no, Chica. This dress was made by my mother. All of the garments here were. You see? I have her name tattooed on my arm."

Chastity looked once again at the name that was emblazoned on his arm in red ink and said, "You mean, that really *is* the name of your mother? It isn't a gang name or something? And your mother made all of these fine clothes? You aren't a filthy drug runner?"

"Oh, such *stories* my sweet senorita," the chuckling boy answered. "Do I look like someone who would be involved in drugs? Of course not. Just look at my face. My handsome, young, innocent face. Look deeply into my eyes, my lovely. Are these the eyes of a criminal?"

"Um, w-well, um, n-no, they aren't," Chastity naïvely responded. "I suppose that it is *possible* that not *all* of you brown ones are criminals. And I suppose it is *possible* that you love your mother just like we do. And cartoons. And flowers. And you aren't a gang member. Yes, as I look into your eyes, I see that you are a kind-hearted young man. My apologies to you sir."

"Oh, that's all right my little Chiquita," the boy replied as his leering eyes toured Chastity's taught frame. His lips curled up into a sinister smile as he continued. "That's *quite* alright. It's easy to make mistakes about us. Oh, I know that there are some bad hombres amongst us. But not me. I'm just a shy, hard-working, God-fearing young man. With tight shirts. And tight jeans. Do you like my jeans?"

Chastity looked down. Her eyes only made it just beneath his waistline and she gasped once again. Before she could respond, the front door opened and three bearded, rough-looking Hispanic men came into the shop. "Just one moment, beautiful," the smirking young man said. "These gentlemen are here for a, um, *special order*." The young man left and the four of them began speaking in what seemed to Chastity to be gibberish. He went behind the store counter and retrieved three brick sized packages wrapped in brown paper. He was presented with a white envelope and immediately placed it into the cash register. The four men continued speaking in gibberish while pointing and laughing at Chastity. The three men continued to laugh and wink at her as they approached the front door. One of the men blew her a kiss before the trio departed.

"Um, what was that about?" Chastity asked as the young man strutted back to her. "Oh, them? They are just neighborhood friends who came in to pick up a special package. That's all."

Chastity held a puzzled look on her face as she asked, "But what *kind* of special package? Those looked far too small to be dresses."

"Oh, looks can be *deceiving*, Chica," the young man responded. "They are *indeed* dresses. Dresses that my mother has made special for those gentlemen's baby daughters. Yes, that's it. All three of those gentlemen have baby daughters and they have bought dresses for them. Little tiny dresses that fit into little tiny packages, heh, heh, heh. I *like* fitting things into little tiny packages."

"Oh, well that makes sense," an embarrassed Chastity stated while covering her red face. "Oh, I'm so sorry. It's just that those packages look just like the drug packages that I've seen on the news. You know. Dear Leader Tonight. Do you watch it?"

"Um, no. We, um, don't get that channel. Probably," the young man responded. "Now, speaking of dresses, how can I help you? Are you interested in this dress? I certainly hope so. You would look so beautiful in it. Would you like to try it on?"

Chastity blushed once again as the young man took the dress off of the mannequin and held it tightly to her quivering body. "Oh, yes," he said as he pressed the garment against her. "Yes, you would look *quite* beautiful in this, senorita. Quite beautiful indeed. You might be the most beautiful woman in the world if you wore this."

"The most beautiful woman in the whole wide *world*?" a delighted Chastity squealed. "Do you really think so?"

"Oh my, yes," the young man lasciviously answered. "The most beautiful woman in the whole wide world. Standing right here in my shop. Right in front of me. Pressed up against me. I must be quite lucky to play host to the most beautiful woman in the whole wide world. Come, Chica. I'll take you to the dressing room. Please. Try it on. Try it on for *me.*"

Chastity took the young man's hand and followed him as her

exhilarated face seemed to be in a swooning trance. She blushed once again, pulled back the flimsy blue curtain to the dressing room, and stepped in. She quickly took off her white gown and held the enticing blue and yellow fabric to her bosom. Behind her, a pair of eyes keenly watched through a peephole in the wooden chamber. The eyes disappeared for a moment, and the young man's voice could be heard saying, "Oh, Chica. I must tell you. My mother made that dress of the finest silk. You really must feel it on your entire body. Take off your underwear so you can feel it on every part of your flesh."

"Oh! Okay! Thanks!" Chastity yelled out as the eyes reappeared in the peephole. Chastity's panties fell to the floor and lay in a wadded heap at her feet. Her bra was then taken off and hung on a tarnished copper hook. She lifted her arms and the dress slinked down upon her pale body. She looked at herself in the mirror while slowly rubbing her hand up and down the smooth silk garment. Her hands caressed every curve that the fabric clung to. The caressing intensified and she bit her lip and closed her eyes as her right hand disappeared under the hem of the dress.

"Is everything okay in there?" the young man asked. "How do you like it? Does it fit?"

"Um, oh my yes," Chastity blurted out as she pulled her hand from under the dress and straightened her hair. "Yes, um, it looks just wonderful."

"Well, come on out," the young man responded. "I want to see it. I want to see the most beautiful woman in the world."

Chastity pulled back the tattered curtain and stepped out of the dressing room. She was immediately greeted by the provocative whistles of the young man. "Damn, Chica. I *knew* you would look beautiful in that dress. But *damn*, girl." He began slowly walking in a circle around her while leering at her adorned body. "Yeah, that fits perfect. It is so tight against your, uh, it's *really* tight. And does it feel good?" He stood with his lips an inch away from hers.

"Does it feel good on your body? Does it feel good on every *part* of your body?" "Oh, Dear Leader, yes," Chastity purred in response as she leaned toward him. "Well good, then," the young man stated as he began walking towards the sales counter. "I'm so glad you like it. I can only accept cash. I hope that's okay."

"Um, um, yeah, I have cash," a confused and frustrated Chastity replied. "Um, here you are." The young man looked down at the brightly colored bills that were laid on the countertop and began laughing. "Oh, I'm so sorry Chica. But you cannot pay for this dress with that. You must have visited the old man across the street, no? He buys things with these bills. This is fake money, senorita. I'm sorry, but you cannot have this dress unless you have some *real* money."

"What?" Chastity cried out. "You mean that old man swindled me? Oh, Dear Leader, I am so stupid. Poppa told me never to do business in the restricted area. And look at what stupid me did. Now I don't have any money, no dress and no eggs! Oh, Poppa and Momma will be so disappointed in me. I'm sorry, but I wouldn't wear this dress even if I had the money for it. I've learned my lesson. No more doing business with the vermin!"

"Hey, hey, hey, calm down, beautiful," the sly young man said softly as he wiped a tear from Chastity's cheek with his index finger. He smiled at her and sucked the teardrop from his fingertip before continuing. "Don't worry about it. Don't let one bad experience spoil everything for you. As I said, not *everyone* here is bad. But that old man is, and I'm tired of his taking advantage of beautiful young women in this way. I'm going to take care of this for you. Don't you worry."

He picked up the receiver of an old rotary phone and dialed a number. He spoke in gibberish for a moment, hung up the phone, and smiled at Chastity. "There. All taken care of. Now, about that dress." He came from behind the counter and stood in front of Chastity. He gently placed his firm hands on her bare shoulders and whispered, "You are the most beautiful woman in the world. And the most beautiful woman in the world must have this dress." His lips slowly approached hers as he continued in a suave whisper. "You are a queen. And a queen must have her royal gown. Would you like to have this royal gown your highness?"

"Y-y-es, I-I-I would," Chastity answered softly through her trembling lips. Her lips continued to shake as he gently kissed her. Their hands began exploring each other's firm bodies while their tongues explored each other's mouths. They began passionately panting as he grasped the straps of the dress and pulled them from her shoulders. The blue and yellow silk dress succumbed to gravity and collapsed around Chastity's bare feet.

A flushed Chastity exited the dress shop. She turned back towards the window and smiled at her lover who was placing a new dress on the nude mannequin. She lifted her arm in the air and waved. He hid his face for a moment to conceal his laughter before waving back.

Chastity was then distracted by a commotion behind her. She turned around and saw the three large men who had bought their daughters dresses dragging the old man from his egg shop. His feet were surrounded by hundreds of following cockroaches as the three men threw him to the ground and began kicking him. He wailed for them to stop. One of the men pulled out a revolver. There was a single gunshot. The smiling Chastity said, "That's what you get for dealing in dirty money, you vermin. I shall never sell eggs in your shop again. But I sure might come back for another dress."

Eight spines had a sharp chill run through them as Chastity's white face turned beet red and dissolved into that of Simone. Her fiery red afro sat proudly atop her head as she intensely stared at the remaining terrified men. She opened her full lips and said, "Alright motherfuckers. We have some shit to talk about."

CHAPTER 15

———

CRACKING

The eight remaining men shivered in their seats as Simone elevated herself and floated through the movie screen and into the theatre. She was wearing a multi-colored, striped gown and was adorned with gold bracelets and necklaces. Her full black afro sat proudly atop her head while her intense brown eyes scowled at the trembling men.

"You twisted motherfuckers," Simone began saying as she hovered above her terrified captive audience. "I must say this to you first. Credit where credit is due. I always considered myself to be one of the strongest bitches on the planet. I never took shit from anybody. Including you assholes. I knew what you thought of me. I knew you were a bunch of racist fucks. And you proved it by calling me all kinds of heinous names. But I was strong. And I knew you couldn't make my film, *Speak No Evil, Hear No Evil, See No Evil* without me. Hell, you put billboards up of me before shooting ever started. Remember those? What a fucked-up ad campaign. 'DEI just came to town. And THIS bitch ain't playin'.

"Wow. White Nationalist propaganda wrapped up in a Black-sploitation flick. You get the racist White audiences *and* the Black audiences. Sitting in separate theatres, of course. Pretty clever. Again, credit where credit is due. So, I was strong, proud, and a valuable commodity to you. And I didn't have to take your shit. I told you exactly what I thought of you every chance I got. You call me a (derogatory term omitted)? I call you a knuckle-dragging pile of shit. You make cracks about me goin' back to the plantation? I make cracks about your motherfuckin' cracker mommas. And I could tell that *my* cracks hit some nerves. Unlike yours. Black don't crack motherfuckers. I stood up to you every fuckin' day on that set. And I sat proudly with you during my screening and watched my performance. I was the only Black person there. The only woman. Sitting proudly and defiantly in a theatre filled with thirteen white devils.

"Even while my movie played you kept making your bullshit, racist cracks. And I sat there. Proudly. I never cracked. That really pissed you off, didn't it? An uppity (derogatory term omitted) never bending to you. Never succumbing to you. And a woman at that. Yeah, you hated that shit. I just never knew how *much* you hated it until the movie ended. You were determined to make me crack. And you did. Like I said. Credit where credit is due.

"Right after the movie ended, you cast me in *another* part, didn't you? Yeah, the opportunity of a lifetime. My very own personal horror flick. You set up cameras and gave your assistant director the chance to direct for the first time. And that's just what Kellen Richardson did. He took full advantage of this shit. He set up the lights. Set the scenes. And gave each of you a part to play. And play it you did. I can still hear your laughter as you demons cut my flesh. Poured bleach into the wounds. Stuck painful objects in every hole that I had. You laughed and laughed as I screamed and screamed. Kellen had that microphone just above my head so he could pick up every fucking whimper I uttered. Every plea for mercy.

"I knew you hated me, but Jesus fucking Christ! What type of twisted fuck gets off on this shit? Stripping pieces of my own flesh from my thighs and making me eat it? Twisting corkscrews into my ass? Cutting my nipples off and hanging them from my ears? I know your White actresses went through some shit. But you saved your best for *me*, now, didn't you? This wasn't just rape, which is sure as fuck bad enough. This was sadistic. This was pure evil. I wasn't human to you. I was a meaningless fuck and torture toy. Yeah, you joyously played the parts that your Kellen handed you. And reveled in my misery.

"But the best part? Making me watch the footage you just shot. Pinning my eyes open and making me relive those horrific scenes while my screams thundered in my ears through the headphones you put on me. I listened to that horrific shit until my eardrums shattered and I couldn't hear a thing. And a small part of my psyche found peace.

"I remembered that moment when I was actually thankful to have lost my hearing when you threw me on that cold stone floor in a tiny cell. I sat there bleeding and shivering and crying. I wanted the rest of my body to feel what my ears now did. Absolutely nothing. So, motherfuckers. As I said. Credit where credit is due. You made this proud Black woman crack. I found a sharp piece of stone and cut off my ears. I used it to saw off my tongue. I jammed it into my eye sockets. And I laid there on that cold floor as I felt the blood draining out of my beaten body, praying to die.

"And die I did. Even when I found my eternal home on Cloud Twenty-Three in Enlightenment, I still didn't speak. You fucked me up so bad that even after I was in literal Heaven, I couldn't bring myself to say a word to anyone. Not even to my fellow fallen sisters. But I still had the urge to act. Yeah, it's in my fuckin' bones. So, when Renata showed up with this opportunity, I jumped at the chance. Once again, I would star in my very own horror scene. But *this* time, *I'm* calling the shots. I'm both the star *and* the director of this motherfucker. The moment I saw this opportunity, my spine stiffened. My strength returned. My pride returned. And I knew just who would be my co-star. Wanna take a guess? Well, of course it's the assistant director that scripted so many torturous scenes for me. So, come on Kellen. You're about to make your big screen debut. And I'm gonna crack your fuckin' mind!"

Kellen Richardson began uncontrollably sobbing as he took Simone's hand and was led into the crimson red movie screen. He sat on a bale of hay in a barn. He anxiously looked around while wearing a confused expression upon his haggard face. There was nothing here to be scared of. A solid wooden structure. Bales of hay. And no Simone. This was not frightening. This was home. He allowed himself to relax for a moment. The serene moment didn't last as Simone entered the red frame.

"Look familiar, motherfucker?" she said as her muscular body strode towards him. "Yeah, this is the type of place you grew up in, right? Barns. Chickens. Cows. Haystacks. Lots of sheep to fuck too, am I right? Yeah, you were just a midwestern farm boy. This is a place that feels safe to you. But you had bigger dreams than milking cows and shit. You wanted to make movies. And you did. You started making movies on your little farm, didn't you? Nasty little films of people who didn't look like you being beaten. Or worse. What gave you those ideas, Kellen? Where did those twisted seeds come from? And not just for you. For *millions* of you White, rural motherfuckers. Man, woman, child. Millions of you. What the fuck happened? How did entire rural communities go from being decent, God-fearing people to hate-filled fucking Nazis?

"Oh, I know the answer to that. It *didn't* happen overnight. And it wasn't by accident. You cracker motherfuckers already had a racist streak in you. Yeah, the Civil War was still just brewing under the surface. And every time you saw a free Black person, your blood boiled. I know. I get it. I get the same way when I see one of you pasty-faced motherfuckers. But you had to hide your racist views. There was nothing you could do about them. And then, a plan by the White Nationalists was hatched. Let's take that racism that already exists in the souls of these simple farm folk and let's exploit it. But let's not stop with the Blacks. We gotta go after the Muslims. The Jews. The Hispanics. The Asians. And every fuckin' woman who won't get on her knees and open her mouth on command. We have a captive audience just driving around in their tractors and combines all day. So, let's give them something to think about. Let's indoctrinate them into believing that the White Christian man is the *real* victim in this society. Let's broadcast hate-filled bullshit that they'll listen to every day. And after days and weeks and months and years of this toxic shit, they won't just believe it. They'll *act* on it. They will worship at the altar of the messengers and their hatred of the other will grow to the point that they would kill if told to.

"You were nothing special, Kellen. Just another wannabe White boy with no talent. But you were *told* you were special. You were *told* that you were being denied your God-given place by the mouthy women. And the Jews. And the Blacks. And whoever they chose to select that week. *You* were the victim. The poor little White boy didn't get everything on his wish list. WAAAA! Everything is being taken from me by more qualified non-Whites. WAAAA! I can't get laid because I have no fuckin' personality. And a small cock. WAAAA! None of this is my fault. It's the Blacks. It's the Jews. It's the Hispanics! It's the LGBTQ folks. For some weird fuckin' reason. What did *any* of these people ever do to you? Come on. Answer me! I'll let you speak. Tell me, what did any of these people ever do to harm you personally? I'll wait for an answer."

Kellen's hands were shaking as his mind searched for an example. His head suddenly lifted when he came up with one. "Well, one time I was at this bar and this gay guy came up to me and wanted to buy me a drink! Plus, he looked at my ass!" Simone burst out in laughter and said, "So? Are you fucking incapable of saying 'No thanks'? Hell, you should have taken him up on it. Your ass isn't that great. You know what I've learned about homophobes? Dudes who act all macho and get pissed about being hit on by a guy have a whole lot of deep-seeded issues with their *own* sexuality. You aren't pissed at the guy. You're pissed at *yourself*. You're ashamed of the urges you feel in your throbbing groin. You're disgusted with yourself for fantasizing about sucking some dude off because your made-up old man in the sky said that it's wrong. Am I right, or am I right? Yeah, I'm fuckin' right. That's some weak shit right there, Kellen. Got anything else?"

"Um, um, well one time this (derogatory term omitted) got a promotion that I wanted." "Oh, I see," Simone answered. "You wanted a promotion and someone with different colored skin got it instead. Because, of course, *that* person couldn't have been more qualified than *you*, right? If you have white skin, you should be *entitled* to *anything* that you want and there's no way that someone with *dark* skin could *ever* be more talented than you. Because they're not really human to you, are they? Yeah, just another fuckin' example of the bullshit propaganda that you've been all too willing to believe. You really are a pathetic worm, Kellen. I'll give you one more shot. One chance to give me an actual example about anything that someone has truly done to you that was unfair and impacted your life."

Kellen thought for a moment and blurted out, "In high school the head cheerleader laughed at me when I asked her out!" "Oh Jesus Christ," Simone chuckled. "You really are pitiful. Yeah, any woman that you want should just bow down and bend over anytime you want, right? You're a man, and you should be entitled to any piece of trim that comes along. Shit man. What the fuck would you do with it? We've *already* determined that you secretly want to suck cock. What a fuckin' dumbass you are. And waste of time. Alright. The quiz is over. And you failed miserably. Just like *all* of you White, bigoted, sexist, xenophobic motherfuckers out there sitting on your farms and being pissed about not getting what you believe you're entitled to. You're all miserable failures who waste your time hating others rather than building something for yourself.

"And then, what do you do? You put the *actual* motherfuckers who are keeping you down in power! You're so fucking stupid that you turn your anger towards groups of people who are *actually* oppressed and lift up *everybody's* oppressors! The exact same rich and powerful motherfuckers who keep wages and opportunities low for *everybody* exploited your bigotry to rise to power! And then you dumb motherfuckers actually pray at their altar as they exploit you again! They fuck you over and you ask for more! Hell, you thank them for it! Because you have been indoctrinated for years into a hate cult! And you're too self-absorbed and stupid to see it. You keep taking it up the ass by the rich and keep blaming the poor Black kid for it. You shouldn't hate that Black kid. Or that woman. Or that trans person. They are just as oppressed, *if not more so,* than you. They are your ally, you dumbfuck. This isn't white versus black or man versus woman or straight versus gay. It is poor versus rich. It is oppressed versus the entitled. Your hatred of others has made you blind to who your true enemy is. And it's really sad how many people are too stupid to see that.

"But speaking of being blind, let's get to our scene, shall we? Yeah, this should be fun. You might get an award nomination or something. If you play your part right. And I'm here to direct you to ensure that you do. We're going to play a little game, Kellen. And it's a game you can win, because I'm going to help you. You see that haystack over there? All you have to do is find my afro pick. It's in there somewhere and all you have to do is find it before you die. If you do, I'm going to let you go. If you don't, well, I guess you're fucked.

"But as I said," Simone continued as she led Kellen towards the haystack. "I'm going to help you. You can ask me questions about where it's at, and I'll answer it." She then conjured a pair of rusty pliers, stuck them into Kellen's mouth, and yanked his tongue out. Blood sprayed throughout the barn as Simone waved his flaccid tongue in front of his face. "Just spit out any question you might have, heh, heh, heh."

"Oh, and I'll point you to where it is. All you have to do is look where I'm pointing and I'm sure you'll find it." She plunged her thumbs into Kellen's eyes. She used her long, painted thumbnails to slice through the membranes around his eyes as though she were pulping a grapefruit. Her laugh was being drowned out by his anguished screams as she popped his eyes out of their sockets and tossed them onto the dirt floor of the barn.

"See? Just look where I'm pointing. You'll find it. And finally, I will *tell* you where to find it. I'll give you instructions. All you have to do is listen to me. But, just in case you can't hear me, I'll help you out in another way. I'll take your hands and put them in the haystack where my afro pick is. Now, listen." She plowed the pliers repeatedly into his ear drums. Kellen's shrieks echoed off of the wooden planks of the barn. After a few moments, he could no longer hear his own screams.

"Speak no evil, see no evil, hear no evil, motherfucker," Simone said in a sinister sneer as she placed his arms into the haystack. His screaming intensified as his hands and bare arms were sliced open by hundreds of shards of glass and razor blades that lay hidden in the hay. He pulled his arms out and Simone thrust them back into the hay. His muffled cries increased as several hidden rattlesnakes injected him with their lethal venom.

Simone laughed hysterically as she pulled his body from the haystack and threw it on the floor. He began frothing at the mouth as the venom began shutting down his internal organs. Blood flowed from his arms, hands, ears, mouth, and eye sockets while he quietly whimpered upon the filthy floor. Simone reached into the haystack and began searching. "Ah, there it is," she said with satisfaction as she pulled out her afro pick. "A girl's gotta look good. Yeah, I might need *these* too." She reached back into the haystack. When she withdrew her arms there were three relaxed rattlesnakes curled around them. She sauntered over to Kellen's suffering body, leaned down and said, "Finish this motherfucker off." The three snakes leapt from her arms and began sinking their long fangs into Kellen's swollen cheeks, lips, and jaw. Simone watched Kellen's final convulsions and hid her face from the audience as she wiped a tear from her vengeful eyes. She then turned around and said, "Here you go motherfuckers. Here's your boy back. But you might want to watch where you sit. Because these fuckin' snakes are coming with him."

Simone disappeared from the crimson screen as Kellen's slashed and swollen body returned to his theatre seat. Three rattlesnakes slithered off of his face and scurried to find safety within the dark theatre.

Eleven teary-eyed women stood at the portal in Enlightenment waiting for their sister to come home. Simone walked through the dense white clouds, approached her sisters, and tearfully embraced them. "Thank you," she whispered in a cracking voice. "Thank you for giving me back my pride. And I'm *never* going to allow *any* mother-fucker to take it away again."

CHAPTER 16

LOOKS LIKE RAIN

Simone straightened her spine and pulled away from her joyfully sobbing sisters. She flashed an evil smile and said in a deep, determined voice, "Yeah, I'm *back* baby. Jesus fucking Christ that felt good. I was shattered. Never thought I'd ever speak another word, let alone off some motherfucker. But somehow, I got put back together. Once I heard about Renata's casting call, my will to fight came surging back. I could feel my muscles tighten and strengthen. I could feel my rage build. And I could see myself acting in that twisted fucking scene. It's my best performance.

"And I'm not done yet. Not even close. My drive for retribution is bursting at the seams and I need more. Yeah, we're immortal, right? I have an eternity to answer prayers on all the parallel Earths and other weird-ass planets throughout the cosmos. Prayers to stop some abusive asshole. Prayers to right some wrong. Prayers to solve murder mysteries. Yeah! That's it! I've *always* wanted to play a Private Dick! This is my chance! Maybe that'll be my specialty! Now, just bear with me for a moment. What if my specialty is answering prayers to solve murders that are being covered up by the rich and powerful? I get the prayer from Central Dispatch. I go to that Earth. I set up an office, wear a trenchcoat, smoke cigarettes, and snoop around. Then, I solve the mystery and bring some assemblance of peace to the victim's loved ones. I return home a hero, and I lounge around by the pool until I get my next prayer. What do ya'll think? I'll need a sidekick, of course. You know. Somebody to get me my coffee and cigarettes and shit. Anybody interested?"

The other eleven ladies looked at one another sheepishly before Sophia spoke up. "Oh *daawling*. It is *soooo* nice to see you come out of your shell. And I absolutely *adore* your idea to have a prayer specialty. But I do believe that we other ladies would prefer to play leading parts as well. I do not believe any of us would be content to be your understudy. In fact, we have all been discussing that very thing. Each of us having a specialty role that we play when we answer prayers. We would make quite the unstoppable team. And we could have a cool name that would be feared throughout the cosmos. Perhaps Brigade of Persistence. How does *that* sound to everyone?"

"I like it," the red-haired Ginger answered. "But I'm sorry Sophia. It's been done."

"What do you mean, it's been *done* daawling?" Sophia inquired while filing her long, perfectly manicured nails.

"Well, there's *already* a Brigade of Persistence," Ginger replied. "There are two parallel Earths so far that have mostly eradicated evil forces from their worlds. Earth Uno took out a cosmic demon named Vetis who was trying to conquer that Earth using some pudgy, smelly, orange-colored moron. It didn't work. A vigilante serial killer conquered him in the heavens, and her Earthbound associates conquered him there. Oh, and the Four Horsemen of the Apocalypse helped quite a bit too."

"Earth Uno, you say?" Renata asked. "Why, that's where Uncle Joe is from! I bet the vigilante serial killer who conquered Vetis's home, Perdition, is his niece that he's gone to get! This is getting exciting!"

"Yeah, and perfectly confusing daawling," Sophia replied while continuing to focus on her nails. "What on Earth, pick one, doesn't matter, does *that* have to do with *my* Brigade of Persistence?"

"Um, well, as I was saying," Ginger continued. "Earth Uno has pretty much been cleaned up from repugnant, oppressive assholes. As has Earth Duo. On *that* particular Earth, witches and mediums were brought together by vengeful spirits lead by Queen Zenobia. The key to *that* working rested with the Ladies Cabot. *One* of whom is also named Sophia, so yeah. Kinda confusing. Anyway, they opened up every woman on their Earth to their natural capacity to be either a medium or a witch. Then, they united them so that they could over-throw the male patriarchy. Evil men were slaughtered. Or enslaved. Or something. Decent men lived alongside their female counterparts in equality. Except the men have to carry papers to prove their decency. A few are pissed about that. Oh, and to make things even *more* confusing, there is *another* version of that vigilante serial killer on *that* Earth as well. Oh, and, um, somehow Jack the Ripper got involved. I don't know why. Seems pointless, but that's what happened. Anyway, that entire group was known on *that* Earth as Queen Zenobia and the Brigade of Persistence. So, um, sorry. It's been done. And we wouldn't want to be a rip-off artist like the so-called writer of DL Studios, now, would we?"

"Perish the thought," Sophia responded. "I would rather be tortured by those brutes for a thousand years than to be associated with a no-talent hack like him. Very well. That name simply won't do. But we'll think of something. Something quite catchy. And cool. Regardless, Simone dear, the point of all of this is that each of us is a star. Which means you will need to find your personal servant under-study elsewhere."

"Huh," Simone said as she rubbed her ebony chin. "Yeah, you're right. You all deserve your names at the top of the marquee. Yeah, alright. I'll just have to find my understudy assistant elsewhere. Surely, there must be *some* spirit *somewhere* in Enlightenment that would *jump* at the chance to assist a big star like me. I'll put out an ad in the classi-fieds of The Enlightenment Enquirer. I bet I'm *inundated* with responses. Now, let me just look up how much that will cost. Holy shit! Six conjuring coins? Just for one stupid fuckin' ad? Ah well. I'll earn more answering my murder mystery prayers. I just need to concentrate for a moment. And there we are. It's in the latest addition that will be coming out today. Just listen to *this*."

Are you bored answering the same old prayers? Are you tired of wasting your talents on getting cats out of trees or helping to open jars of pickles? Are you ready for some real excitement? Then join one of the greatest actresses from Earth Tres as she answers prayers to solve murder mysteries. Duties include, but are not limited to, providing all necessary items from a carefully prepared rider. Being at my beck and call at all hours of the day and night. The occasional massage. You must be enthusiastic, intelligent, and have a zeal for righteousness. Send inquiries, references, and your head shot to:

Simone
Cloud Twenty-Three

"Sounds pretty good, huh?" Simone proudly stated while the other twelve ladies attempted to hide their laughter. "What?" Simone yelled out. "What is it? What's so fucking funny?"

"Oh daaawling," Sophia answered. "The spirits in Enlightenment typically don't waste their energy on cats in trees and other such trivialities. Such prayers really don't pay that much but you still have the overhead of conjuring your wardrobe, travel expenses from here to that particular Earth, food, and so on. So, the spirits that answer prayers are already doing things much more exciting than that. But perhaps you'll find somebody a bit, um, gullible."

"Fuck yeah, I will!" Simone roared. "I have to! I have to find an assistant for my murder mystery work. You'll see. I'll find someone. I just hope they aren't too mouthy. And no ego. I can't stand that shit. Just come to work, do your job, and keep your thoughts to yourself. Yeah. I'll find someone. Don't you worry."

"Hey!" Renata then yelled out. "This is all interesting and everything, but the scene from my movie where Chastity supports her brother again then is driven home in shame is coming to an end! The screen is about to turn red! Skipper! Skipper! Are you ready? Places everybody!"

"Oh, fuck", Pug said as a dark red hue encased the movie theatre once again. The seven remaining men began sweating in the frigid theatre as a blurry female form began walking towards them on the screen. The closer she got, the more in focus she became until the petite Skipper was in full view. Her blonde pigtails bounced around her perfectly round, cute face while her patriotic stars and stripes bikini left very little to the imagination. The seven men were petrified and turned-on simultaneously, leaving both of their heads swirling in confusion.

"Hiya fellas!" Skipper enthusiastically squealed as she levitated out of the movie screen and into the theatre. "Well, here I am! In all my firecracker glory! Your perky star of *Star Spangled Firing Squad*! I really must say, James, that this was probably your *worst* script ever. I mean, it was just a mash-up of every patriotic musical mixed in with fascist propaganda. How did you describe it to me? Oh yeah. You said, 'It's like *Yankee Doodle Dandy* meets *Birth of a Nation!*' I had no idea what the fuck you were talkin' about. I was just thrilled to be cast in a movie written by the great James Proctor.

"But man, if I had known what *Birth of a Nation* was, I don't think I would've done it. What a racist piece of shit *that* is, I have since learned. And you fuckin' copied it. Except, instead of Klansmen being the heroes, it was the militant masked thugs of The Regime. And instead of Black people being made to look like rapists and idiots, they were Hispanic folks. Really fuckin' disgusting. But hey! That's what you were watching at the time, so that's what you wrote. Or, ripped off, actually. And the songs! Taken note for note from *Yankee Doodle Dandy*! And with such original names like, "Give My Regards to Wall Street," "Dear Leader's a Grand Old Name," "Over There is an Illegal," and who could forget the big hit? Yeah, "The Grand Old Swastika" sold quite a few units to the knuckle draggers out there in fly-over country. It was a huge hit that was listened to in millions of tractors and combines throughout this once-great nation.

"And it made me a star. I mean, sure, you had to dub somebody else's voice in for the songs, but I got the credit. If there's one thing that The Regime is good for, it's lies. And, I must admit, I did enjoy lip-syncing that song on various TV shows on State TV. Those personal appearances gave me a break from the beatings and the rapes, y'know? Which, was *also* copied by you, James. You'd just beat me or rape me in the exact same way that the previous dick had done. I mean, it got to the point where I thought to myself, 'Ah shit. Here comes James. He's gonna beat and rape me the same way that this dude just did. How boring.' I mean, dude! You know you're a hack when your *victim* gets bored by your copied shit!

"But hey. Let's give you a little credit. It *was* your idea to cast real people from the concentration camps as extras in this film. You told them that all they had to do was play their parts and they would be released. So, they did. And they were. They ran around trying to escape the masked thugs. They allowed themselves to be beaten. They allowed themselves to be tied up in front of the firing squad in the movie. And then they were released. From their fucking lives. Those people weren't acting on that screen as the firing squads shot at person after person while some patriotic bullshit rhythm played underneath. That wasn't acting. Those were *real* people dying from being shot by *real* bullets. I didn't know until after the movie was released. And by then, I was so beaten down by being tortured by you assholes, that it just all made sense to me. I was disgusted by your abuse and even more disgusted to have been associated with this fucking film. So, I found myself a gun and BLAM! Ate a fuckin' bullet. Another starlet dead. And another box office bonanza for you boys. Well, enough of my rambling. We really should get to the point, shouldn't we? Come James. Take my hand. And let's see if we can't do something original for our scene together."

The bound and naked body of a sobbing James Proctor was projected on the crimson screen. As was the bubbly, bikini-clad body of Skipper who was bouncing around him in a dark tool shed. "Well, we only have one shot at this, James, so let's come up with something cool. Hey, hey, stop your crying. It'll be okay. We'll come up with something. I bet that if we put our heads together, we can make this the best scene in the entire film. Right?"

Skipper leaned forward and lightly placed her forehead upon that of James. She smiled at him tenderly and softly said, "Okay, James. Just come up with an original idea of how to kill you. I'll tell you what. I'll make you a deal. If you can come up with an original way of killing somebody, I won't use your idea on you. I'll grab somebody else from the audience and do it to them. You can sit here and watch the scene play out, then I'll release you. You will be free. I will open the theatre doors for you, and you can walk right out of here with nothing more to fear from any of us. Okay? Deal? Just give me *one* original idea. Come on James. You can do it. I have faith in you. Just look around this shed. There's tons of shit in here."

James furrowed his brow as his mind searched for a unique way to murder someone. He stuck his tongue out of the side of his slack-jawed mouth and intensely stared at the walls of the shed while his few brain cells bounced against one another. He then smiled, looked at Skipper and yelled out, "How about hanging?"

"Got that all on your own, huh?" Skipper said. "Just by looking at this old rope on the wall? Well James, I'm pretty sure that hanging has been done before. Anything else you can think of that you could do with a rope? No? Alright. Try again."

He looked around once again and came up with a brilliant response. "There's an old umbrella over there! How about if you beat him to death with that?"

"Seriously?" an exasperated Skipper replied. "How in the hell are you going to kill somebody by beating them with an umbrella? I mean, the best you could do is give him a headache or maybe cause some bruising! No, that won't work, James. Try again."

James thought for a moment and blurted out, "Firing squad!"

"Oh, fuck man," Skipper stated after slapping her forehead in disgust. "That's just stealing your own idea from *my* movie. And using guns is like the least original way to kill somebody. It's unimaginative. Plus, guns are for pussies. No, I'm sorry James. No guns allowed in this scene. And since I'm going to have to write this myself, I guess you'll end up being my co-star. But the rope and umbrella *does* give me an idea."

Skipper lifted James's quivering body over her shoulder, then threw it over two sawhorses. "You know, James, when you're writing fiction, you can do anything that you want. I mean, fucking *anything*.

There's *nothing* outside the realm of possibility. Like this. Check this shit out."

The smiling Skipper uncurled the rope and stuffed one end of it deep into James's ass. "Ow. I bet that hurts, huh?" she said as she stood in front of his wailing mouth. "Now, that's not so original. But how about this?" She took the pointed end of the umbrella, tied it to the rope, and placed the pointed end against his anus. "There. The scene is set," she said as she showed him her delicate hand. It began expanding in front of his dismayed eyes until it was three feet long and the fingers had merged into a hook.

"Alrighty then," she said while smirking. "Now just open your mouth up wide for me. That's it. And don't move. This is going to be a delicate operation." He began squealing as he felt Skipper's hook hand going into his mouth, down his esophagus, and snake through his intestines.

"There. Got it," Skipper said with satisfaction as her hook hand grasped the end of the rope. "Now, just a bit of a tug and..." He shrieked with agony as he felt the umbrella penetrate his body all the way up to the handle. Skipper was being pelted by his spittle and tears as his screams bounced off of the wooden walls of the shed.

"Fuck! You're getting me all wet!" Skipper exclaimed as she bounced around to his exposed backside. She looked at the handle of the umbrella sticking out of his posterior, smiled wickedly, and said, "Good thing I brought an umbrella." She pressed the button on the umbrella's handle and pushed the metal mechanism up. The umbrella opened and sliced its way through James's abdomen and back. He let out a tortured squeal as the metal rods and attached fabric tore through his organs, bones, and flesh giving his midsection a blood-soaked awning.

"Now, *that's* fuckin' original James! See? You can do anything that you *want* with fiction! Even pull an umbrella through a guy's ass and open it so he looks like a...um...looks like a...well, I don't know. I guess you look like a guy who has an opened umbrella sticking out of him. Anyway, why couldn't *you* have not thought of that? Oh yeah. 'Cause *you're* not *me*. Right James? James? You still with us? Well shit. I guess he's dead. I'd like to say that your work will live on James, but we *both* know better than *that*, don't we?"

Skipper wiped blood and pieces of organs from her exposed flesh and skimpy fabric. Her sparkling blue eyes then looked at the astonished faces of the six remaining men in the audience as she said in a perky cadence, "Hey fellas! Good news! If the sprinklers go off in there, you'll have an umbrella to use! All you gotta do is collapse it and pull it out of the asshole of this, um, asshole! Alright guys! Gotta go! But don't go anywhere, cause we'll be right back with ya in a moment! Right after this next scene from *Take My Hand*. Enjoy! Okay! I need hair, make-up, and wardrobe *immediately*. This shit is fuckin' gross!"

           # CHAPTER 17

CHEESEBURGER FROM PARADISE

Chastity glared at her brother as he drove them both back from the city to their rural home. The amber sun was setting over the golden waves of grain as their father's perfectly waxed sedan rumbled over the graveled path. "You didn't have to be so mean about it," Chastity said through her pouting lips. "I said I'd support you. I didn't say I'd support you, um, back *there*."

"Oh, I bet you let your new (derogatory term omitted) get supported back there, didn't you?" Chad tersely replied. "Hey! He was nice to me!" Chastity argued. "He was sweet and tender and made me feel special!"

"Yeah, I *bet* he did," Chad scoffed. "Of *course* he made you feel special. That's what those (derogatory term omitted) do. They are sick illegals who seduce stupid girls like you into doing stuff so that they can have anchor babies. Do you know what an anchor baby is? It's a half-breed. Half master race and half (derogatory term omitted). And they make stupid girls pregnant so they can have an anchor baby and have an excuse to stay in our glorious nation. Then they can take all of our tax money for welfare and take all of our jobs. That's why Dear Leader, in all of his love for us, has declared all pregnancies caused by an illegal to be demon babies. They aren't a sweet and innocent life. They are demon spawn who are born to take our great nation away from us. And you fell for it. You let that (derogatory term omitted) into you. And now you're probably pregnant by his demon seed. Since you made me promise not to tell Momma and Poppa, *I* had to teach you a lesson myself. So, you should thank me."

"Well, I guess you make a good point," Chastity replied as the sedan pulled into their gravel drive. She looked up and shed a single tear as she saw her country's flag proudly flapping in the light summer breeze. "Oh, I don't know how I could have been so stupid, Chad. What I did goes against all of the teachings of Momma and Poppa. It goes against everything our savior, Dear Leader, stands for. You're right. All of you are right. Women are stupid and can't be trusted to make important decisions. That is for the men to do. And we women are here to serve our divine purpose to support our men. In any way they wish. I'm sorry that I was cross with you, Chad. I truly am. I know that you, and all men, are here to protect us women from making such foolish mistakes. And I will support you however you want."

Chad smiled at his sister as he turned the car ignition off and said, "Good. I'm glad that's settled. Now, just go in and give Momma the money from the sale of the eggs and go straight to your room. Hopefully they won't notice the money is fake. And make sure they don't see that new dress. It is so colorful and provocative that they'll know that you got it from a (derogatory term omitted).

Chad entered the creaky, screened kitchen door first followed by his red-faced sister. Chastity held her head down as she rushed up to her mother, placed the money on the kitchen table, and said, "Um, here you are Momma. Here's the money from the eggs. I'm going to my room now."

"Alright dear," her mother said as she turned from the boiling pot on the stove and looked at her proceeds. "But just one moment. Don't be rushing off. Why *this* seems to be a bit much. And why are the bills different colors? Just where did you sell the eggs? This seems to be considerably more than the oligarch market pays."

"Um, um," Chastity stuttered. "Um, I just sold them at a shop and that is how much they paid me."

"Yes, I understand that," the mother countered. "But what shop *exactly* did you sell them at? And what is that behind your back? Come, come. Did you buy yourself something with our egg money?"

"Um, um, just a little something, Momma," the panicking Chastity answered. "May I please go to my room now? Please?"

"No, you may *not*," the mother sternly responded. "Not until you answer my questions. Where *exactly* did you sell your eggs? And *what* are you hiding?"

Chastity looked straight at the floor and pulled the vibrantly colored dress from behind her back. Her mother gasped when she saw the garment and yelled out, "Poppa! Poppa! I'm sorry to disturb you, but you *must* see what our daughter has brought home from the city!"

The plain-dressed, bearded father entered the room and looked at his daughter's slumping head. He then looked at what she was holding in her hand. "Oh, Dear Leader," he said softly. "Oh, Dear Leader. Please don't let this be what I believe it to be. Chastity. You had better tell us where you got that...that...hideous garment. Why, only a (derogatory term omitted) whore would wear such a thing. It is the uniform of floozies and tramps. And it is in the hands of my very own daughter? My sweet, innocent one? Chastity. We cannot begin to cleanse your soul until you tell us everything that happened in town."

Chastity dropped her new dress to the floor and kicked it away from her. She then buried her head into her hands and began sobbing uncontrollably. "Tears aren't going to help you now, girl," her father scolded. "Dry your eyes and tell us now. Where did you get that blasphemous garment?"

Chastity looked up and mournfully looked at her father through her red, puffy eyes. A streak of drool fell from her trembling pink lips as she reluctantly opened her mouth to speak. "Oh, Poppa! Momma! I'm so sorry! I was so stupid! I saw this dress in a shop window in the restricted area! I thought it was so pretty! I didn't realize that it would make me look like a whore! I went into the restricted area and sold my eggs, then bought this dress from a (derogatory term omitted)! I'm so sorry, Poppa! Please forgive me!"

Her father reached down and lifted the brightly colored bills from the table. He examined them briefly before wadding them up and throwing them at her daughter. "And just how did you pay for this hideous dress, Chastity? How? You sure as Enlightenment didn't pay for it with these! This is phony currency Chastity! This is fake money that is used by those devilish (derogatory term omitted)! That is where you sold your eggs, wasn't it? You sold them to a (derogatory term omitted)!

"Yes, Poppa! Yes! That is where I sold them!" an anguished Chastity admitted. "They were offering so much more than the oligarch shop, and I wanted that dress so badly! I'm so sorry!"

"Haven't I told you time and again, Chastity?" her father yelled back. "Haven't I told you that the (derogatory term omitted) may have the same color skin as us, but they are not to be trusted! They are the spawn of demons who can change into human form from cockroaches! To deceive us! To take all of our wealth! To control *everything*! The (derogatory term omitted) are demons walking amongst us! And now, our own daughter has had business dealings with *them*? Oh, the shame you have brought upon our pious household. The shame."

"I'm so sorry, Poppa! I promise! I'll never do it again!" Chastity pleaded. "I now understand just how dishonest they are and how wonderful our glorious oligarchs are! I'm so sorry! Please forgive me, Poppa!"

"Back to the dress!" her father yelled. "If you had no real money to pay for it, just how did you get it? Oh please. Tell me that you stole it. It would serve those (derogatory term omitted) right to have something stolen from *them* for once. Tell me, girl. How did you get this dress?"

Chastity burst into tears once again. She averted her pained blue eyes from her reddening father as she blubbered. "Stop stalling, girl and answer me!" the father demanded. "How did you get this dress?"

"Oh, Dear Leader, what have I done?" Chastity screamed. "I'm so sorry, Poppa! The boy at the dress shop was so nice to me! He told me I was the most beautiful woman in the world! He gave me this dress, Poppa! He gave it to me! Right after I…right after I….right after…"

"Right after you did *what*, girl?" the father yelled. "What did you do with this (derogatory term omitted) boy?" Chastity's pitiful face looked at her father as she stuttered softly, "Right after I let him have his way with me, Poppa."

"Oh, Dear Leader!" Chastity's mother declared before fainting and collapsing into her astonished husband's arms.

"Can you blame us for wanting to rape this bitch?" Pug pompously said to his five beleaguered colleagues. "She played a stupid whore on screen. Hell, that makes her *ripe* in our world. Fuck, that scene where she undresses and then fucks that (derogatory term omitted). That was fuckin' hot. I've been looking forward to tonight for months. Tonight, we were all going to have our fun with little pure Angel Feathers. And instead, this stupid bitch and her fucking friends are killing us off. One by one. It isn't fair. We're the men. We have the right to do whatever we want to these stupid bitches. Grab 'em by the pussy. Anything. And we're being punished for that? Punished for doing what we were put on this Earth to do? It's bullshit. But maybe we can get out of this. Maybe there's still a way that we can get out of this alive."

Chastity's sullen face turned dark red on the screen, and the six remaining men began mournfully hanging their heads as the grinning Renata said, "And just how are you boys going to do that? Huh? The doors have been rigged. Nobody else will be here for hours. And your cell phones are useless. We've seen to that. You are mortal. We are eternal. We can travel through portals throughout the universe to any planet that we want. Any planet in any parallel universe. Shit man! We can literally go from hell and back! But sure. You're going to find a way out of this. How are you going to do that, Pug? Talk your way out of it? It seems to me that you don't really have much credibility with us. Isn't that right, Veronica?"

The raven-haired Veronica entered the scene wearing a skin-tight black vinyl cat suit. And a devilish smile. "Yeah, that sounds about right. You can go now, Renata. I'm ready for my scene." The pair hugged before Renata blew a kiss and winked at the six trembling men.

"Alright guys," Veronica said in a bored tone. "Let's get this shit over with. I'm here to kill one of you motherfuckers. I really don't care which one. I just want to shoot my scene, then go take a nap. Yeah, I was perfect for my part in *Meatgrinder Mayhem*. That character was a disinterested, bored bitch. Just like me. Of course, I started paying much more attention after you assholes began abusing me. Yep. That kept me up at night. Always wondering when you would return for me. Wondering what twisted shit you were going to make me do. Or do *to* me. I went from sleeping at every opportunity to not being able to sleep at all. The sleep deprivation probably contributed to my depression and eventual insanity. I mean, it's not like a *sane* chick would throw herself into a meat grinder, am I right? That's some hardcore shit. As you're about to find out, um, now which one should I choose? Not Pug. He's Renata's finale. Probably Ezekial too, so you two assholes are safe. For the moment. So, two off the table. Four to choose from. I'll just do it *this* way. Eenie, meenie, miney, Sam. Sam Shutter. The Director of Photography."

Sam began weeping uncontrollably as his body lifted itself out of his velour chair and marched up the stage steps and into the crimson screen. "Welcome to my little slice of hell, Sam," Veronica said as she took him by the hand. Their surroundings changed from Chastity's kitchen to a butcher's shop. There were metal hooks, cleavers, knives, and meat grinders spread throughout the dingy room. And blood. There was lots and lots of streaks of blood.

"No, please, no," Sam sobbed as Veronica lead him to a chair next to a small meat grinder. "Now just calm down, there, Sam," Veronica said in a detached tone. "I'm not going to do anything that you haven't seen before. And see it you did, didn't you? I saw you from my cloud in Enlightenment. I saw the thrilled expression on your face as you filmed what was left of my mangled body after it was spit out of the industrial sized meat grinder that I threw myself into. I saw you taking still pictures, too. Hell, I watched from my little perch in the sky as you jacked off to them. I mean, I kinda get guys wanting to see inside a girl, but that's fucking *ridiculous*, man! How does human hamburger meat turn you on? I know there's a lot of shit you can put on a burger, but your own jizz? That's *definitely* doing it wrong, Sam. Ketchup I can tolerate. But slathering your own cum on a bun, then eating it? You are one fucked up bastard. And don't try to tell me that you didn't. I *saw* you. I watched you do it after all of you assholes fried up my remains and had one hell of a cookout.

"But that *did* make me curious. Not the eating cum part. I *know* what *that* tastes like, and it *definitely* should *not* be used as a condiment. I should know. You motherfuckers made me eat enough of it. No, I'm talking about being curious about what human flesh tastes like. It seems unfair that you have experienced that and I haven't. So, let's have a little taste, shall we?"

Veronica let out a dark chuckle as she placed Sam's hand into the feeding tray at the top of the meat grinder. Sam let out a loud wail as his fingers pressed up against the corkscrew blades within the cold, metal chamber. His screaming harmonized with Veronica's laughter as she began churning the handle and pressing his hand deeper into the grinder. And deeper. And deeper. Until thin shreds of bright pink Sam flowed into a large metal trough.

"Huh. This thing's pretty wide. Wanna go up to the elbow? I'm pretty hungry," Veronica said as she continued to push Sam's arm into the churning grinder. The sounds of wet glop being torn apart by merciless metal blades could be heard just under Sam's tortured shrieks.

Veronica stopped turning the handle and looked into the metal trough. "That should be enough for a double burger," she said as she took a large wad of Sam and began enthusiastically balling it up between her palms. "Fuck man, you're really greasy," she said darkly to the screaming Sam. "You're really going to cook down. I might need a little more." She began turning the handle once again and more ground Sam came snaking out of the grinder. The preparation of his meat continued until he was stuck in the grinder up to his bloody shoulder.

"Alright, now into the skillet. What do you think? Medium rare? Yeah, that's how I like my meat. With a little pink in the middle. Remember when you said that to me as you were raping me? Yeah, I bet you do."

Sam's flesh patties sizzled for a few minutes in the frying pan while Veronica concentrated on conjuring lettuce and tomato. Some Heinz 57 and a french fried potato. Then, a cold kosher pickle and a cold draft beer to wash it down. "Yeah, perfect," she said as she placed the condiments on top of the Sam Burger. "This is the way to eat a fuckin' cheeseburger. Got the recipe from a song. Now, let's take a bite."

She straddled a chair at the front of the screen and stared at the astonished audience in the theatre as she chewed. And chewed. And chewed. She wiped Sam's greasy juice from her chin and smiled at the disgusted men before saying, "Fuck yeah! Now, *that's* some good eating! Why pick on poor innocent cows when you've got all these asshole men in the world that we could be chowing down on? What a great idea! I wonder if I could get in touch with Satan. Maybe he could let us have a few damned souls and we could get him some fun angel girls to party with once in a while. It takes a village after all. Am I right Sam? Shit, are you still alive? Fuck man, are you okay? You want me to call you some help?"

Veronica reached into Sam's back pocket and pulled out his cell phone. "Who should we call?" she asked as the phone's screen began glowing. "I know! We'll call Wendy! Get it? Wendy? Because of the burger joint? Oh, fuck it." She laughed as she looked at the phone's screen. Her smile faded and turned into an expression of horror as she watched images from Earth Tres. And heard a very disturbing subliminal message under the annoying voice of Dear Leader.

"Okay, fuck off Sam. I've got bigger things to do," she said as she took a meat cleaver and buried it into Sam's skull. She then looked off-screen and yelled out to her sisters. "Hey guys! I don't know *what* the hell is going on with the cell phones, but we'd better look outside the theatre. Everybody on our Earth has gone batshit crazy!"

CHAPTER 18

ISLAND OF ONE

"What the fuck is *happening* down there?" Renata yelled out as Veronica rejoined her eleven sisters in their perch in Cloud Twenty-Three. "I dunno," Veronica answered as she continued to scroll through Sam's phone. She let out a slight burp and wiped Sam's grease from her chin before continuing. "But there's some bad shit going down. Take a look at these images from dickwad's phone." Veronica lifted the phone and concentrated until its images were projected on a nearby wall cloud.

The twelve actresses gasped as they witnessed scene after scene of cities in ruin. Explosions. Fires. Collapsed buildings. And *most* disturbing, images of stark raving mad people cannibalizing each other. "The whole world is collapsing. They are destroying *everything*. And each other. But listen. Listen really closely. Do you hear that? It's Dear Leader's annoying voice bragging about his sexual conquests and how he's the greatest leader ever and how everybody loves him and blah, blah, blah. Same shit we heard every night on State TV. But tune in closer. Listen to what is being said *underneath* fucknut's word salad diatribe. Do you hear it? Do you hear that evil whisper?"

"Yeah, so?" Skipper chimed in. "It's a subliminal message. Probably to get people to buy Dear Leader's stupid cologne or something. Remember *that* shit?

YOUR DEAR LEADER PRESENTS
GROOMING
A Scent For The Distinguished Man Who Likes Them On The Younger Side

Jesus Christ! Just the *thought* of it makes my skin crawl! It smelled like sweaty pubes mixed with rotting flesh wrapped up in a shitty diaper! And all those assholes from DL Studios wore that shit all the time! It was everything that I could do to prevent myself from vomiting every time I was around them! Good thing we're not impacted by bullshit subliminal messages up here. Otherwise, we'd be conjuring gallons of that shit up, wearing it, then hurling all over Enlightenment!"

"Yeah, it's a subliminal message alright," the violet skinned Violet contributed. "But this isn't about buying his shitty cologne. Or gold tennis shoes. Or worthless trading cards. Or stupid hats, shirts, flags, or banners. Jesus Christ. His entire reign has been nothing but one giant grift. Brainwash his people, oppress them, then make them buy his worthless shit. But that's not what *this* is. *This* subliminal message that is buried in all these videos on this cell phone is darker. It is evil. Oh fuck, you guys. *This* subliminal message is turning people into cannibalistic zombies!"

Violet grabbed the phone and began opening app after app. "And it's on fucking *everything*! Dating app? Dear Leader's voice with the subliminal message. Stupid cat video? Same thing. Word games? Yep. On here too. This subliminal message is on every fucking thing that is on this cell phone! And *everybody* uses a cell phone! That's what is happening on our Earth! Somebody implanted evil subliminal messages into the cell phone networks and it's turning everybody into mindless, violent fucking zombies!" (AUTHOR'S NOTE: Wanna know the backstory to all of this? Check out *Island of One*. Or don't and be left in the dark. Not my problem).

"Oh, Dear Enlightenment," Ginger said as she watched the horrific violence that had been unleashed upon her terrestrial home. "They did it. They actually did it. They found a way to destroy all of humanity. But why? Why would somebody do this? Why would somebody intentionally destroy the world? It makes no sense. Whoever did this has to live on Earth too. What are they going to do? Just sit in some mansion and hide from billions of zombies? This couldn't have been intentional. It had to have been a mistake. A really *deadly* mistake."

"So, you think that everybody who looked at their cell phone is now one of these...these...*things*? Or have been *eaten* by these things?" Renata asked. She was greeted by eleven solemn nodding heads. "Oh, sweet Jesus," she said as she buried her weeping face in her trembling hands.

"Hey, hey," Ginger said softly while enveloping Renata in a comforting embrace. "It's okay. You're okay. You don't have to worry about this. You don't *have* to return to your body on Earth Tres. You're safe here with us. Just allow your deceased body to remain on our Earth and your soul can live here with us free from any burdens. It's all over for our Earth now. But it isn't over for you. You can stay here and answer prayers from the parallel Earths and other planets."

"And, like, collect conjuring coins!" a delighted Virginia chirped. "And then you can go shopping on Cloud Nine and drink cocktails by the pool and then, like, fuck the pool boy! Plus, we're gonna need the extra help. Just think of all the souls who are going to be arriving in Enlightenment from our Earth. Shit. And we thought there was a housing crisis *before*."

"Well, they shall not be invading *our* perfect little cloud, daawlings!" Sophia yelled out. "Why, we have the most elegant cloud in all of Enlightenment. We cannot have these sad creatures ruining what we have here. Of course, *Renata* is welcome to stay. She is one of us. A fallen angel just as we all are. Plus, she has given us this wonderful opportunity to resurrect our acting careers. Yes, *she* is most welcome. But not the others. We do not need their kind here."

"Do you know who you sound like, Sophia?" Ginger replied in a serious tone. "Do you? You sound like every bigot who walked our Earth. Every 'not in my neighborhood' asshole who looked down upon others in need. Just because they weren't exactly like themselves. It is that callousness towards our fellow people that has driven all of this. This uncaring attitude of the plights of others. *That* was the fuel that led to the rise of Dear Leader and his sadistic regime! And it is an attitude that is *not* welcome *here*, my dear friend. But do you know who *is* welcome? Everybody. Every soul that was good enough to be welcomed into Enlightenment is good enough to live here with us. In peace. In harmony. And with unconditional love and caring."

A grinning Virginia nudged Sophia in the ribs and whispered, "Plus, *some* of them might be hot pool boys, heh, heh, heh." Sophia looked down at her young friend and smiled. "Oh, daaawling. I have no interest in hot pool boys. But perhaps a few bathing beauties that Randi and I could play with might be fun. My apologies everyone. I suppose I *have* become a bit jaded and overly protective of my home. Of course we shall welcome new souls. It isn't as though we have a choice anyway. The Keepers of Enlightenment shall assign the newly arrived as they see fit. I do hope that they are people with artistic inclinations, though. With good taste in music. I really do not think that I can survive living next door to a clan of hayseeds and listen to their twangy country music as they throw yet another hootenanny."

"I don't think that we need to worry about that," a laughing Ginger responded. "Most of *those* types of people won't be coming here. And the ones that *do* will be assigned to Cloud Thirty-Five. I must admit, though. They do conjure some powerful moonshine there. But, oh! The Banjos! When they really get going, you can hear their infernal picking nearly to Cloud Sixteen. But they are good hearted. That is why they are in Enlightenment. Anyway, this isn't the point."

Ginger turned back to the sobbing Renata. "You see, dear? You are safe here. You are with *us* now. And *we* are with *you*."

Renata lifted her face as tears flowed from her grieving blue eyes. "No, it isn't that," she stuttered. "I know I have a home here. It isn't me that I'm worried about. It's my sister. And…and…my darling *niece*!"

"Please Mom! Please stop!" a terrified six-year-old Anastasia Miazga was screaming. Outside of her closet door, she could hear her enraged mother growling at her and pounding upon the wooden barricade. "Please Mom! What is wrong? Why are you so mad at me? Why did you try to bite me?" She screamed as her mother's head came crashing through the door. Her dead, white eyes scanned the darkened closet until she found what she had been smelling. The ripe flesh of her daughter sat trembling on a pile of pink tennis shoes, white sandals, and a menagerie of well-worn stuffed animals.

"Get out, Mom!" Anastasia yelled as she threw a large pink frog at her snarling mother. Her mother shook her head, growled, and began gnashing her teeth at her desired meal. "Mom, please! Please, stop! I love you!" the hysterical young girl screamed as her mother's shoulders broke through the splintered wooden door.

Anastasia then looked around her closet and said, "What? Find a sharp object? I can hear you Aunt Renata! Where are you? There's something wrong with my Mom! Please help me! I don't have anything sharp like that, Aunt Renata! Please help me! She's getting closer!" Anastasia's pale face was filled with pure terror as her mother's slobbering mouth came within inches of her. "I don't have anything sharp, Aunt Renata! *Please*! She's getting closer! Oh! What's this in my hand? How did you do this? How did you give me this knife? What? I *can't* Aunt Renata! I *can't* hurt my Mom!"

Her mother's body burst through the closet door, sending shards of cheap plywood flying over Anastasia's pretty dresses and colorful toys. She curled her lips upward and emitted a low growl as she approached her trapped meal. She then lunged at the screaming morsel. She grabbed Anastasia by her blonde ponytail and began lifting her squirming body towards her biting jaw. Anastasia screamed again, "Please, Mom! Please stop! Please!" As her tiny toes left the plush carpeting, she instinctively swung her right hand and was immediately dropped to the floor. She looked down at her trembling hand that was gripping a bloody knife. She then looked into the dead eyes of her mother.

Anastasia's mother began making gurgling sounds while she clutched her throat. She stumbled backwards out of the closet and collapsed in a bloody heap on Anastasia's pink princess bed. "What have I done!" Anastasia yelled out as she ran to her mother's side.

"Please, Mom. Please. I'm so sorry," she pleaded as she tried to wrap a bright blue blanket around her mother's sliced throat. "Please, Mom. Please don't die. I'm so sorry," she wept while looking into her mother's white eyes. Her mother turned her face and her eyes returned to a dark blue. She reached her trembling hand up and lightly stroked her daughter's blonde hair. The loving smile on her face became frozen as she let out her final breath.

Anastasia collapsed upon her mother's bosom and wept uncontrollably. "No, Mom. No. I'm so sorry. Please come back," she said as her confused, young mind tried to absorb this horrific tragedy. She then looked up once again and said, "What is that Aunt Renata?" Her mother's blood dripped from her ponytail as her confused blue eyes searched for where the voice of her beloved aunt was coming from. "Aunt Renata! Please come get me! I'm all alone! I'm all by myself! Please! Mom's dead and I'm scared! What? You *can't* come get me? I have to come to *you*? But how Aunt Renata? Where are you? How will I find you? Look out my window?"

Anastasia jumped onto her bare feet and ran to her window. She opened her pink curtains and stared in horror as she saw hundreds of frenzied men, women, and children pounding at her house. "There's more of them Aunt Renata! They're coming for me! Please help me! Okay, Aunt Renata. I'm breathing slowly. I'm trying to calm down. Yes. Yes, I remember playing hide and seek with you. Yes, I remember when I hid in the vent in the basement. You told me to never go there because it's dangerous. You want me to go there now? But why? Why do I need to hide my body? I don't understand. Okay, I'm being calm. I'll go there. But why do I need to take the knife?"

Anastasia shrieked as she heard her downstairs front door being smashed in. She ran out of her second-story bedroom and down the stairs of her home. She screamed as she whizzed past bloody, flailing arms that were desperately trying to grasp their next meal through the partially broken front door. She reached up and turned the cold doorknob to the basement. The door opened with an ominous creak. "I, I can't reach the light switch, Aunt Renata," she said as the growls of approaching zombies grew louder. Suddenly, the entire basement was illuminated by a soothing glow. "Thank you, Aunt Renata. Okay. I'm going downstairs now."

She closed the basement door and locked it as her aunt's voice had instructed her to do. She carefully placed one tiny foot in front of the other as she descended the rickety wooden staircase. She could feel dirt particles stick to her bare feet from the cold, concrete floor as she approached the metal vent. She grabbed the sides of the vent and grunted as she pulled it off. She silently crawled in and pulled the cover tight behind her. Through the slats in the vent, she could see the glowing light dissipate. She could also see hulking, dark silhouettes coming down the staircase. The growls of her tormentors echoed in the dank basement as Anastasia covered her mouth to stifle her fearful cries.

"I don't understand, Aunt Renata," she whispered. "Why do you want me to hurt myself? Why is it the only way I can join you?" The hideous growls were growing louder as several dark figures approached the vent. Anastasia closed her eyes, bit her light pink lips, and slashed each of her wrists with the knife. She laid on the cold metal of the vent and felt her life draining out of her while her vicious pursuers were letting out confused and frustrated grunts. Just before she closed her eyes for the final time, she whispered in her childish voice, "Release me from my flesh so that I am free to take the flesh of those who would do me harm."

"Oh, Dear Enlightenment! You're here!" an overjoyed Renata yelled out as the soul of her beloved niece appeared in the dense fog at the entrance of Cloud Twenty-Three. Anastasia squealed with relief as she saw the blurred figure of her aunt rushing towards her. Renata picked up her niece and spun her around causing the clouds to swirl around them in a protective vortex.

"I'm so sorry, my love," Renata said as tears flowed down her porcelain cheeks. "I'm so sorry to have done this to you. I wanted to appear to you, but I couldn't. I can only go back in spiritual form to exact *retribution* on others. Not to *save* them. But with the help of my sisters, I was able to make contact and speak with you. I know that was scary. I'm so sorry. And I'm so sorry about your mom. But it was the only way. It was the only way I could save you from her. And all of those things. The world has gone mad, my darling. But you are safe here. You're not alone anymore. We are together. It's just you and me now."

"And us," Ginger interjected. Renata and Anastasia turned to look at eleven pairs of tearful, sympathetic eyes that were staring at them. "Neither of you are alone. You are with us now. And it is so nice to meet you, young lady. Why, I'll bet we can conjure up all of your favorite toys. And candy. And would you like a puppy or a kitten? Well, we can get that for you too. You are safe now. And you are going to love living here with us. And we will love having both you and your aunt in our little family.

"But Renata, this new development raises a question. We still have five assholes to deal with. They have no idea what's going on. We disabled their cell phones and locked them in the theatre. They don't have a clue as to what is happening. What do you want to do with them? Should we just open the theatre doors and let them meet their own demise? Or should we..."

Ginger fell silent as a thinking Renata lifted a single finger. Her piercing blue eyes stared at her hopeful sisters. They then fell upon her beloved niece's tender, pretty face. She looked back at her eleven co-stars and said in a determined voice, "Oh, no. We're not done with these assholes yet. I don't fucking *care* what is happening outside those theatre walls. These motherfuckers are *ours*. And we *still* have several actresses who haven't been in their scene. No. The fucking Earth can burn all it wants. But it can't take *them* from us. *We* will be their executioners. It's in the fucking script. Ladies, get into hair and make-up. This fucking show goes on."

Twelve women burst into laughter after hearing an innocent, angelic voice say, "Aunt Renata? You *really* shouldn't say those bad words."

CHAPTER 19

LET'S MAKE A DEAL

"What the fuck is going on?" Pug stated to the four remaining dignitaries of DL Studios while nervously pacing up and down the carpeted theatre aisles. "The projector's not going, and there's nothing on the screen. No movie and no red screen with one of those evil bitches. It's just blank." He then turned to the movie screen and yelled out, "Hey! Bitches! What's the deal? You run out of ideas about what you're going to do to the rest of us, or what? You think we're scared? Well, we're not! You just wait. Just wait. Just put *me* in one of your scenes. I don't give a *fuck* what type of voodoo mojo you might have. I'll break free of it. I'll murder whatever bitch is there with me. Then I'll find my way to your cloud or wherever the fuck you are. And then? Then I'm going to kill every fucking one of you. You think you're tough? You haven't *seen* tough. I've gone through all kinds of shit in my life and come out on the other side just fine and dandy."

"Hey, Pug," Ezekial Winthrop III whispered. "Maybe we shouldn't piss them off any more than they are. I mean, what the hell are you going to do? Our cell phones don't work. The doors are boobytrapped or something. And they can paralyze us. Maybe there's a way out of this. Maybe there's a deal we can cut. I know we're not the dealmaker that Dear Leader is, but we're no slouches, either. Listen to me. Being a bull in a china shop isn't always the best approach. They're women, right? Let's sweet talk them. Appeal to their gentler nature. Maybe tell them about *other* men who do way more nasty shit than we do. We offer *them* up in exchange for our release. We promise to be good little boys from now on. And we sweeten the pot by giving them any part in any production we make. Assuming they can come to Earth and perform. It's a win-win. They get their revenge on men and coveted movie roles and we get to live. C'mon, man. Think about it. Pissing them off is a death sentence."

"Yeah, maybe you're right," Pug conceded as he wiped sweat from his bald scalp. "Okay. I know just what to say. Hold on a second." He looked again at the blank screen and yelled, "Hey! Angel! Or, um, what's her name again?" "Renata," Ezekial answered. "Yeah, yeah, Renata! That's a really pretty name you got there. I don't know what we were thinking when we changed it. Anyway, Renata, please just appear on the screen. We want to talk with you. We have an idea that might work out for all of us."

The men shivered as they heard the hum of the projector starting up once again. And once again, the screen turned blood red. Renata's crimson face appeared upon the screen as she was wiping a tear from her eye. "She's been crying," Ezekial whispered to Pug. "Something's up. She's vulnerable. Make this good and exploit her feelings."

Pug nodded in understanding, looked up at the screen and flashed his most manipulative smile. "Renata! *There's* my favorite little starlet! We thought that maybe you had forgotten about us poor schleps down here. Hey! That's okay. We needed a little intermission. And I've gotta hand it to ya. This film you're putting together is brilliant. Just brilliant! I know I said it was a piece of shit. But, hey baby. You know me. I can get all temperamental and shit. Especially when I see real talent. Makes me a bit jealous. And baby, am I jealous of you! Wow, do you have a keen eye for talent and great story telling. Every scene that you have produced has been perfect. Just perfect. The lighting. The camera angles. The casting. And the special effects have been out of this world! Literally, I guess. Yeah, baby, we fucked up. We fucked up by not seeing that you had more than acting chops. You're the whole package. You can act, produce, direct, and write. We never should have planned to do that nasty shit to you. And I never should have threatened your family. That was a dick move on my part.

"No, we should have recognized your talent and embraced it. We should have made you a primary player in our studio. We could have made a lot of money and a lot of movie magic with you, kid. And we still could. Listen, baby. I don't know how you're doing all of this and I don't care. All I know is that we all have an opportunity here. An opportunity to work together to get everything that we *all* want. You fine ladies want revenge on bad men, right? Well, we can offer that to you. We have names. Lots of them. And film. We have film of very bad men doing very bad things. And we're just tiny fish compared to these assholes. You want to make a difference in this world? Well, *nothing* will change by killing *us*. But how about some oligarchs? Some cabinet members? Some congressmen? Heads of state? How about... Dear Leader himself?

"Yeah, we have *plenty* of evidence on him. And hundreds of others. Just think about it Renata, baby. You and those other eleven brilliant, beautiful actresses could produce and star in your very own snuff films. And take this entire cruel patriarchy down in the process. *You* could be the change that is needed in this country. You could collapse the entire oligarch system and the entire government just by producing your films. You could kill them all. Even Dear Leader. And then, just think of how joyful that emancipated women and other minorities will be. You have the power to free them *all*. You have the power to build a new society. And, hey, make a shit-ton of money in the process. Waddayasay, baby? You let us live so we can help you produce your snuff films, and you get to change the entire fuckin' world. And I promise you. We'll never do *any* of that nasty shit ever again. The power just went to our heads, I guess. Plus, that shit's encouraged by Dear Leader, you know? It's like that fat prick brainwashes you into becoming something completely evil.

"Hell, we're as much victims as you are, if you think about it. We used to be really nice guys. We really were. Until Dear Leader and all his asshole friends came along. The things that we have done are just disgusting. *We're* disgusting. And we're so ashamed of what we allowed that blobby orange fuck to turn us into. What I'm trying to say to you, Renata, and to all those other actresses is, we're sorry. We are truly deeply sorry for what we put all of you through. Okay, baby? So, come on Renata. Help *me* help *you*. Let me help you clean up this shit-hole country. You want blood on your hands? Well, baby. I can deliver it to you. Enough to bathe in if you want. So, do we have a deal?"

There was a nervous, hopeful tension that filled the theatre as the five remaining men anxiously watched for Renata's reaction. They studied her eyes and her face for any indication of amnesty. What they could *not* see was what was happening in her mind. The horrific images of their Earth on fire. Images of frenzied people tearing each other apart. Images of cities collapsing and explosions and cries of frightened children. The image of her own beloved niece having to slice open the throat of her own mother to survive. They could not see the brutal complexity that would impact her response. If they could, they would have known that their efforts to strike a deal would have been futile.

Renata took a deep breath and forced herself to smile wickedly before she calmly responded. "Oh, boys. You really think you're cute, now, don't you? You think that you can deal your way out of this? You think that we're interested in becoming a commodity? Well, we're not. Let me address a few points that you raised there, Pug. First, you do *not* think my name is beautiful. That is why you changed it to Angel Feathers. You wanted me to sound like a missionary stripper to fill Christian men's minds with all sorts of twisted fantasies about me. No one's gonna jack off to someone named 'Renata'. Despite how cute I am. Am I right?

"Secondly, you can give us all the names of evil fucking men that you want. I can't do *anything* to them. I can only exact revenge upon those who have harmed *me*. Which is only *you* thirteen assholes. As much as I would *love* to bring down Dear Leader and his entire sadistic regime, I am powerless to do so. Besides, I have a feeling his downfall is a helluva lot closer than you know.

"Thirdly, you say you are just as much of victims as *we* are? Are you fucking *serious*? Did somebody put a fucking gun to your head and *force* you to do all that twisted shit to my sisters? Are you incapable of free thought? Are you incapable of saying no? Just admit it. You performed those heinous acts on these women because you enjoyed it. You got off on it. And if we let you go, you'll do it again at your first opportunity. You perform cruel acts because you are cruel men. It is as simple as that. Which leads me to my fourth point. You can take your apology *and* your deal and shove it straight up your tight asses, hold it there, let it mix around with whatever you just ate, then shit it out into each other's mouths. Have I been clear enough? Do you have any questions? No? I didn't think so. On with the show, motherfuckers."

Renata's face dissolved into the smirking image of Ursula. Her muscular frame towered over them on the deep red movie screen as the five men slinked back into their seats. Her tightly braided dirty blonde strands bounced around her face and shoulders as she began laughing at her cowering subjects. "Really, motherfuckers?" she asked while continuing to laugh. "You really thought you could make a deal with Renata? You really thought she would sell us out? But that's the thing with you pompous fucks, now, isn't it? In *your* world, everything and everybody is a commodity. Everything and everybody are for sale. You have no concept of loyalty. Because you aren't loyal to *anyone*. Every relationship in your life is transactional. You buy people and use them. And once they can no longer be of service to you? You throw them overboard and feed them to the sharks. It doesn't matter what that person may have done for you or who they were in your life. It doesn't matter if they are a business partner, neighbor, supposed friend, or family member. Every interaction with them is 'what can they do for me'? And when the well runs dry, you toss them aside and move on to the next gullible son of a bitch. You move on to the next *deal*.

"Which is what you did with all of us. You beat and tortured and raped each one of us until we no longer had anything left to give in this life. So, we killed ourselves. And instead of reflecting on that, and mourning our loss, you rejoiced in it. You fucking loved that your punishment was so harsh that you drove us to our own demise. And you think you can make a deal with *us*? Let me clue you in on something, boys. Not *everybody* lives in your fucked-up transactional world. Not *everybody* is for sale. In fact, *most* people aren't. Most people actually care about others and have a sense of loyalty to those that are loyal to them. You know the old saying, 'the world is run on relationships'. That's so very true. Healthy relationships, healthy world. Toxic relationships? You get the fucking Regime. And you sadistic pricks are nothing but the sprinkles on this shitty ice cream cone.

"No, not everybody is for sale, which means not everybody is open to make a deal with worms like you. Especially Renata. What *are* you assholes? Blind? Yeah, maybe you are. I sure as hell know *one* of you who is *about* to be blind. And he's a big name, too. Crash Collins. Leading man for DL Studios. And star of some pretty twisted gay porn too, am I right? Wow. I'm actually really honored. Honored that Renata wrote this scene for the two of us, Crash.

"I had such a crush on you. Well, before I met you. But once we started the table reads for our movie, *Blind Bondage*, I knew you were a fucking creep. I knew it was a S&M flick, but it was supposed to be acting, Crash! But you got off on those scenes where I was all blindfolded and tied up and helpless, didn't you? You really got off on being a little too rough with me. And that was just the coming attractions for what you and the rest of these little pricks would do to me *after* the screening. I was decimated. No matter how hard I scrubbed myself in the shower, I could still feel the sharp stings of the whip and the throbbing pain in my ass and vagina from your repeated rapes. My psyche was shattered. My soul was extinguished. And I could think of only one way to find peace. I blindfolded myself, opened my twenty-third story window, and stepped out onto the ledge. It only took me three steps before I lost my balance and splatted onto the pavement. Or should I say, *crashed* into it? So, come now Crash. I have recreated our little set from our movie. Do you recognize it? Do you recognize all of the toys? No? Do you need a closer look? Then join me onscreen, won't you?"

Crash's muscular, bound, and naked body appeared in a wooden chair in the middle of a S&M torture chamber. He frantically looked around at the black leather walls that were affixed by shiny silver studs. Snot began dripping from his nose as he began whimpering at the sight of all of the various sadistic toys that were neatly displayed on silver metal shelves.

"No fair cheating," Ursula said as her black latex-clad frame sauntered behind him. "No fair looking at my toys. Let's just put this black blindfold on you, shall we? Makes it more fun. More exciting. Maybe not for *you*. But certainly, for *me*. There. Tight enough? Good. How does it feel, Crash? To be tied up? Blind? Helpless? How does it feel to know that I can do anything that I want with your body? And, I must admit, you certainly were built for porn. No dad bod on you. Which makes it kind of curious how you were cast to be Chastity's father in Renata's movie. You should be playing a gladiator or something. Whatever. I'm not a casting director.

"Now, just what should I *do* with your body? Should we be leather? Or lace? Harsh? Or sweet? I'll tell you what. I'll leave that up to you." She went to a metal shelf and retrieved two items. "Now, in one hand, I have a feather. You pick that hand, and I'll just tickle you a bit. In my other hand, I have a whip. I think that it's pretty obvious what will happen if you pick that one. Okay, Crash. Which one will it be? Left or right?"

"Um, um, um," Crash began mumbling before yelling out, "Right!" Ursula looked down at her right hand and said, "Well, shit." She hastily switched the feather to her left hand and the whip to her right. "Okay, good choice. Harsh leather. You get twenty-three lashes. One lash for every story that I plummeted. Ready? Here we go."

Crash screamed out as the first lash sliced through his right ear. Then the second, causing a deep gash in his chiseled face. The third shredded his hairy chest. And the fourth sliced his penis nearly off. His screams grew louder with each subsequent strike from the harsh whip while Ursula laughed maniacally. Blood flowed from every part of his body. There were deep lacerations in his legs, arms, torso, face, and scrotum. The sticky red coagulates pooled at his shaking feet as his tortured face suffered the twenty-third merciless strike.

"Damn, I never knew you were so funny, Crash!" the enthralled Ursula stated. "But you really are a cut-up! Get it? Cut up? Because of all the cuts and shit? Never mind. Let's try this again. One hand has a feather. The other has a spiked ball gag. Left or right, Crash? Left... or...right?"

"P-p-please," crash began pleading. "I-I-I-'m so s-sorry. P-please. Stop." "Oh, fuck it," Ursula said. "It doesn't matter which one you pick. I'll just cheat like last time. You're getting this spiked ball gag no matter what you say. And here we go."

Crash shrieked as the metal spikes in the ball gag pierced through his lips, gums, tongue, cheeks, and roof of his mouth. His teeth ground against the spikes as he muffled pleas for mercy. "Damn, dude, you're a mess," Ursula observed. "I mean, I'm into piercings, but *that* shit's ridiculous. You got metal sticking out from every part of your mouth. Okay. This is boring. I'll tell you what. I'll make a deal with you. But I have to change the scene first."

Ursula waved her arms and the pair were instantly standing on the ledge of a snow-covered mountain. "Let me set the scene for you Crash!" Ursula yelled over the frigid howling winds that swirled around them. "You are still blindfolded, obviously, and your hands are bound behind you! You are standing on a narrow rock at the top of this mountain! You can step in any direction you want! There is one step that you can take that will lead you back to me! If you choose *that* step, I'll end this and let you go! If you choose any of the *other* three directions, you will plummet to your death! Now, take your step! And if you don't, I'll whip you again and cause you to fall! Now choose!"

Crash blindly moved his head around in an attempt to pick up on any clue as to where safety may lie. He cautiously moved his bare foot behind him and felt a sudden drop off. He did the same with his front and felt the same deadly nothingness. To his left, he could feel the rock disappear beneath his searching foot. He let out a relieved breath and confidently began stepping sideways to his right. With each step upon solid, jagged stone, he felt increasingly safe. That feeling was short lived.

"Are you fucking kidding me?" Ursula cried out over the swirling winds. "How in the hell did you pick the right direction? Oh, fuck this!" she yelled as she gave Crash a slight shove forward. She looked down the cavernous side of the mountain and watched his tumbling, naked body being torn apart by unforgiving rocks. She began laughing as one arm was nearly snapped off. Then a leg. She was bent over holding her ribs and nearly hyperventilating from her elated squeals as she watched his face explode on a sharp stone twenty-three feet beneath her. His shattered body finally collided with an overhang and came to a merciful, albeit messy, rest. The pure white snow appeared to transform into a cherry snow cone as his blood flowed from his body and into the once-serene landscape.

"Well, I guess Crash was an appropriate name for him, huh?" Ursula said as she walked toward her viewing audience. "You see, boys? We always have a choice in the deals we make. But sometimes we don't have a choice on who we make deals with. Like you mother-fuckers. I thought I was making a deal with decent people who cared about me and my career. That's what you told me. But you lied. And he thought he was making a deal with somebody who would keep her word. And usually, he would be right. But not in his case. Fire with fire, motherfuckers. You want to deal with me? Fine. I'll keep my end of the bargain, and you keep yours. But if you fuck me over just once? If you lie to me? Then I will do everything in my power to ensure you never do it again. To me, or anybody else.

"It was nice dealing with you boys. You're down to one final cast member. Lance Thruster. Or should I call you by your character's name, 'Chad'? Yeah, I hear there's a special guest coming to watch *your* scene with Randi. You're *really* gonna love her new pink hair. It looks *especially* cool if you drop acid. Just sit tight boys. The show is just beginning."

CHAPTER 20

——————

WELCOMING UNWELCOME GUESTS

In the darkest corner of the cosmos, there lies The Realm of Perdition. It was originally conjured by The Keepers of Enlightenment to be a state of eternal punishment and damnation into which a sinful and impenitent person passes after death. It was where the Dark Souls from throughout the various planets in the multiple universes would be sent to be tortured for their sins and was fiercely ruled by a demon named Vetis. From his cold, sadistic perch, Vetis would attempt to harness the strength of his Dark Soul army to invade and conquer Earth Uno. He had vastly overestimated his insipid, Earthly pawn and vastly underestimated the strength of humanity to fight back against his dominion. He was decisively defeated both on Earth Uno and in his own home of Perdition.

And Perdition was converted from a sadistic and cold outer realm into a... tourist resort? Upon her victory over Vetis, Madeline Ruth Sommers, or 'Maddy', for short, invited her friends and family to live with her in Perdition. They pooled their conjuring coins and transformed the darkness into light. Where there was once jagged, black stones, there were now intoxicatingly beautiful botanical gardens. Where there had been treacherous lava flows, there were now tranquil streams of clear blue water gently trickling throughout the lush land. Where there had once been the hellish screams of tortured souls, there were now the delighted squeals of vacationing souls frolicking in the sun-soaked pools. And where horrific torture chambers once stood, there was now, um, well, she kept those. There were still plenty of torture chambers in Perdition.

For Maddy had been an unrelenting vigilante serial killer upon her Earth. And her death and subsequent invitation into Enlightenment did nothing to suppress her more violent tendencies. She, along with her friends and family, was now tasked to oversee the day-to-day operations of Perdition. And should a Dark Soul happen upon this galactical oasis? Well, that was what the torture chambers were for. And knives. And axes. And razor wire. And…well, you get the point. Plus, she made a killing, figuratively speaking, by charging tourists for tours of Perdition's more macabre offerings. Most would leave the experience feeling as though it was overpriced and the tours received their fair amount of negative reviews which were published in the *Enlightenment Enquirer*.

Perdition was now Uncle Joe's destination as he journeyed through the cosmos to entice his niece to join him and watch a killer scene from a movie on Earth Tres that was being produced by his young friend, Renata. He smiled as his soul flew past bursting super-novas, raging red stars, and majestic comets. He was filled with pride as he thought of his beloved niece. His Maddy had followed in his rather large footsteps. In fact, she had outdone him, both on their Earth, and in Enlightenment. Her lust for justice was only matched by her lust for drawing the blood of the unjust. Well, and her lust to be constantly entertained, which was often satiated by her reading *The Enquirer*. And what didn't entertain her, usually just pissed her off.

"Hey Erick!" Maddy shouted to her beloved husband as she lounged in the couple's swanky living room in Perdition. Her straight, copper bangs quivered with anger while her intense green eyes scanned the latest review of her torture tour in *The Enquirer*. Her light mauve lips curled up into a sinister sneer as she yelled out to her husband. "Listen to *this* fuckin' shit!

SAVE YOUR CONJURING COINS! My son and I just vacationed in Perdition. And while the exotic décor, guest houses, and frequent concerts by some of music's greatest dignitaries were well worth the expense, I cannot say the same for "Maddy Sommers's Tour of Torturous Travesties." For starters, entry into the John Lennon concert was only ten Conjuring Coins. But to take the tour of torture chambers? Eighteen Conjuring Coins. That's right folks. For eight more Conjuring Coins, you can skip one of the greatest songwriters from Earth Uno regale you in his finely crafted work in an intimate setting and settle for a self-ingratiating two-hour ill-conceived diatribe by a self-important, pompous imp. Was there a discussion about the history of Perdition? No. Was there a discussion about how The Keepers came to be? No. Was there anything of importance ever presented? Absolutely not. Just story after story about how this egotistical little bitch murdered this person. Then that person. And then her triumph over her own mother and Vetis. Her ego, of course, would not allow her to give any credit to any of the other people and souls who contributed to the defeat of Vetis. No! According to her, she did it all on her own! Story after story was nothing more than egotistical half-truths and lies. And her language would make a sailor blush! Every other word was the F-Bomb! And her jokes? Well, let's just say she shouldn't quit her day job. Whatever that might be. And then, there were the demonstrations of the torture devices which were unnecessarily cruel. We finally had to leave after she tried to entice my five-year-old son onto the rack. The entire presentation was disgusting, overbearing, and a complete waste of time. And a complete waste of Conjuring Coins. Next time you vacation in Perdition, skip this utterly distasteful tourist trap. Oh, and also skip Howard's House of Pegging. Don't ask. Just don't go in there.

"What the fuck, man?" Maddy roared. "I *remember* this bitch too! She had this stupid fuckin' brat that wouldn't ever shut up! Every time I was in the middle of telling one of my great stories or one of my great jokes, this little fucker would ask me a question! *What is this for? What is that for?* Blah, blah, blah. Totally threw my presentation off. So, I put a ball gag on the little fucker and tried to put him on the rack just to shut his little ass up. I'm sorry that she and her son died in a fiery car accident on Earth Uno, but that's not my fuckin' problem. Maybe try not texting and driving, bitch! No reason to rain on *my* fuckin' parade! Whatevs. Fuck her. And fuck her brat kid, too. What else do we have in the ol' *Enquirer* today?"

She turned the page of the newspaper with disgust, and her sneer began to change into a smile. Her bright green eyes softened in intensity and widened as she burst out laughing at her discovery. "Oh, my fucking God! Hey baby! You *gotta* listen to *this* bitch! Check *this* shit out!

Are you bored answering the same old prayers? Are you tired of wasting your talents on getting cats out of trees or helping to open jars of pickles? Are you ready for some real excitement? Then join one of the greatest actresses from Earth Tres as she answers prayers to solve murder mysteries. Duties include, but are not limited to, providing all necessary items from a carefully prepared rider. Being at my beck and call at all hours of the day and night. The occasional massage. You must be enthusiastic, intelligent, and have a zeal for righteousness. Send inquiries, references, and your head shot to:

Simone
Cloud Twenty-Three

"I have the best idea! I think I'm going to answer this ad just to fuck with this stupid bitch! Come take my picture! She wants a head shot!" Maddy paused for a moment while awaiting Erick's response. She began lightly tapping her crossed size-six bare feet in frustration while listening to the silence. "Are you listening to me? I need you to come down here and take my picture so I can go to Cloud Twenty-Three and fuck with this bitch! I'm gonna apply in person, ace the interview, then turn her down cold. She'll probably cry, 'cause she'll know she'll never get a better candidate. But I'll actually be doing her a service. You know. I'll be showing her what the perfect candidate looks like, so she'll have something to go on in the other interviews.

Will she be disappointed? Well, sure. Nobody will come close to my qualifications. But I'm sure she'll find *somebody* who won't fuck up the job *too* much. So, hurry up! Get down here and take my picture!"

"I'm busy!" Erick's irritated voice came from the second story of the home. "Doing what?" Maddy yelled back in response. "What the fuck is so important that you can't immediately take my picture so I can fuck with this bitch?"

"I'm taking guitar lessons!" Erick angrily responded. A sharp chill ran down Maddy's spine as she slapped her forehead in frustration. "Ah, shit, not this again," she muttered to herself as she hoisted her five-foot-four-inch frame from her chase lounge and began stomping up the wide staircase towards Erick's "rehearsal room". She opened the door and immediately clasped her hands over her ears as she was bombarded by the high-pitched shrieks of Erick's guitar. She was also greeted by a pair of smiling guests. "Hey!" Erick excitedly stated. "Malcolm Young and Bon Scott are over and they're teaching me the chords to "Highway to Hell"! Listen to this!" He swung his hand down upon the guitar strings. Maddy's teeth felt like they were about to shatter as the ungodly noise penetrated them. He stopped playing, looked up at his beloved wife, and smiled. "I'm getting pretty good, huh?"

"Baby, you know I love you," Maddy answered tenderly. She wanted to be supportive of her husband but felt the need to be honest about his obvious lack of talent. She searched for the right words that she could say to not offend him. She knew that she could not fuck this up. Maddy fucked it up.

"But Jesus Christ man! You fuckin' *suck* at guitar! Face it! You have no talent for it! Hendrix couldn't teach you! Prince couldn't teach you! Eddie fuckin' *Van Halen* couldn't teach you! Why do you think these blokes from AC/DC will be able to? No, sorry. Time to go fellas. Always nice to see you, Malcolm. Bon. All good things must come to an end. And really shitty things too, as it turns out. I'll walk you to the door. Get the fuck out of Perdition and drink a Fosters or play with kangaroos or whatever the fuck you Aussie's do. Just don't do it here. I've got important shit to do like having my husband take my picture so I can fuck with this stupid bitch on Cloud Twenty-Three." The pair of confused rock gods followed Maddy through the exotic flora of Perdition to The Great Gate. Maddy cordially shook their hands, opened the gate, and immediately smiled broadly. "Uncle Joe!"

The huge iron gate slammed behind Bon and Malcolm who looked at one another and shrugged. "You wanna get a drink?" Bon asked. "Sure," Malcolm replied. "Alright. What'll ya have?" Bon inquired. "I believe I'll have a gin and tonic," Malcolm answered. "Right," Bon replied with a huge smile. "Two Jack and Cokes."

"Uncle Joe! I haven't seen you in *forever*! What are you doing here?" Maddy squealed as she jumped into the brawny arms of her uncle. "Hiya Buttacup!" Uncle Joe shouted while spinning his niece around. "Let's go back to your place and I'll tell ya all about it!"

Uncle Joe stood in Erick and Maddy's living room and excitedly told them about what was happening on Earth Tres. A pouting Erick sat slumped in a large red chair with his arms folded while Maddy's enthralled face looked at her uncle. "So, ya see," Uncle Joe began. "There are these actresses from Earth Tres who are producing their own movie. They have all these motherfuckin' douchebags trapped in this theatre, and these actresses are sucking them into their movie one at a time and killin' 'em off! Fun, right? And the best part? The entire movie is being produced by my young friend, Renata! You remember me talkin' about her, don'tcha Buttacup?"

Maddy's face immediately turned from enthusiasm to disgust. She folded her arms and lifted her nose to the ceiling before saying in a jealous tone, "Nope. Never heard of the bitch." "Why sure ya have!" Uncle Joe responded. "She can slice her wrists, say some spell or somethin' before she dies, then get her revenge on motherfuckin' douchebags from up here in Enlightenment. Then, once she's done, she can re-enter her body back on her Earth. She's been comin' up here since she was six and I've helped her learn the tricks of the trade. She's a really nice young lady, Maddy. I think you'll really like her."

"Nope," Maddy said defiantly. "She sounds like a stupid bitch. Not interested in meeting her." "Oh, come on," Uncle Joe replied. "Listen, I know that tone. Buttacup, she is not your competition. Yes, I care deeply about her. But nobody is as important to me in this life, or afterlife, than you are. You have nothing to be jealous about, alright? You're really gonna love this movie. And they have a scene coming up where they're gonna kill some actor who plays a guy named 'Chad' in Renata's movie. Come on. I know you're enticed. Watching someone named 'Chad' get tortured and murdered? Then we can go get some ice cream? Just you and me? I can see that you're interested. I see your lips moving up. See? You're about to smile. And there it is!"

"Oh, fine!" a giggling Maddy exclaimed. "It *has* been a while since I saw a 'Chad' get fucked up. And this Renata bitch can't be as cool as *I* am. And she sure as fuck isn't getting ice cream with us. Okay, I'll go. But first, I gotta take a picture for my head shot. I'm going to Cloud Twenty-Three to fuck with some bitch named Simone. Can we stop off there, first?"

"First?" Uncle Joe responded gleefully. "Hell, Buttacup! That's our *only* stop! That's the cloud where all the actresses are!" "Oh cool!" Maddy yelled out. "This is like, the greatest day ever! Come on Erick! Let's go to Cloud Twenty-Three and watch a murder and fuck with this stupid bitch!"

"I'm not going," the still-pouting Erick said as he began pounding up the stairs. "You go have your fun. I'm going to stay home and practice my guitar." "Like *that's* gonna do any fuckin' good," Maddy muttered while rolling her green eyes.

"Well, hello everybody!" Uncle Joe exclaimed as he and Maddy appeared in the dense fog on Cloud Twenty-Three. He was immediately greeted warmly by the twelve women there. The final woman to hug him was Renata. "Oh, Uncle Joe! You're right on time!" she said as her blue eyes met his. Maddy folded her arms and lightly tapped her left, tennis-shoe adorned foot while witnessing the scene. "We're about to show a scene from my movie, *Take My Hand*, then it's gonna be Lance Thruster's turn to be a, um, star, of sorts. But in *my* movie, he plays my brother named 'Chad'. And I guess that's why *you're* here, right? Maddy is it?"

Renata extended her hand in greeting and was immediately met by the icy stare of Maddy. "Yup. That's my fuckin' name. Maddy fuckin'

Sommers. And Uncle Joe's *real* niece. I'm not some cloud-hopping poser like *some* people around here. I rule Perdition. I've murdered hundreds of motherfuckers both on *my* Earth and up here in Enlightenment. And in all sorts of creative ways, too. So, I thought I'd show up here and see what amateur hour was all about. Oh, and I'm lookin' for a job. I saw an ad in the paper. Is there a Simone around here somewhere?"

Uncle Joe turned bright red, shrugged, and looked at Renata apologetically. A voice came through the clouds. "I'm Simone. What can I do for you?" an ebony woman said as she walked toward the group. "Check *this* shit out, Uncle Joe," Maddy whispered through her ornery giggles before turning to the approaching Simone.

"Hi there, Simone," Maddy said as she extended her hand. "So nice tameetcha. So, I would like to apply for your position as your, um, assistant. Well, I think that *assistant* probably isn't the best title for it. Not for somebody with *my* impeccable qualifications, as you'll soon see. Here's my head shot. Pretty cute, huh? And here are my qualifications." Maddy reached into a bulging black duffle bag and began retrieving large black binders. "Here is my resume. Each of these ten huge binders contains my murders. As you can see, there are quite a lot of them. And the bloodier, the better, am I right, Simone? And I'm *very* versatile. I can murder on any Earth or planet, or I can rid the entire universe of evil demons. So, as you can plainly see, I'm actually *over*qualified for this position. So, the title of *assistant* really isn't appropriate. I was thinkin' something like, Chief Executive of Operations. Or, how about *this*? Why don't *I* just be the lead investigator, and *you* can be *my* assistant? Yeah, that'll probably work out better. Now, I can see by that shocked look on your face that you love that idea, so I'll just take that as a yes." Maddy turned to her embarrassed uncle and gave him a knowing wink.

"But I *do* need to tell you something," Maddy continued as Simone began furrowing her brow in disgust. "As much as I would *love* to be lead investigator and have *you* be *my* assistant, I'm sorry to tell you..." Maddy was abruptly cut off by Simone.

"No," Simone said bluntly. "What the fuck do you mean, 'No', bitch?" an incredulous Maddy replied. "I mean, no," Simone answered while defiantly folding her arms. "No. You are not going to be lead investigator. And no, I'm not hiring you to be my assistant. In fact, I wouldn't hire you to be my assistant if you were the last fucking soul in Enlightenment. You are arrogant and brash and loud. You'll never take my orders and will have to be the center of everything. Which means, you will completely fuck up my investigations. So, no. You are not hired. But thank you for your interest in the position."

"Why you arrogant little bitch!" Maddy roared. "Are you fuckin' kidding me? Did you not hear me earlier? I'm Maddy Sommers! Maddy *fuckin'* Sommers who pretty much took down Vetis all on her own! Yeah, a few people helped a little, and there *were* The Four Horsemen of the Apocalypse, but they're just a bunch of upstaging little brats who didn't do much. I was both the brains *and* the brawn behind that entire operation, sister! If it weren't for me, Earth Uno would be hell on Earth! Literally! Oh, I see. You're jealous aren'tcha? Yeah, well, you have reason to be sister! I'll tell you what! I wouldn't work for your skanky ass if my life depended on it! And here's *another* thing! You think you got what it takes to be a Private Dick? Well, you don't! But I sure as fuck do! *I'm* the one who's gonna set up my *own* murder mystery prayer service! Yep, lil' ol' me! And I'm gonna leave *your* ass in the dust. So, get out of my way, bitch. I have a fuckin' movie to watch or something. Where do I sit? Here. I'll take *this* cloud. Thanks for moving, whoever you are. Nice pink hair, by the way. Come on, Uncle Joe! Come sit next to me! Sorry, Renata, there's really not much room for *you*."

Uncle Joe and Renata shrugged, shook their heads, and gave one another a knowing smile as they each sat next to Maddy. "Um, it's kinda tight, Renata," Maddy observed. "You wanna maybe move to another cloud or some shit? I mean, not to get personal, but your big ass is kinda taking up some valuable real estate, if you know what I mean, and I think that you do."

Renata gave Maddy a disingenuous smile. The meaning of it was unmistakable. She was definitely saying, 'Fuck you'. She then placed her hand on Uncle Joe's broad shoulder, looked into his eyes, and said,

"I hope you enjoy this scene from my movie, Uncle Joe. Oh, would you like for me to conjure some ice cream for us?" Renata stared back once again into Maddy's seething green eyes and gave her the same smile. 'Fuck you.' Maddy smiled back. And the meaning behind *her* smile was *also* quite apparent, if not a bit more verbose. 'Oh yeah? Well, fuck you too, you stupid fuckin' bitch. You think you're gonna steal my Uncle Joe? Well, think again sister! It's gonna take more than conjuring up some fuckin' ice cream to steal my uncle away! You probably don't even know his favorite flavor!'

Renata calmly smiled at Maddy once again and thought *'My God. She is so fun to fuck with. This should really piss her off.'* She held out her hand and concentrated. A bowl of ice cream suddenly appeared in her outstretched palm. Uncle Joe looked down into the bowl and yelled out, "Hey! Butter Ripple! My favorite!"

Chapter 21

Hanging Chads

"The movie's almost over," Pug stated to his three remaining friends in a despondent tone. "We're so fucked. I wonder who will be next. Not me, apparently. Sounds like I'm the grand finale. The final scene, as it were. I guess that's fitting since I'm the head of the studio and leader of our little band of sadistic bastards. I wonder if they feel what we feel? I wonder if they get the same excitement from torturing us as we got from torturing them? Maybe they aren't different from us at all. Maybe *everybody* has these twisted impulses buried in them. It's not whether we can derive glee from the pain of others. I think *everybody* has the capacity to do that. The difference seems to be the motivation behind it. Their motivation is revenge against us. Our motivation? Pure lust for power. The drive to dominate another human being so brutally that they succumb and wilt under our fuckin' boot. It gets us hard. And they get fuckin' wet getting their sweet revenge upon us.

"Yeah, *everybody* has the capacity for this shit. I don't give a fuck if you're as pure as Mother Teresa. Deep down inside, we're all animals. We're still nothing but a bunch of fuckin' cavemen bashing each other's skulls in to get next to the fire. Or eat that last fish. Or fuck that cavewoman. We're all just animals trying to survive. And thrive.

We all live to be the king of our respective caves. They're no different. They're doing to us the exact same thing we did to them. They aren't holier-than-thou. They're just a bunch of cave bitches doing what comes naturally."

The screen turned red and Renata's beautiful, smiling face appeared. "You are so wrong, Pug." Her red gown flowed behind her as she sauntered toward her audience. "We are *nothing* like you. You are right about one thing, though. We do all have the capacity to unleash unspeakable cruelty against others. But, unlike *you*, *we* are not *driven* to do so. We do not wake up in the morning thinking about cruel ways to fuck somebody up. Physically. Emotionally. Psychologically. We don't dream about doing this shit. You do. You wake up every morning and make a little sadistic to-do list. Complete with the name of who you will do it to. Like my niece, here."

The camera zoomed out to reveal the six-year-old Anastasia holding Renata's hand. "This is my niece. This is who you threatened to murder. This sweet, innocent child. I told you I wasn't coming to your torture-fest, and you threatened to put a bullet in her. We would never do that. We would never threaten to murder someone just because we didn't get our way. But that was your first response, wasn't it? To murder my niece. Because you have absolutely no capacity to empathize with others. You have no capacity for remorse or regret. You have no humanity in your dark souls. Which makes you not human. It makes you fucking demons."

"There's that bad word again, Aunt Renata," Anastasia said in a sing-song voice while looking up at her aunt. "Sorry, sweetie," a chuckling Renata replied. "I'll try to do better. But sometimes, that word is necessary for emphasis. Now. Back to you to you, Pug.

"As I was saying, you are a fu...um...damned demon. I mentioned earlier that we all have the capacity to inflict pain upon others. The difference is, you are capable of inflicting pain upon *anybody*. We do not have the capacity to inflict pain upon other people. Other *humans*. We only have the capacity to inflict pain upon the *inhumane*. The *soulless*. The *demons*. Organisms like yourself. So, yes, we derive great pleasure out of torturing and murdering you thirteen twisted fu...

uh…peop…uh…assholes. We thoroughly enjoy righting wrongs. Tipping the scales of society back towards justice. Ripping power away from evil and giving it back to kind-hearted people. Yeah, you are right about one other thing, too. It does make us wet."

"Are we going swimming, Aunt Renata?" Anastasia innocently inquired. "Um, well, maybe later," a confused Renata answered. "But I hadn't planned on it. Why do you ask?" "Well," Anastasia replied. "You said we're going to get wet. And swimming makes you wet. So, I thought we were going swimming." Even the dark red screen could not conceal Renata's blushing face as she said, "Oh, yeah. Yes, that's right dear. Swimming makes us wet. And when we're done with our movie, we're all going to go for a celebratory swim. Okay?" "Yay!" Anastasia squealed.

"Nice save," Pug stated. "But if your niece is there, that means she's dead, right? She's on some fuckin' cloud with you. So, how did *she* die? It sure as hell wasn't *my* doing."

Renata let out a light, evil chuckle before replying. "Oh, never mind about that. That's none of your concern. But it is *definitely* something you should be concerned *about*. Just settle in boys and enjoy the last couple of scenes from *Take My Hand*. The reason for my niece's visit will be revealed to you in due time. When my movie is over. Bye, boys. Randi will be here soon. And she's *really* looking for her scene with Lance Thruster. Or should I call you by your character's name, *Chad*?"

The screen dissolved back to Chastity's kitchen. Outside the windows, the glorious sunset had been replaced by dark, ominous clouds. A shaking Chastity stood sobbing with her head buried in her hands. "Just look at what you've done girl!" her father yelled out. He gently placed his unconscious wife upon the white linoleum floor and proceeded to unlatch his black leather belt.

"You're pregnant. I can tell already. You're knocked up with a (derogatory term omitted) baby. You have disgraced our family, girl. You have disgraced us in the eyes of our lord, Dear Leader. And there's only *one way* our family can redeem itself. I'm going to beat that demonic life right out of you. And I'm going to beat *your* life out of *you*. It's the only way to get back on the road to our salvation. Ours, and if you pray hard enough for forgiveness while I'm taking your life, *your* salvation as well. Chad. Grab your sister. Take her to the basement. Her mother doesn't need to see this."

Chad began approaching his sister with an evil smile upon his face. Chastity screamed, pushed her brother to the side and went running out the back door. The screen door slammed and her father's face immediately appeared behind the metal mesh. "There ain't nowhere to run to girl! We'll find you! And when we do, we're going to reclaim our family's name! Run while you can! You're only delaying the inevitable! You're going to hell for this, girl! And me and your brother are going to send you there!"

The scene shifted to a soaking wet Chastity crawling through the mud in an opening in the gate that entered the restricted area. Lightning flashed and thunder boomed as torrents of rain soaked her nearly sheer, white dress. Her beleaguered blue eyes darted around the dilapidated neighborhood for signs of danger. She then sprinted to the dress shop and began banging on the door. "Oh, please! Please let me in!" She cried out.

The young man opened the dress shop door and said, "Well, hey there Chiquita. You here for another dress? You got money this time? Or will you paying in another way, again?"

"Please, hide me," she stuttered as rain pelted her desperate face. "Please. They know about us. I had to tell my parents. And they know. And they say I'm pregnant with your child. Please. You told me I was the most beautiful woman in the world. I'll be *your* most beautiful woman in the world. I'll do *anything* to support you. Just please. Hide me. Save me. Save our child."

The young man scratched the back of his tan neck and said, "Yeah, gee, I don't know about *that*, Chica. I mean, I never really wanted a kid, y'know? And you're cute and everything, but there are tons of cute chicks in the world. Plus, if they find you with me, they'll..."

He was cut off by a man's voice from behind them. "It's not *if*, you vermin. It's *when*." A large, masked man dressed in the black uniform of the Regime's security forces turned to his companion and said,

"Call her parents. Tell them we've found her. And we'll be bringing her home soon."

He turned toward the shaking couple and said, "As for you. You know the punishment for consorting with a White girl, don'tcha boy? Yeah, I can tell by the look on your face that you do. Grab him boys." Five security officers grabbed the young man and dragged him into the street while Chastity was handcuffed and lead away to an awaiting black SUV. She heard her paramour screaming for mercy as he was being brutally beaten and kicked. She then heard a single gunshot. And his screaming was silenced.

The screen turned dark red once again. There was a swirling kaleidoscope of colors on the screen while psychedelic music thundered through the sound system. In the distance, there was a gyrating figure. She danced closer to the camera until her shapely form that was draped in a striped, multi-colored mini-dress and white go-go boots came into focus. She approached closer, revealing her smiling, pierced face that was framed by her flowing pink hair. Randi looked at her shivering audience and said with a smile, "Ah, yeah. I just totally dig this. This whole vibe. Reminds me of my film, *Acid Test*. You remember that one, don't you fellas? All the psychedelic colors and music. And the drugs. Yeah, there were a lot of drugs on that set. And even more at the after party. Yeah, you boys just kept putting acid on my tongue. I was so totally tripping while you were raping me and beating me. I didn't even know where I was. I had no idea what was happening to me. All I remember were a bunch of pink animals laughing at me and sticking shit into me.

"And I remember feeling a need to take a bath after your henchman took me home. I remember thinking I needed something really strong to cleanse my skin with. I didn't know why. I just knew some bad shit had just happened to me and I wanted to cleanse my body before I left it. I needed to cleanse my soul so that I would be welcomed into Enlightenment. So, I found some acid. I poured it into the bathtub, got undressed, and laid down in it. I was so high that I didn't even feel anything as my flesh dissolved off of me. Then my bones. I think I finally died after my internal organs burst out of my dissolved abdomen, but I'm not sure. All I know is that the next thing I remember was being greeted by Ginger and these other amazing actresses. How I've longed to give one of you the same experience that I had. How I've wanted to give one of you your very own acid test. But our personal prayers can't be answered in Enlightenment.

"Until now. Renata is the answer to our prayers. To *my* prayers. She is directing this scene. And she is producing my opportunity for revenge. So, I think we all know who is going to co-star with me. The author has already foreshadowed it. So, yeah, Lance Thruster. What a wild made-up name that is. Since we're using made-up names, I think that I prefer your character's name from Renata's film. So, Chad. Come on down."

A confused Lance, or Chad, looked around at his crimson surroundings. He was paralyzed and sitting on a stool in a hot dog shop. The floor was a shiny, checkered linoleum while the walls were adorned with rock and roll movie posters from the fifties. Randi stepped up to the counter, smiled at him, and said, "What'll ya have? Want a hot dog? You know, Chad, I thought it was really curious that you got cast in this Christian, White Nationalist flick. Not really what you're known for. I was used to seeing you deep throating guys in gay porn films. Yeah, you were a master with taking sausages down your gullet. I thought maybe you missed those days, and since I don't have a dick, I thought maybe you'd enjoy a hot dog. One of *my* hot dogs. Yeah, we'll just put this wiener between these hot buns here. How do you like it? You look like a ketchup man. It's my own special recipe. I think you'll like it."

From offscreen a loud woman's voice began shouting. "No, no no! Cut! You're ruining this scene! You're doing this all wrong! I shoulda known you fuckin' amateurs would fuck this up. Well, never fear, for Maddy's here!" Maddy came strutting into the scene and sat next to Chad on an adjacent stool.

"Um, Maddy, what in the hell are you doing here?" Randi asked in a terse tone. "This is *my* scene. I've waited a long time for this and I'm *not* going to be upstaged."

"I'm not here to upstage you sister!" Maddy yelled back. "I'm here to save this movie! Which, if I'm being honest, is a helluva lot better than Renata's movie, am I right? Wow. That Chastity bitch sure is stupid. And, just between you and me, kid, I'm not sure that Renata's a very good actress. She was *supposed* to be frightened of her father in the kitchen, right? Well, I didn't buy it. Totally not believable. But you. You got some acting chops. You coulda been a star. But not if you fuck up this scene. So, I'm not here to upstage you. I'm here to save this scene and save your acting career. Oh, and make sure your performance blows Renata's out of the fuckin' water. Stupid bitch. I really have no idea what these movie assholes saw in her. Or Uncle Joe, for that matter. Anyhoo, I'm here to just give you a couple pointers."

"And just *what* about this scene needs to be fixed?" Randi asked as she defiantly folded her arms. "Well," Maddy began softly before exploding. "You're putting ketchup on hot dogs! What the fuck are you thinking? Putting ketchup on hot dogs is doing it wrong! Here, let me show ya." Maddy leaped over the counter, took the hot dog from Randi's hand, and began surveying her options. "Yeah, here we go. A little mustard. Some relish. A few diced onions. Yum. Here ya go kid. You're welco…"

Maddy was cut off as a large gold hook came from off-screen, was placed around her waist, and yanked her back to Enlightenment. Randi shook her head in bewilderment, stared at the hot dog that had been given to her and promptly threw it in the trash. "Goddammit," she said. "Now we've got to start over. Okay. New wiener. New hot buns. And now for the ketchup."

The top of the jukebox opened up, and Maddy came crawling out of it. "Nope! Cut! Doing it wrong!" she yelled as she stomped back toward the counter. "This isn't really difficult, kid. Mustard. Relish. Onion. That's how to dress a fuckin' hot dog. I don't know why you can't get that through your head. Oh! I bet I know! It's in the script, right? Well, fuck the script, Randi! Renata wrote it! And if we've learned anything today, it's that Renata doesn't know shit about shit. Okay, just throw that ketchup covered monstrosity away, and we'll start over."

"I will *not* throw this away!" Randi yelled out while a bewildered, sweating Chad sat helplessly on his stool. "Don't you get it? I'm murdering him with the *ketchup*! I died by acid! *He's* going to die by acid! The acid I put in the *ketchup*! I didn't put it in this other shit! Just the ketchup! If I feed him a hot dog with *your* shit, all he'll get is heartburn!"

"Well, shit, why didn'tya say so?" a laughing Maddy answered. "Okay, I guess on this *one occasion*, I'll allow ketchup on hot dogs. But if you ever do this shit again, do it right. Put the acid in the mustard. Okay, sister. Shove that shit down his throat. Aaaaaand, action!"

Randi looked up in disgust and mouthed 'why'? She then reoriented herself, stared Chad in his pitiful, puffy red eyes, and said, "Oh, fuck it. Open your mouth you sadistic perv." Maddy's gleeful face was inches away from Chad's reluctantly chewing mouth as the hot dog was forced into him. "There you go," Randi said with a sadistic sneer. "Yeah, be a good boy and take *all* of it. Every last inch. Just like in your movies. Yeah, take it until it explodes inside of you. You like that burning sensation going down your throat? Oh, I know you do. Is it all the way down now? Can you feel it eating at your insides? Burning through your organs? Burning through your…"

"Oh fuckin' gross!" Maddy yelled out as Chad's internal organs burst put of his abdomen and sploshed onto her shoes. "And how fuckin' cool! Nice job Randi! Just one more little thing, though. Yeah, this'll make for a perfect scene."

Randi and Maddy stood proudly with their hands on their hips as they looked at Chad's decimated body hanging from the rafters of the hot dog shop. As they looked at blood pouring from Chad's exposed abdominal cavity, Maddy elbowed Randi and whispered, "Okay, now we need a great joke as the punchline for this scene. How about this? Cut off his dick, shove it in his mouth, then say, 'As the saying goes, two heads are better than one!' Get it? Pretty good, huh?"

"Uh, yeah. Really funny," Randi answered unconvincingly. "But haven't you used that one before? Like in your first book?" "Oh fuck! You're right!" Maddy shouted in response. "Nice catch! Man, I've been in so much of this shit, I sometimes forget about all of my great jokes. Okay. How about this?" She leaned in and whispered into Randi's ear.

Randi grinned widely, placed her hands triumphantly on her hips once again, and yelled out, "This is a public service announcement! Just remember, kids! The next time you have a hot dog, make sure to dress it correctly, or else you'll end up just like this poor schlep. Because, and say it with me now, putting ketchup on hot dogs is doing it wrong!"

CHAPTER 22

CUT!

"Brilliant. Fuckin' brilliant," a giddy Maddy was saying as she and Randi re-entered Cloud Twenty-Three. They were greeted by the other actresses with boisterous applause. Randi and Maddy looked at one another, clasped hands, and took a big bow. Maddy began shaking the actresses' hands. Once she got up to Renata, she turned up her nose and said snottily, "See? *That's* how that shit is done. Maybe you need to take some more writing lessons. And directing lessons. And a few acting lessons wouldn't kill ya, either. Well, not anymore."

Renata looked at Maddy with her soft blue eyes, smiled, and hugged her. "Thank you, Maddy. That scene *definitely* wouldn't have been the same without your input. I am in your debt. And please. Do not think of me as your rival. Uncle Joe is just my *friend. You* are his family. The most *important* part of his family. Please. I would just like for us all to be friends. We are all on the same side, right?"

"Well, of course we are!" Maddy exclaimed as she stepped back from Renata. "We *are* all on the same side! Well, except for that bitch, Simone. *My* murder mystery prayer answering service is going to be *way* better than hers. Anyhoo, thanks for the kind words. I'm glad you can appreciate real talent. And you're welcome. Happy to be of service to ya. Anytime you need some pointers on writing. Or directing. Or acting, well, just give lil' ol' me a ringy-dingy in Perdition."

Renata smiled broadly as she glanced at Uncle Joe. He smiled back and mouthed, 'Thank you.' Renata nodded, and said, "Well thank you again so much for coming to our little show. I hope you enjoyed it. And Uncle Joe, it was so great to see you again. Next time, we'll have to spend more time together. And by 'we' I mean *all* of us, Maddy. I really would like to go on your torture tour in Perdition."

"And for you, sister, I'll give you my friends and family discount!" Maddy gushed. "Only twelve Conjuring Coins! Okay, Uncle Joe. Say your goodbyes. I gotta get back home before my husband blows out all the windows with his fuckin' guitar."

Uncle Joe walked up to Renata and gave her a long embrace in his massive arms. He said to her, "Yes, I'm really looking forward to next time. But that won't be for a while. I know your Earth is in flames, but your work isn't done there yet. Nor is your niece's. Or another that you two will soon meet. I have seen it. And I've also seen us eating ice cream once again together. But before we can do that, I need you to listen very carefully." He leaned in further and began whispering something into Renata's ear. She gently nodded her head in under-standing as she listened intently to his instructions. Uncle Joe took a step back, adoringly looked at his friend, and turned to leave. He then caught himself and quietly said, "But you *might* want to skip Maddy's torture tour. It really *is* overpriced."

"Come on, Uncle Joe!" an impatient Maddy yelled out. "Chop, chop! I got shit to do!" "Alright, let's go home, Buttacup," a chuckling Uncle Joe answered as he placed his arm around his niece's shoulder. "But on the way, let's get you some ice cream." The pair dissipated into the dense white fog and Renata turned to her final actress.

"Okay, Candace," she said. "You get the last scene before the finale. You ready?"

"I was fuckin' *re-born* ready," Candace replied. She stepped forward and exited Cloud Twenty-Three, only to reappear on a certain movie screen in front of three trembling men.

"No rest for the wicked, boys," Candace said with a sneer as she appeared on the deep red canvas. Her short, spiked hair was on full display. As were her various tattoos and piercings. "Renata thought she'd throw another one of our more, um, *violent* scenes in before we watch the conclusion to her movie. And it is quite the honor for me to stand before you three tonight. And soon, it will be only two. Yes, we believe it is time for your director, Justin Scallop, to join me on screen. You know, Justin, before I got involved with your studio, I was a really sweet girl. I really was. And I really hesitated to get involved in my movie, *Skin Tight, Up All Night*. I wasn't raised that way, and I really didn't want my first movie to be a soft-core porn flick. You said you understood. That there was *another* part for me that you would prepare me for. The part of Chastity in a wholesome White Christian Nationalist movie called *Take My Hand*. Yeah, you told me the part was mine, but it wouldn't start shooting for over a year. So, you took me under your wing and became my personal tutor.

"And, oh my, the things you taught me. I was young, naïve, and ambitious. I was the perfect little student for you, wasn't I? At first, you introduced me to drinking. A little bit at a time at clubs or parties. Then a bit more. And a bit more. Until I was embalmed pretty much every hour of every day. But getting me drunk wasn't enough, was it? No, in order for me to act in my *real* part, you needed to introduce me to something stronger. A little white line here. A little red pill there. Then the needles. I was so out of it, I didn't even know we were shooting a movie. Suddenly, my hair was cut off and spiked up. I had tattoos all over me. And piercings. I remember looking at myself in the dressing room mirror through my blurry eyes. I didn't even recognize myself. But you know what? I liked it.

"I liked what I saw. I liked this hard-core don't-fuck-with-me rebellious bitch that I was staring at. Of course, all of the booze and drugs probably played a part in all of that. But for the first time in my life, I felt powerful. And I accepted the role in *Skin Tight, Up All Night*. Well, I didn't so much accept it as I sleep-walked my way into it. And I relished my scenes of being a badass bitch. Telling dudes off. Kicking their asses in some dingy dark alley. Hell, I was even looking forward to the sex scenes. I thought, 'Why not? I've got the bod, the attitude, and the acting chops. And this is a soft-core flick. The sex isn't weird or anything. This will be fun.'

"Yeah, that's what I thought. I wasn't aware that there had been a rewrite. And I was so fucked up on every substance known to man, that I barely even remember the rape scene. Or should I say, *scenes*. You, as the director, had us shoot *several* of those, didn't you Justin? I remember you coming into my dressing room before each one of them. You'd come up behind me and give me something and say, 'Here ya go, Candace baby. Just take these. It'll help you get into character. So, I did. Gulped down the pills or slammed the drinks or shot God knows what into my arm. And my compliant little mind and body were ready for my scene. But *those* scenes weren't just graphic. They were *brutal*. Not that I felt anything. Shit. I was barely conscious.

"But I definitely felt something the night of our special screening. Yeah, you made sure I was perfectly sober that night, didn't you Justin? And this wasn't a screening of the film that would be distributed. This was the Director's Cut. With all the brutal rape scenes included. The scenes I had no memories of. I sat there and I watched in horror at what you directed those actors do to me. Over and over. And in places that I never had interest in being penetrated. I was so drugged up at the time, my body never felt the pain of the rapes and beatings. But on *this* night. The night that was supposed to be my *special* night, I felt *everything* in my very soul. I felt it *in* my body and *on* my body and in my fucking mind. I felt every lash of a whip and every thrust of an unwelcomed cock. Or worse. I was living it for the first time, and I was horrified by it.

"But not as horrified as I would feel about what you did to me *after* our little screening. You thought my reaction to anal was so funny, didn't you? Even in my fucked-up, drug-addled state, you knew that it was hurting me. Both physically and emotionally. And now, it was time to experience that for yourself. The things you did to me. And directed all of these other twisted fucks to do to me. Over and over. The more I cried, the harder you fucked me. The more I pled, the harsher the beatings. For hours. Until I was dropped off at my apartment. Beaten. Humiliated. Shattered. In the span of a few short months, I had gone from a pretty strait-laced chick, to a badass, to a shell of a human.

"I was once again in a dream-like state. Nothing felt real. I was out of my own head. I saw a plunger and I did to myself what you had done to me all night. Over and over until I went too far and something burst. I bled out on my bathroom floor. And just to rub salt in my wounds? You got the police photographs from the scene and used them for publicity. There I was, naked on a bathroom floor with a plunger handle up my ass, lying in my own blood. Nice tag line, too. 'Now THIS little bitch knows how to party 'til she drops! Meet Candace in DL Studio's latest release *Skin Tight, Up All Night*. She'll be cumming soon.'

"I was fucking mortified when I saw that from my new home in the clouds. I spent days crying on the shoulders of my newfound sisters. Even in death, you managed to fuck with me. I prayed constantly that this wouldn't be my legacy. And my prayers were never answered. Until Renata joined us. And she told us about her new production. And I realized that I had an opportunity to re-write my legacy. And here we are, Justin. You destroyed me on Earth Tres. You destroyed me physically and you destroyed me emotionally. Then, you destroyed my reputation. And now, you are going to help me reclaim it. Take my hand, Justin. Come with me onto the screen. And together, we'll restore what you destroyed."

The crimson screen dissolved into a bare, concrete room. A naked Justin sat sobbing on a hard, metal chair while a smirking Candace circled him. She was wearing torn jeans, a black, safety-pinned T-shirt and pink spiked hair. Her nose and lip piercings glinted in the subdued lighting while she slowly walked around the sniveling man like a shark circling her prey. "This is fuckin' *dingy*, isn't it?" Candace remarked. "Just bare concrete walls. Nothing in here but the two of us. Oh, and this."

Candace focused for a moment, and a rusty hacksaw appeared in her hand. Justin's body began to heave uncontrollably as his sorrowful eyes saw the sharp, jagged, rusty teeth of the hacksaw. "Hey, hey, hey, just calm down there, buddy," Candace said feigning empathy. "It's going to be okay. I'm going to take care of *you*, just like *you* took care of *me*. You won't feel a thing. I promise. Here, baby. Just take these." Candace placed two red pills into Justin's mouth and held her hand there until he swallowed.

"Good boy. We'll just wait a moment for those to take effect. They are pretty powerful. Makes you amenable to any suggestion I make to you. You'll be quite relaxed as you do everything and anything that I tell you to do. There, now. Nice and calm? Good. Now, take this hacksaw."

Justin's eyes widened in sheer panic as his hand grasped the hacksaw. "P-p-please. D-don't." he mumbled as snot and drool dripped from his chin. "It's okay," Candace said softly. "You want this to be a good scene, don't you baby? Good. I knew you did. I knew you'd do *anything* to make this picture a success. So, just lean forward. Good. That's it. Place the hacksaw up against your right ankle. Good. You're taking my direction really well. Do you feel the teeth biting into your skin? Let me see it. Let me see the pain and trepidation in your face. Perfect. You look absolutely petrified. And now. Begin sawing."

Justin screamed out as he involuntarily began sawing through his ankle. The sound of metal tearing through skin thundered out of the theatre speakers. As did his high-pitched shrieks. He continued pushing and pulling the saw until it cut through all of his flesh. And tendons. And bones. He let out one final cry for mercy as his severed foot flopped onto the cement floor.

"Really good, baby," Candace praised. "Really nice. I can't even tell if you're acting. You're a natural, kid. Yeah, you're going to be a star. Now let's just shoot that scene again. I want to make sure we get a good take. Do the same thing to your left ankle."

Justin's screams resumed as he sawed through his left ankle until it joined its mate in a bloody heap upon the cold floor. "Nice. Really nice," Candace commented. "And I think I have the *perfect* tagline for this scene. 'Meet Stumpy. Stumpy is a bad man. But he will do absolutely *anything* for his love of anal!' What do you think? Oh, right. It doesn't quite make sense yet, does it? Well, it will in a moment. Now, just one more time, baby. Put the teeth of the hacksaw up against your left shoulder. Yes, that's it. Press down so the teeth are cutting into your shoulder. A little bit more. I need to see a trickle of blood. Good. Now, begin sawing."

Justin wailed while slashing through his shoulder with the hacksaw. Blood, skin fragments, small pieces of bone, and cartilage flew about the confined cement room as he yanked the saw back and forth through his appendage. Finally, he let out one final hellish gasp as his arm plummeted upon the floor. "And, cut! That was awesome, baby. Really awesome," Candace enthusiastically said. Justin looked up at her through his swollen red eyes and allowed himself a breath of relief. "That's it. You're all done for the day. You don't have anything left to do but sit in this chair."

She retrieved the fallen arm and bent under the metal chair. "Yep. Just sit in this chair. This chair that has a large hole in the seat. And a chair that has a hydraulic lift under it. I'll just plop your arm on this hydraulic lift like so. And *then*, we'll ball your hand, um, I mean your *former* hand up in a ball like *this*. Damn, dude. You have a *really* long arm. And a *really* large fist. But I guess you'll find that out in a *moment*, won't you?"

Candace's blood-stained body emerged from under the chair. She was wearing a sadistic smile and holding a metal controller. "Now, as I said," she began explaining. "You did really well today, baby. You really took it like a trooper. Now all you have to do is sit there. Just sit there and relax. I'm just going to push this little button." There was a low hum that emerged from the theatre speakers as the hydraulic system became engaged. Justin's former arm began lifting up towards the bottom of the seat. And towards Justin's bottom.

"There it goes," she gleefully narrated. "Up, up and away, my little superman. Right up into the dark side of the moon. Oh, it's almost to the hole in the bottom of the chair. Yes, there it goes. Into the hole in the chair. And, judging by that pained look on your face, it's beginning to enter *your* hole, isn't it? Yes, that big, balled up fist is beginning to stretch you out. The hydraulics are really straining, but it will get there." Candace burst out laughing as she heard the loud POP of

Justin's stretched anus finally give way followed by his high-pitched wails of agony.

"Oh shit, that's perfect man," Candace commented. "Yeah, keep screaming like that. Keep screaming as your arm and fist impale you. Keep screaming as it keeps going up. Up into your intestines. Up into your abdominal cavity. Yes! Keep screaming, you twisted motherfucker! Scream for me as you made *me* scream for *you*! Make it convincing! Scream as your own arm fucks you right up to your ribcage! Scream as it lodges up against your heart! Scream as you…"

Candace stopped speaking the moment Justin's pathetic howls ended. She cocked her head and looked at him for a moment. She then smiled, turned to her two-man audience, and yelled out, "Cut!"

Just as the remains of Justin's impaled body reappeared in his theatre seat, Renata's face appeared on the screen. Her beet red face glared at Pug and Ezekial for a moment before turning sullen. Her beautiful face drooped as her skin tone changed from red to her natural, pale skin-tone. Her head bobbed silently as the camera panned out, revealing two masked men dragging her handcuffed body up the stairs of Chastity's family home. She looked up at the camera, winked, and said, "Final scene, motherfuckers."

CHAPTER 23

CURTAIN CALL

A distraught Chastity fell into her mother's arms sobbing. "I-I'm so sorry, Momma," she sniffled as her tears soaked her mother's drab housedress. "I-I just didn't know what to do. I was so afraid. Afraid of being beaten by Poppa. But I know I deserve it. I'm so sorry how I've tarnished our family. P-please forgive me."

"It is not *our* forgiveness you should be asking for," her mother sweetly replied. "We can forgive you. But we do not hold the power over your eternal soul. We do not have the ability to welcome you into the heavens. Only our lord and savior, Dear Leader, can do that. Come girl. Let us sit on the couch. And do not worry about your father. He will not lay a hand on you."

"No, I won't," the father stated in a choked-up voice. "I'm so sorry, Chastity. I don't know what got into me. I was just so shocked that you had been with one of those (derogatory term omitted) and are now carrying a (derogatory term omitted) demon baby. I reacted too harshly, and for that I am sorry." He nervously chuckled before continuing. "You know, women cannot be trusted with major life decisions. They are simply too emotional to be able to deal with finances and politics and all of the complexities that fills this world. That is a man's business. But I must admit, in times like these, it sometimes takes a woman's compassion to come up with the right solution. And your mother has come up with one."

"Yes, I have," the mother answered softly as she laid her daughter's blonde head on a pillow that leaned against the arm of their dowdy sofa. "I believe that I have come up with the perfect solution. Chad, darling. Please go into the kitchen and retrieve the pitcher of coolaid. But do not drink it. I have made it for our Chastity."

"Y-you have, Momma?" Chastity inquired in a confused tone. "You have made me a treat? Despite what I've done? I've brought shame upon our entire family, Momma. I do not deserve a treat."

"Oh, but you do, my dear. You do," her mother answered as she poured a tall glass of orange coolaid for her daughter. "You *do* deserve a treat. The treat of salvation. The treat of your soul being blessed by our lord, Dear Leader. You deserve the treat of redemption. And you shall have it, my darling. Let us read from the holy scriptures. Poppa, if you would please do the honors."

"Of course," the father said as he opened his gold Bible, Dear Leader Edition, to the perfectly selected scripture. "Ye, WOMEN cannot be Trusted with deciding who to fuck! They are TOO EMOTIONAL and must be Looked After by their MEN! Any LOW IQ WOMAN who fucks Vermin MUST be Redeemed! Only by MY HAND, your Favorite DEAR LEADER, can your Soul be Saved! Offer yourself to ME, your Favorite DEAR LEADER, and ALL will be Forgiven! Thank you for your attention to this matter. DL."

Tears of joy ran down Chastity's youthful face as she looked up at her loving family. "I now understand, Momma. I understand how wrong and sinful I have been. I understand that in order to redeem my family's name, that *I* must be redeemed. And I understand that it is only through the love of our lord, Dear Leader, that my redemption is possible."

"Good, dear," her mother softly responded. "Good. Now, take this glass of orange coolaid. Good. Place it up to your lips, my darling. Yes, that's right. And now, drink. Drink it all up." A slight trail of orange liquid dripped off of Chastity's pink lips as she swallowed the sugary drink. She finished the last drop, smiled, and handed the glass back to her mother.

"Thank you Momma. Thank you Poppa. Thank you Chad. Thank you for your love. Thank you for my chance at redemption. But most of all, praise be to Dear Leader for allowing my soul to live on in his golden kingdom."

"That's right dear," her mother said. "Now, just close your eyes. It is time to sleep now, my darling. Here. Take my hand. Take my hand and allow your mother to guide you to redemption in our lord's kingdom."

Chastity's breathing became heavy for a moment before stopping. Her proud, smiling parents looked down upon their serene daughter as her soul was lifted from her body. They continued smiling as they watched their daughter's soul drift upward, then out the window. Chastity's translucent essence drifted upwards into the pure white clouds. She looked down and smiled as the brilliant rays of the sun beamed down upon her nation's flag that was flapping in the light breeze outside of her family's modest home. The camera zoomed into her tranquil face and her smile widened as billowy clouds, and a lush orchestra, swirled around her. The credits began rolling over her beautiful, static face. Her smile then faded and she furrowed her brow. Her lips curled up into a vengeful sneer. And the screen turned dark red.

The credits for *Take My Hand* were replaced by still images from Renata's production. A smiling Ginger with Jake Johnson's decimated body trapped in the wreckage of a crashed car. Violet beaming as she is pissing into a bag covering the drowning Phillip Phillip's head. Sophia smirking while watching the dismembered Kyle Splicer flailing in the ocean. Virginia mixing a drink for the panicking Bob Lemmings. A laughing Claudia playing *Pac-Man* with Arpeggio Dante's severed head. A pensive Simone carefully watching as snakes are biting the face of Kellen Richardson. An enthralled Skipper opening an umbrella that is sticking out of the posterior of James Proctor. A drooling Veronica stuffing Sam Shutter's arm into a meat grinder. Ursula taking a selfie as she is giving Crash Collins a slight shove over a cliff. Randi force feeding a hot dog into Lance Thruster's mouth. And finally, Candace bent over laughing as an arm is going up Justin Scallop's ass. The final credits then rolled while Renata continued to smirk. 'Written, Produced, and Edited by Renata Miazga. The Producers would like to thank every cruel, misogynistic man out there in the world for their inspiration for this work. We truly could not have done this without you. And we look forward to producing movies with each and every one of you in the future. We would especially like to thank every survivor out there for your courage, conviction, and relentless pursuit of justice against your abusers. It is through your truth and strength that evil shall be defeated. Special thanks to Uncle Joe Argento and Maddy Sommers. Copyright 2026, Renata Productions.'

And the screen turned black. Pug and Ezekial's eyes widened as they looked around the dark theatre. They each began sweating profusely and panting while awaiting their most certain grisly fate. Suddenly, a spotlight appeared on the blank movie screen. There was the sound of fabric ripping as twelve proud actresses emerged from the torn open movie screen and onto the stage. They were each wearing long, flowing white robes and donning blood-soaked angel's wings. They clasped hands, raised their arms into the air, and took three long, deep bows. They began applauding their work before embracing one another. Tears of joy ran down their exuberant faces as celebratory red roses rained down upon them from the rafters.

Renata wiped her tears from her piercing blue eyes and looked around the theatre. Her face wore an electric smile as she looked around at the eleven corpses that littered the theatre. She then stared at the trembling faces of Pug Homleyman and Ezekial Winthrop III. "And there you have it, boys," she said as she stepped down from the stage. "That's our little movie. What do you think? Do you think we might get some award nominations? Yeah, I think we might. We're really proud of it. So, that's it. Thanks for watching. You're free to go."

Pug and Ezekial looked at one another with shocked expressions. Pug then said, "What do you mean, we're free to go? And why is that the end of your movie? Aren't we going to be in it? Aren't you going to torture and kill us like you did to the rest?"

"Naw," Renata replied. "I'm pretty sure you learned your lesson. You can go. The doors aren't booby-trapped anymore. Hit the bricks. Go rejoin the world that you helped to create. *That's* your punishment. To have to live in this cesspool of your own creation. Now, get out of here. Before I change my mind."

Pug and Ezekial let out joyful yelps, high-fived one another, and ran out the theatre's exit. "Dumbasses," Renata chuckled before turning to her spiritual sisters. "Well, there's my body. All dolled up. I'm going to need to put on some jeans and shit. And just look at my make-up! Christ! Did they have to make me look like I'm ten years old? Fuckin' pervs. Fuck it. Alright ladies. It's been a blast, but I have to go home now."

Ginger approached Renata, tenderly placed her hand upon her shoulder, and said, "No, you don't. Please, Renata. Please stay with us. Your Earth is destroyed. *Our* Earth is destroyed. It's been overrun by zombies. There's nothing you can do here."

"Yeah, that's what *I* thought too," Renata replied through a slight chuckle. "But Uncle Joe told me that it isn't my time. He said that Anastasia and I still have work to do here. And he gave me some very specific instructions. But thank you. Thank you all. I love you all so dearly. Please take care of Anastasia until I can get to her body, okay? Watch me through the universal portal. Once I get to her body that is hidden in her basement vent, have her say these words. She will then join me. And our adventure together will begin."

"It will be our honor," Ginger replied as she fought back her tears. "Come on, ladies. Let's watch what our new friend is going to do. There's certainly one thing that we know. It won't be boring." Final hugs and good-byes were exchanged before eleven women were absorbed back into the torn movie screen.

Renata looked down at her still body, shook her head, and recited her passage. "Jesus fucking Christ! I never get used to that!" Renata yelled out as her soul reentered her stiff body. "Oh, fuck. My neck hurts. I bet they twisted it carrying me down from the projection booth. Assholes. Alright. First things first. I brought a duffle bag. Now, where is it?"

Renata rushed up to the projection booth and found her black duffle bag. She stripped off her pink babydoll dress and replaced it with black jeans, a black T-shirt, and black canvas tennis shoes. She then ran to the restroom and scrubbed the gaudy make-up from her pale face. "There. That's better," she said as she recognized her reflection once again. "And now, time to go shopping."

She shielded her eyes from the sun's harsh rays as she exited the theatre. She looked down and began laughing. "Wow. Those motherfuckers didn't even make it five feet," she said as she watched zombies tearing apart and eating the flesh of Pug and Ezekial. "Yeah, I bet *that* was quite the surprise. Feel the elation of being free, step outside, and BOOM! Attacked by motherfuckin' zombies! There's nothing that I could have done to them that would have been worse than that. So, fuck you, boys. You created this fucking world. You can die in it. And speaking of dying, I gotta get the fuck out of here. First stop, a toy store. For *some* weird reason."

Renata ducked past throngs of zombies for three blocks until she came upon a toy store. She grabbed a large plastic bag and filled it up with brightly colored squirt guns. "Okay, now a perfumery. Right next door." She dodged three more zombies before jumping through the smashed picture window of the neighboring perfumery. "Oh, fuck, Uncle Joe. Why in the hell did you want me to fill these guns with *this* putrid shit?" She grabbed several bottles of *GROOMING* from a shelf, ran to the back of the store, and locked herself in the office. She began gagging as she opened one of the bottles and began pouring it into a squirt gun. "Oh fuck! This shit stinks! It smells like a sweaty ball sack that's been dipped in horse shit! And, oh! Goddammit! This bottle just spilled all over me! I guess I'm not getting laid tonight. Not that I'm into fucking zombies or half-eaten corpses, anyway. Methinks my options on *that* front are going to be *pretty* limited. Alright. I've got a bag full of filled squirt guns, and a few more bottles of this horrid shit in my duffle. Uncle Joe told me that this will protect me from the zombies. Well, I guess we'll see."

She emerged from the back office and was immediately confronted by six snarling zombies. "Oh, fuck! This shit had *better* work!" she yelled out as she began squirting the grasping marauders. They began sniffing the air, stopped snapping their jaws, and proceeded to vomit. And vomit. And vomit. Until their internal organs were being wretched up. The zombies collapsed into a large pool of their own puke, blood, and intestines within seconds. "What the fuck is *in* this shit?" Renata asked as she looked at the bottle.

YOUR DEAR LEADER PRESENTS
GROOMING
A Scent For The Distinguished Man Who Likes Them On The Younger Side

"Oh, fucking gross!" Renata yelled out. "I mean, everything *about* that motherfucker screams out pedophile! It's one thing to be in a cult, but those motherfuckers are complete morons! And Made in China. Sure, sure. Makes sense. Whatever. It sure as hell kills *these* motherfuckers. Thanks Uncle Joe. I hope the rest of your instructions are just as accurate. Okay. Time to get my niece."

Renata stood in her niece's basement and stared at the vent. Her mind was torn between the anxiety of waiting for Anastasia to be reborn, and the ghastly images of her world on fire. On her drive to her niece's house, she had seen hordes of vicious zombies tearing people apart and eating them. The streets were filled with blood. And collapsed buildings. And fires. She had literally just witnessed hell on Earth. Her attention snapped back to the vent when she heard a young girl's voice say, "Oh, gross. What is that *smell?*"

Renata burst out laughing as she dislodged the vent cover and embraced her beloved Anastasia. "Yeah, sorry kid. That's me. Maybe *you'll* be better at filling the squirt guns. Yeah, let's both jump in the shower, pack some bags, grab some food and water, then hit the road."

"Where are we going, Aunt Renata?" Anastasia asked as her confused blue eyes looked up at her aunt. Renata looked lovingly at her niece, hugged her, and whispered, "Colorado. Pueblo, Colorado."

"Well kid, here we are," Renata stated as she pulled her "borrowed" SUV into an overgrown field. "That was a helluva trip. Burning cars.

Burning towns. And a fuck-ton of vomiting zombies. How many did we squirt, there, squirt?"

"Well, let me just look," Anastasia answered as she pulled out a pink notebook from her princess back-pack. "According to this, we have squirted one hundred and twenty-six zombies. I guess that's a fuck-ton, right Aunt Renata?"

"Okay, listen," Renata said as she tried to hold back her laughter. "You see, that's a bad word that only adults can use and…oh, fuck it. It's armageddon. You can say whatever you want. Who's gonna judge you?"

"Cool!" Anastasia shrieked. "I'm gonna say 'fuck-ton' a fuck-ton of times!" "Yeah, great," Renata answered as the pair got out of their black SUV. "Okay, this is where Uncle Joe told us to look for a flash drive. He said it would be in some weeds near a collapsed cell tower in Pueblo, Colorado. Well, we're in Pueblo. And there's the cell tower. And there's a lot of weeds here."

"There's a *fuck-ton* of weeds here, Aunt Renata," a giggling Anastasia said. "Well, I really shouldn't have started that," Renata muttered to herself. "Okay, kid. Why don't you look over there and I'll look over here and…"

Renata was cut off by her niece yelling out, "Is this it?" "Shit yeah, kid!" Renata exclaimed. "Damn, you're good at this!" "I've *always* been good at finding things, Aunt Renata," a jubilant Anastasia answered. "All I have to do is concentrate on what I'm looking for, and it's like this little voice in my head guides me to it. I've found a *fuck-ton* of stuff that way. Pretty cool, huh?"

"Yup," Renata agreed. "Okay, kid. How about this? You think you can focus on finding some Black chick? And, I mean, a real woman. Not a zombie."

"Well, maybe," Anastasia answered. "Do you know anything else about her?"

"Not much," Renata replied. "She's, like, thirty-two-years-old. Six-foot tall. Really tone. Oh! And she has a big fuckin' afro!"

"Okeedokee then," Anastasia said before closing her eyes. "Um, I think we need to go *that* way."

Renata and Anastasia walked through the dense forest as quietly as possible. The crisp air was filled with the sounds of birds chirping and small woodland creatures scurrying through the thick brush. The one thing that they did *not* hear was any sound made by humans. There were no automobiles. No music. No jets flying overhead. Just the tranquil sounds of thriving wildlife. Then, there was another sound. The peaceful sound of water trickling in a stream. They emerged through a grouping of trees and stood several feet from the shore of a beautiful shallow waterway. There were two large Black Bears fishing in the cool water. Their two cubs were joyously splashing about just a few feet away. In the middle of the stream, there was a small island that housed a blue tent. Renata stared at the tent for a moment and slightly gasped as a small Hispanic boy, a tall Black man, and an Asian woman with a protruding belly emerged. They looked at something behind a nearby tree and began waving.

Renata motioned for Anastasia to stay where she was, then cautiously crept around a tree on the stream's edge to see what the people were waving at. Standing on the soggy bank was a tall, tone, Black woman with a large afro. She was smiling and waving back to the island people. Renata took in a deep breath, stepped forward, and quietly said, "Um, excuse me?"

The Black woman spun around and pointed a yellow squirt gun at Renata. "Oh shit, I'm sorry," the woman said. "I shoulda known. Zombies can't talk. But this shit has me on edge, y'know?"

"Yeah, how I know," Renata replied. "Um, are you Payekha? Payekha Poopala?" "Well, kinda," the woman answered tersely. "It's Payekha Po*poola*. I don't understand why that's so fucking difficult for you fuckin' crackers. Anyway, yeah. That's me. How do you know my name? Who the fuck are *you* bitch? Whoa! Wait a minute! You look familiar! Yeah! I recognize you! I've seen you on billboards and shit! You have a shitty movie coming out! You're Angel Feathers!"

"Well," a chuckling Renata replied. "I *used* to be. My *real* name is Renata. Renata Miazga. And if there wasn't an audience for that piece of trash movie *before*, there *definitely* isn't one now. Anyway, I don't think that movie will be coming out. And as for how I know you, um, well," Renata pulled the flash drive from her jeans pocket and showed it to Payekha. "Um, is this *yours*? This is probably going to sound crazy, but, um, I was told by a spirit from Enlightenment to find this, then give it to you. I was told that you'd know what to do with it and to tell you to not give up on humanity. And my niece and I are to help you with whatever you're supposed to do with this. So, um. Is it yours?"

"Yeah, it's mine," Payekha answered while wearing a shocked expression. "But I never thought I'd see it again. I dropped it in the weeds. And I never thought that there would be a reason to look for it. There didn't seem to be a use for what's on that flash drive. Until now. Until seeing you. And those other people. Okay, Angel or Renata or whatever the fuck your name is. Go get your niece. And let's go talk to those *other* three over there. Something tells me we're all about to go on an adventure together."

THE END
IS JUST THE BEGINNING